THE

SMALL

HOURS

THE SMALL HOURS

A Novel

By

Edward Averett

The text of this book is set in Georgia 11-point font.

The Library of Congress has catalogued this book as follows:

Edward Averett 1951 -
The Small Hours/Edward Averett
First Edition October 2025

Summary: As Michael Virtue grapples with his friend's untimely death and the end of his marriage; his lifelong obsession with the unresolved disappearance of his uncle in the Spanish Civil War gains traction. Thanks to an unlikely source, he embarks on a risky quest to solve the mystery. Once in Spain, he and his unconventional travelling companion become embroiled in a village steeped in tragedy and retribution after 50 long years; Michael learns that war never ends for its victims.

ISBN 978-0-9989359 - 7-3

FICTION; GENERAL 1. Historical/20th Century. 2. Multiple Timelines. 3.Epistolary (Letters, Diaries, etc.)
1. Spanish Civil War 2. Mid-life journey/crisis. 3. Female fugitive 4. Lost family member. 5. Seek and find

Wellborn Books USA
Wellbornbooks.com
Printed in the United States

ACKNOWLEDGEMENTS

While I lived in Spain, during the 1980's a, man came out of hiding in the village just up the hill from us. He had been ensconced in the wall of his home for the 42 years since the end of the Spanish Civil War. Most in the village knew of his existence but chose not to expose him because the consequences of hiding from the Franco regime were extreme. The idea of these *topos*, as they were called, never left my thinking and this novel is the result.

In response to amazement at the feat of the *topo*, I read many stories about the Spanish Civil War, including George Orwell's account of his own experience as a fighter for the Left, *Homage to Catalonia*. I also read *The Battle for Spain* by Antony Beevor, *The Spanish Civil War (Revised Edition)* by Hugh Thomas, *Spain In Our Hearts: Americans in the Spanish Civil War, 1936-1939* by Adam Hochschild, and *Letters From The Spanish Civil War: A U.S. Volunteer Writes Home* by Peter N. Carroll and Fraser Ontanelli.

I'd like to thank Elizabeth Smythe Brinton for reading the manuscript in the early going. Her comments were invaluable I am eternally grateful to Maria M. Morton for her assistance in many aspects of the publishing of this book, not the least of which were her fine-tuned editorial skills. Having a group to rely on for reaffirmation to continuing on as a writer is extremely important and I would be nowhere without my Zoom group, which meets from all over the world on every other Sunday of the month. I am grateful to Blair Miller, Gregory Leddy, Mary Ann Murphy, Jim Price, Sheila Collins, Jan Hopwood, Mary Averett, Don Jensen, and Debbie Jensen, who may have sold more of my books than anyone else. I love them all and they may not even know the places they each have in my heart.

For my Spanish family

The best time to plant a tree was 20 years ago.
The second-best time is now.
—Chinese Proverb

Chapter One
Robert, 1937

January 10, 1937 On the Empire Builder

Dear Mom and Dad,

I didn't think there was any other way to do it. Forgive me for not letting you know, especially so soon after the holiday. Mom, I knew you would try to dissuade me. And Dad, I knew you would look at my idea as a fool's mission. Anyway, it's done, and here I am, sitting in the observation car on the Great Northern Railroad, observing, as they say, with a group of disinterested newspaper readers. I'm not to Chicago yet, but I think we're getting close. The Midwest is mostly boring but the weather is wild, so much snow, I thought the train would fly off the track, but I guess that's what the cowcatchers are for. Please don't be mad at me. I'm still your same old son. I haven't turned into a Wobbly or a Communist, or anything. I'm doing this for Max. Remember him? My best friend? He was in my class at Lewis and Clark before his parents decided to move back East again. Jewish kid. Horrible swastika on their lawn? We've kept in touch. He's much more political than I am. He says it's a man's responsibility to know what's happening in the world and to do something about it if it's wrong. He thinks what's going on in Spain is wrong. He promises to fill me in on the way over. He says it's the right kind of learning, "en vida real" is what he calls it, which means "in real life." He may be right. It didn't feel like

I was getting much of anywhere the last year or so. Dad, even you have to agree; a guy can't make a living just dancing. It made me itchy when I realized it. This could be just what the doctor ordered. Something to pin my hopes and dreams to. I will keep you posted. In the meantime, think of me as being on aN adventure and look forward to the stories I'll tell when I get home again. Don't worry. I'm in good hands. I'll mail this before I set sail.

Your loving son,
Robert

Chapter Two
Michael, Andalusia, 1969

Michael Virtue bulleted down a narrow, rutted track with the warm Spanish wind whistling in his ears and warm Spanish wine slogging through his veins. He thought about his dead uncle. The uncle he never met. The uncle no one talked about anymore. He overheard the stories as a child, late at night when he was supposed to be fast asleep, and held them carefully to his chest. For a while he heard them resonate in his blossoming soul, and then heard nothing as his interests turned to carnality and behavioral science.

Michael roared into a small village, negotiated a tight curve, saw the milk truck directly in his path, and saved himself at the last moment by jerking the handlebars roughly to the right. But he quickly came upon a steep concrete stairway and had no time to throw on the brakes. Yelling for his life as he bounced over the first step, he thigh-clutched the sloping seat of his old Oso and clamped onto the handles until his hands ached from fighting to stay astride as this bucking bronco caromed down the wide vertebral steps.

His teeth clashed and his eyes bounced as he battled the vaulting cycle. When he thought he could hold on no longer, the ground rose up and smacked him and his mount slid out from under him at the bottom of the flight and threw him clear of the wreck. Before falling over a precipice plumed with fragrant broom, he grasped a pair of root clumps which saved him as the Oso kept twirling sideways in the dirt and soon crashed through the broom and somersaulted over a bluff.

A dog barked and then another, but there was nothing to keep them singing save their own familiar yapping, so they soon stopped. Michael waited for the pain to come, or to feel the thick trickle of blood, but all he felt was an urge to pee and to vomit, which he performed simultaneously, never once loosening his grip on the sturdy roots of the Spanish Broom.

"I promise to whoever's listening that if I make it through this I will never do a foolish thing again as long as I live," he vowed in the seconds after the retching ended and he could let loose of at least one of the clumps and wipe his face with the back of his hand.

Once said, he could picture himself letting go the other hand and righting his body enough to free him from his precarious perch. Instead, fearing that the roots were the only thing saving him from the fate of the Oso, he held onto the last clump for the rest of the night, enduring the riotous pain and fright until the sun rose and a goat chewed on a belt loop at the back of his trousers.

"Who's there?" he asked brazenly. Truly he said, "*Quién es?*" But his language and his accent were not well-formed, and he wished he had not given Miss Jones, his junior-high Spanish teacher, such short shrift.

The goat snorted, shocking Michael enough so he turned his head and stared into the steely gray eyes of the beast. It craned its neck and dabbed a raspy tongue against Michael's cheek. Michael did the only thing he could do, since most of his appendages were occupied with keeping himself from falling over the cliff. He spit.

The goat pawed at him as if he were thick underbrush covering something tastier.

"Get!" Michael shouted, and the animal backed up. Emboldened, Michael commanded it again. "Get out! Get off me!" The goat cocked its head and retreated another step, and as it did, another goat peeked around its rump, followed by another. Now there was a herd of them.

As his arms grew weaker, Michael at last let loose of the clump of broom. He waited to slide down into obscurity. Instead, nothing happened. His shoulder throbbed and his elbow was on fire. After a beat, he sat up, waving his aching arms wildly so as to finish scaring off the goats. At that moment, he noticed the woman sitting on a rock not fifty feet away. She picked up a pebble and tossed it in his direction. It plunked next to the hooves of the most offensive goat, which whirled away from him, its tail bobbing.

The woman clucked her palate with the flat of her tongue and chided her animals. "*Harre!* Go now! Leave this helpless man alone!"

Michael only understood a single word of what she said: man. He gazed at her. Her skin said sixties, and she sat with authority, as if she and the stone had a lifelong understanding. She hurled another rock and her goats scrambled over the hill and down toward Michael's pitiful wreck of a motorcycle.

The woman rose. The morning sun shined on her face, its rays lacing through her steely gray hair. She advanced toward him in all her black-dressed handsomeness.

When she stopped a few feet away, Michael was suffused with a sense of her otherworldliness. He said to her what he practiced the whole time he was packing for his trip, albeit with thoughts of one younger, prettier, and less seasoned than this woman appeared to be. "You are the Virgin Mary incarnate. Thank God for you."

She puzzled over this for a moment before saying in English, "You've urinated on yourself."

Shame climbed on Michael's face. "I had an accident."

She walked to the edge of the hill and peered over. "Good. One more dead. These motorcycles are like giant hornets; all day and night they buzz along the roads."

"How is it you know English so well?"

"The language is not difficult."

His head pounded as he squinted to keep the sun from burning into his brain.

"Do you need help?"

"I think so."

She came closer. "You're American, aren't you?"

"It depends on how you feel about them."

"Oh, you're American all right. Always the easy diplomat."

Looking down on himself, he said, "I can't tell if I'm hurt. Did you say my motorcycle is dead?"

"My goats are now chewing on the seat." She turned once more and peeked down the hill where they were indeed making short work of the remains. "Why are you here?"

"I guess you'd say I'm on a mission." He flexed his muscles, one by one, to ascertain the damage. "I graduated. I was gifted some money. I had an interest in Spain, so here I am."

"From where in America?""The Northwest. Washington."

"The city?"

"The state."

"Seattle?"

He tipped up his head and battled again with the sun. "Spokane. You know an awful lot about the states."

"For a woman of little means? No, don't apologize. I understand. Contrary to what you said earlier, I am not a vision of riches."

She heard a noise below and quickly picked up another rock that she flung with precision, scaring one of her charges back into the herd. Meanwhile, Michael tried to stand. His connectors creaked and throbbed as he shimmied and swayed like a newborn colt. At last he was up and, hands on hips, stretched out his back. Bones popped and crackled into alignment. The wandering wet stain on his front had picked up a cake of dust and now resembled the map of Texas. He scraped a hand clean and offered it to her.

She shook it boldly. "Do you have plans now?"

"I suppose I should find someone to help fix my motorcycle."

"There are plenty in town who would jump at the opportunity."

"I'll find somebody," he said.

"Do you want my help?"

He glanced at the wreck of himself once more. "It probably seems like I need a lot of it."

"Come, we're almost through for the morning anyway. Follow me."

This woman spared little time scrambling along the sides of the hills and over the rocks her animals treated as playgrounds. They skirted the village as she allowed her goats to dine on what was left of the low shrubs. Michael could now see a town, including a spot where it was framed by the sparkling blue waters of the Mediterranean in the deep background. A light-gold church dominated the skyline; one faded red tile hung precariously from an edge. Michael sucked in a rich and thirsty breath.

She lived within shouting distance of the village in a long, low stucco building she shared with her goats. They were kept in a covered wire pen to the left of her house. A crumbling stone and mud wall, long abandoned by whitewash, separated her from them. She tucked them away while Michael stood on the buckling terrace that tried to contain the snaky roots of a eucalyptus towering above him. The song of its sagging branches was encouraged by the breeze. A few goats bleated. A dark dog growled a warning from the doorway. Michael stepped back and eyed it warily.

Soon the woman emerged from the house, stopping to rub at her knuckles. "You think I'm odd because I'm not like the others."

He quickly shook his head, lying, for he had just been thinking that very thing. "I only wonder why you can talk so well."

"We'll start over." She walked up to him and extended her hand. "I am Maria del Carmen Escobar. You may call me Carmen, as most do. What is your name?"

He told her as the rough edges of her palm rubbed against his own.

"Your motorcycle is not as important as you think," she said. "I know you're wondering about it."

"It could get me back to the States."

"Now you think you can drive on water. Tell me, why have you come here? The tourists spend their time and money on the other side of the capital."

"I'm looking for a grave," he replied.

"Whose?"

"A man. An American. One who came here a long time ago."

She studied the leaves of the eucalyptus and, as she began to hum, Michael thought their voices were similar. "How long?" she asked, once again leveling her eyes on him.

"During the war."

"I see," she said with delicacy. "And you believe he was buried here?"

Michael realized the daunting nature of this search of his. The hollow part was he never expected to find a grave or even a headstone, much less anyone who remembered his uncle.

"You are too young to be looking for bodies," she said.

Michael shrugged.

Carmen seemed to be struggling with something. Her tongue washed her lower lip, her hands trembled.

"What is it?"

"Nothing. Just thinking about the war."

"It was bad, I know."

"Perhaps you know and maybe you don't."

Halfway through her sentence, Carmen changed to a clear Spanish, none of which he understood. She stood on her toes to do it, not all at once, but slowly like a ballerina preparing for a long siege on point. By the pensive look on Carmen's face, Michael felt she was delving somewhere into her own past.

When she stopped, he said, "Okay, now I'm lost. What did you say?"

"I told you a secret I've never spoken in my language before. I must say, it was the right thing to do."

"Do you know where my uncle Robert is buried? Is that the secret?"

"What I said is indelicate. And I have a reputation for indelicacy. Women become this way after years of inactivity."

He shook a finger. "You're avoiding the question."

"No," she said curtly. "The answer is no. I was young. And poor. The war took away my life."

"I'm sorry," Michael said.

She sat down on the edge of the terrace and shaded her eyes. "It was chaos back then. So many were lost."

"It must have been horrible."

"For some, yes."

"Can you tell me anything more?"

"Listen, we Spanish are not like you Americans. We don't talk and talk about things better left unsaid. It is not proper to treat something with less reverence than it deserves."

He wiped a thin film of sweat from his forehead. "Sorry. I should know better. I guess, now that I'm here, I don't even know what I want."

"You're in want of a motorcycle. You'd best decide about the one in the arroyo, or it will be decided for you."

He stood. "I think it's beyond repair."

"You'll leave it as a monument to your presence here?"

"Yes."

"I'll find you a ride back."

"I'd be grateful. But I don't have anything to give in return."

"Answer me a question and that will be my payment."

"I'll try."

At last she stepped down from her throne. "Is it true that in America you can find your heart's desire?"

"I guess so."

She quickly began to cry. Tears rolled from her eyes as she dug in a pocket for an exquisitely embroidered hanky.

"Yes," he said. "Yes, of course you can find your heart's desire."

Then she said something that stayed with him for the next twenty years. He thought of it at night when he couldn't sleep because babies had ear infections or swollen gums. He thought of it when the voice of a boss snapped at him in his dreams and he ended up tossing and turning over some bit of work he'd forgotten to complete the day before.

She said to him this: "Say hello to Mr. Roosevelt."

And he answered: "I sure will."

Chapter Three
Michael and Mason, Spokane, 1989

"You're living in the past," Michael's friend, Mason, once said to him. "Spain, Spain, Spain. Haven't you done anything since?"

This was a reasonable question and Michael had a dozen pat answers. Sure he had. He'd gone to graduate school. He'd decided not to become a teacher of elementary students and chose psychology when he couldn't make up his mind about anything else. And he'd done well. He'd met Eva in class and secured her quickly. They'd traded Winstons and notes on child development and vows a year later. He'd eschewed private practice and set to work in one of those government clinics where the pay was low, as were the rewards, and ended up wondering after a few years what he was doing there.

"You're probably feeling the inertia of real life," his darling Eva had said. She had entered the consulting wing of the field and was now impressing the business world while Michael could be found on the phone with a disgruntled mother who wondered why her schizophrenic teenager was still up in his room masturbating his penis to a raw red stick.

"Maybe he's looking for pleasure in his life," he tried. And then he set out on one of those psychological sojourns that therapists are so expert at over the phone, explaining this and noting that, pulling a quote or two from memory and tying it up with a flawless recommendation.

"No," the disgusted mother said. "None of that works. You'd be singing a different tune if it was you who had to wash the damn sheets every day."

Which was certainly true. Psychologists didn't do the sheets part very well.

Time brought Michael to his senses. He quit the agency-go-round, launched a private practice that eventually turned lucrative, and latched onto some pretty decent friends in the process.

Most of them were in the same business, all blessed with grace and cynicism, a winning combination for shrinks. Of all his friends, Michael liked Mason the best. There was so much of him in every way. Mason was gaining about ten pounds a year – the rest of the group, a pound or two. All that Mason was made of passed through his mouth. He ate, he barked out soliloquies when drinking too much, he sang ancient fundamentalist hymns on key, he breathed laboriously when walking up the stairs. And he would not let Michael be. He remembered conversations they'd had years earlier and would conjure them, like a loyal spouse, and use them, either for or against, depending on what was needed.

Michael enjoyed the times he had to defend himself against his friend. "If you want me to change, you should start with yourself first," he might say in frustration. "Lose some weight." But the truth was he didn't want Mason to change at all. The guy was an inspiration at beating the odds. Like the rest of them, Mason had a yearly physical and had his cholesterol levels and blood sugars and his ever-increasing hypertension checked. Unlike the others, he never made a pretext of giving a damn. He never reached way back in his closet to drag out a dusty pair of running shoes he'd had for years. He didn't bring sack lunches to work and spend the afternoon picking carrot and apple out of the widening spaces between his teeth. Instead, Mason perused the doctor's report, said, "Hmmm" and promptly lost it in the pile of other important material that grew over time on his desk.

"We were meant to grow wider and slower the older we get," Mason said. "Why fight it? Why not enjoy the life we have?"

Indeed.

Michael often thought of his times with Mason. The best talks, the best times. He had yet to talk with Mason about the big thing that had happened along the way. Somewhere, he'd lost his darling Eva.

§

"There once was a man from Nantucket," Michael said. He paused. "How does the rest of it go? Whose cock was so long he could suck it."

"Are you sure about that?" said Mason.

"Yes. There once was a man from Nantucket, whose cock was so long he could suck it. That's how it goes."

"I suppose there's more," Mason said. He glanced down at his watch and whistled. "Is it really two?"

"It's one," Michael said, "and the bartender's looking nervous."

They turned their heads and studied him for a moment.

"Impotent," Mason said.

"Right," said Michael. "Unless her armpits are unshaven and she recites *Howl* while he's doing her."

"Who cares?" Mason said. "We're wasting our time. Last call's coming up and we haven't toasted anybody dead yet."

"I've been waiting," Michael said. He reached for his briefcase.

"Are we going to say prayers for your uncle again?" Mason said. His words were slurred from drink and exhaustion.

"Yes, Uncle Robert," said Michael. He opened the briefcase and pulled out a piece of paper, which he snapped open. "I've got something different this time."

"What?" said Mason.

"Just listen." Michael cleared his throat and began to read:

January 5, 1937, Brooklyn, New York

Dear Robert,

Stop everything. Have I got a plan for you. I suppose you're wondering why a train ticket dropped out of the envelope along with this letter. Well, wonder no more, my boy. As you can see the ticket is for Spokane-New York. My friend, you can't live your whole life trying to win another bunion derby. The one was pure luck. And don't waste any time figuring out what you should do about this request and for God's sake don't talk to anyone about it. Just pack your bags and get here. The ship leaves a day after you arrive. We'll hash it over on the crossing, but I feel so strongly about what's going on in Spain, it would be immoral not to do something. I already know what you're thinking, but relax, I'm not a Red. We'll have the time of our lives and do good for the world as a bonus. And don't tell me you can't come because things are going too well. I've been hearing how bad the crunch affected you guys up there. I can't wait to go. So, get a move on, will ya?

Your Comrade,

Max(well)

P.S. Franco hates Jews. All the more reason.

Glasses clinked in the background, but silence invaded the table as Michael carefully folded the paper. He felt a bit woozy and was sure it was not entirely the fault of the drinks.

"Is that real?" Mason finally said.

"It's a copy."

"Where'd you get it?"

"My mom, or her caregivers actually. They told me my dad always wanted me to have them, the few letters my uncle actually wrote, but that all got put away when he died and, well, you know my mom's brain now. But anyway... Isn't it great?"

"You always told me there were others."

"Yes, a few more."

"Well, let's hear them."

Michael chewed on his lower lip. He thought one would do, now felt possessive. "Maybe not. I guess the thought of losing their son was pretty gruesome for his parents. I don't want to overdo it."

"Well, at least give me an idea of what they said."

"Not much. Observations. Descriptions. That sort of thing."

"That was cool," Mason said, raising a glass. "Here we go. Here's to Uncle Robert."

After downing his glass, Mason checked his watch. "I'm never going to get up in time."

"You got something early?"

"Court. Custody case." Mason smiled big.

"Look at you," Michael said. "You dog. You love it, don't you?"

Mason nodded. "Why don't you do it? I mean, what more could you ask for? A chance to show off your talent. To snatch the decision-making from people who don't understand. I would think you would jump at the chance to testify."

The bartender finally came over and signaled for last call. Mason shook his head and stood. That was their sign.

"I Don't Care." Mason.

"Nor do I." Michael.

§

Outside, Mason stood by his old Volvo and looked across the top of it. Michael was doing pushups against the frame.

"You never actually say it, do you?" Mason said.

"Say what?"

"That you don't care. Don't think I haven't noticed. You don't say it. You just agree."

"Hmmm. Sometimes I do care."

Mason checked the giant illuminated clock dial over the door to the restaurant. It winked out. "You going to tell me or what?"

Michael stopped pushing against the car. "Tell you what?"

"Something's got you. I could see it when you were reading the letter. That uncle of yours…"

Michael shrugged and pushed away. "I got a lot going on. Me and Eva." Should he tell him now?

"I can sense it." Mason said. "And you'll spill when you're ready. But what's that got to do with your uncle?"

"It's all complicated," Michael said.

"Ain't it though. You know, in a few hours I'll be sitting in a courtroom, and attorneys will be asking me contrived questions to which I will respond with brilliant answers, and we all will call it the process of justice. Talk about complicated."

"You do a bang-up job of it, bud," Michael said. "Better than the rest of us."

"I guess I am. It's Ramey."

"Help me with it. That little blonde girl who got deeked by her father?"

"Truth be told, I'm not all that confident. It was never proved, you know. He got to her. She gave a beautiful deposition, at least for a seven-year-old, but recanted the next week. I know in my heart he did it and I'll rot in hell before that man gets custody of her."

"It'll work out," Michael said. "You'll save the day."

"I know." Mason opened his car door. "And Eva's waiting for you."

"Not really."

Michael backed away as Mason crawled into his car and started it up. Before he left, he rolled down the window.

"You really should go back."

"Where? To Spain?"

"Yes. Like I said, your eyes told the tale while you were reading. It's a whole different Michael."

"Maybe."

"We should do the things we crave before it's too late."

Michael waved and watched his best friend drive across the lot. But as soon as he reached his own car and stabbed the key in the lock, a screech of tires brought his attention back to the old Volvo.

Its taillights flashed red and there standing next to it was a tall, angular woman. She leaned over, glorious butt out, and stuck her head in the window. A few muffled words were exchanged before she opened the door and slid in. Mason took off again and Michael stood puzzled a moment longer before he got into his own car.

He pulled the letter from his briefcase and stuffed it in the glovebox, along with several others he kept hidden there.

§

It was a while before Michael could come fully awake the next morning. He listened with his eyes closed as Eva went about her business. She was up early most days now, stealing from bed so as not to rouse him. At least he thought that for a while. Later, when he actually sneaked down and saw her dancing about the house, flinging open windows and doors, watering plants, calling friends, he realized she hadn't actually slept with him and didn't want him to disturb *her*. Here was a woman with a whole life lived in the small hours.

Now, she came to the bedroom before she left. She wore a crisp mauve suit, professional but with a ceramic pin of a clown's face to break up the polished terrain. "You were sure late," she said.

"You know IDC."

"I know IDC," she said. "But I don't understand it. I think people should actually care."

"Where to today?"

"In one hour, I'll be in the air headed for Seattle."

"You coming back tonight?"

"You're slipping, Michael. I told you I won't be."

"Have I mentioned I think you're gone too much?"

She slipped to the closet, pulled out a small plump travel bag. "What's up for you today?"

"Same old," he replied. "If I'm lucky I'll get a couple of cancellations so I can sleep this off."

"As a private practitioner you should hate cancellations."

He tried to sit up but failed. "It's hangovers I hate. Where are the kids?"

"It's summer vacation. They're still in bed. They have some seminars later. Also, Carmen wants to know when does she get a car. I told her to talk to you because I don't make the little decisions." She started for the bed, thought better of it, and blew him a perfunctory kiss instead.

"Be careful," he called after her.

She stopped at the doorway and patted the jamb. "Michael?" But she hesitated and the feeling it gave him made him rush to say something to quash the moment.

"I'll pray for your safe return," he said as she turned and headed down the stairs. He heard her open and close the door, listened for the distant rumble of her car starting up and drifted a little as she rattled out the driveway.

Chapter Four
Eugenio, Andalusia, 1989

Eugenio Robles was a man of high honor and attention to detail. In the United States, he might be said to be afflicted with Obsessive-Compulsive Disorder, but in Spain he was seen as a man who focused on the small things. He was a good son and a better grandson. Even though he never met his grandfather, because the man was gunned down during the war trying to do the sacred work of *El Caudillo*, and even though he failed only one time, that one time changed the entire history of the Robles family forever. They found someone else's blood near his body, but it was always the same in these Republican villages, some Red invariably was ready to drag away the carcasses of the enemy and leave the real patriots to rot in the Andalusian sun.

Eugenio's father, Carlos, was a storekeeper and a decent man, albeit ambivalent about the war itself, even though his own father had been on the winning side. It was the fact that Eugenio's grandfather had missed the victory celebration because of his untimely death that most likely turned Carlos off to the whole idea of war, revenge and the like.

In fact, Carlos Robles couldn't even tolerate harsh words with his wife. He often showed mercy where mercy wasn't due in order to keep the peace. Sometimes his son was there to observe him, and Eugenio developed a disdain for the man who would not push ahead and try to win when winning was the most important outcome in life.

It was expected of Eugenio, being the elder of Carlos's two sons, to train in the store so that when the day came, he would run it himself. He did try, even grew to enjoy some of the customers, but he was fidgety and unfocused and soon realized he had no desire to lead the family business. He didn't want to be on the premises at all, would never have been if the family hadn't lived above the store and he had to pass through it to make it out to the street.

He was seven when he first heard the story of his grandfather. His mother was telling a customer, a woman new to the city of Málaga, about the family's history. Because it was a slow day, they had moved out to the chairs in front of the store and there they sat and drank chamomile tea while Eugenio cracked the window overhead so he could hear them better.

"It was a dark night," his mother began. "Darker than most. It has been said that the Republicans had covered the moon because they needed all the advantage they could get. One of the foreign groups – what did they call them... the International Brigades – was reported to be as close as Motril, and while they weren't the best shooters, they made up for it in their enthusiasm for killing. You can see them now, these foreigners, when they come to visit our country. You can see the look on their faces, the one that says, we are better than you.

"But that night my father-in-law was tired. He had been on patrol for two straight days without sleep and with little bread. You can imagine! He was a dedicated man, as all men should be, and he did not let this circumstance influence his decisions.

"It was in La Jolla... you may not know this village, but if you visit it still, you must be careful, just as was necessary in *La Guerra*. The people who live there have long memories."

"Ah," said the new customer, "the memories."

"I have told you it was a dark night, have I not? One could barely make out his own hand in front of his face. The air was warm; a *terral* would blow in within the next few hours and cover everything with the Sahara's orange sand.

"La Jolla was Leftist; everyone knew that. And after Málaga fell to the Right, even though many of them fled to the main highway, there were always pockets of subversion. Francisco usually rode his horse proudly, but this night he had dismounted and was leading it by its long reins along the road between Lo Puerto and La Jolla, a road pitted by wagon wheels in the winter mud. Even the horse had to step carefully for want of a broken fetlock.

"It was a boy who caused my father-in-law's death – not even ten years old, crying. Who could resist that, I ask you? The cries of a boy in distress. Food and play and the touch of a loving mother are the true politics of the young. How can you or I blame the babies for the faults of their parents? My father-in-law heard this cry and stopped his horse with a tap on its nose."

Above them, with his head lodged in the crack of the window, Eugenio listened to his mother's story, breathless.

"My father-in-law, like many men of the strongest nature, had a soft spot for children, and he took up the reins again and led the horse off the road and into the green flat field that he knew from his daylight rides was filled with an army of brilliant yellow oxalis. The horse's hooves clumped through the flowers, scaring off a hare, which made my father-in-law draw his weapon from his saddlebag. But he and his horse kept creeping along.

"And suddenly they came upon the sound again, this time much closer, as if he could reach out and stroke the poor boy's head and calm his fears.

"'*Quieto*,' said Francisco. 'It will be all right. Come to me. Would you like a ride on my horse?'

"There was movement in the bushes and my father-in-law's grip tightened on his rifle. Of course, he did not want to make a mistake and shoot the boy, but neither did he want to play the fool with the Leftist assassins. He looked up to the night sky and tried to will the stars to shine brighter. And when he looked down, he could see a shape. To be safe, he aimed the weapon at this profile.

"'*Venga*,' he said. 'Come closer so I can see you.'

"But the figure did not move, rather stood as still as a statue of the Virgin of Guadalupe."

A customer rounded the corner and stopped in front of Eugenio's mother. "I need diapers," this woman said. "And a cake of soap."

Eugenio's mother patted her new friend's knee and took great pains to stand up and hobble into the store. In a few minutes she came back out, counting *pesetas* laid out in a row on her palm.

"Now where was I?" she said, sitting carefully back down in her chair.

"A child crying. A figure in the darkness," said the new customer.

"And the rifle," Eugenio whispered from his perch above them.

"Ah yes. In the darkness. He could have crawled out of the pages of an old novel, this figure. My father-in-law felt the nudge from his horse, smelled the chewed grass on its heavy breath. He grew skeptical of this boy's intentions. Could whomever it was see him more clearly than Francisco could see? What was he waiting for?

"'I will give you this chance,' said my father-in-law. 'You will come forward with your hands in the air. You will identify yourself and if you do not do these things, then sadly you leave me no choice but to use my weapon.'

"What is the appropriate time to wait for a boy to do your bidding? One full minute? Ten seconds? I am here to tell you my blessed father-in-law waited a total of twenty seconds before he made his decision. And in those twenty seconds, he struggled with his own beloved conscience over what he must do. But you need to remember, it was also wartime and decisions must be made that one would not normally make, say, at the market at closing time.

"He lifted his rifle, which by that time was heavier than his aching heart. 'I do not want to shoot you,' my father-in-law said. 'But if I must, I must. And I will.'

"And this pronouncement stirred something in the figure standing in the dark. It troubled the horse who snorted and bobbed his head. But before the gun could be raised all the way, another sound broke the darkness.

"'No, you won't,' said a second voice. This voice came out speaking a language from a different country. English as we found out later. 'No, you will not shoot this boy.'

"And this strange voice surprised my father-in-law, who swung his gun and fired. And in a split second, he saw a splash of flame jump from the bush and felt a thump in his chest, felt the lead as it dug its way into his fine-toned body, pierced his lung, and lodged next to his spine."

Above them, Eugenio gasped with the news. "Oh, grandfather," he said. "*Pobrecito.*"

The new customer patted her leg now. "*Jesús y Maria.*"

"My father-in-law was stunned, but awake. The boy and another man knelt at his side. Blood dripped from this other man's fingers and spotted the ground beneath them. 'The sound will draw others,' the boy said. 'What must we do?'

'Why have you killed me?' Francisco said.

"The wind was picking up. The olive trees were whipping their ancient branches. My father-in-law listened to the sounds of his life as they slowly faded and he wept with the impending loss.

'You can't stay,' the other man said to the boy. 'You are in grave danger.'

'*Yo?*'

'You see his uniform? He's of a high rank. This won't be a simple death. It will be regretted for decades.'

"And the boy understood. He stood up and saluted the man before he dove into the bushes and was gone."

Here, Eugenio's mother wiped at her eyes and reached in her dress sleeve for a handkerchief, which she dabbed at her nose. "Each time I tell this, it is closer and closer to me. I can imagine I am there myself. But how could I have been? I am still so young."

"You are telling a painful story," the new customer said. "But might I have permission to ask one question?"

"Of course."

"How is it that you know this in such exact detail? You've already told me your father-in-law didn't live. How did the information come to you?"

Eugenio's mother might as well have been shot in the darkness of La Jolla herself, she was so shocked by the impertinence of the question.

"Why, it is the story of our family. This is our legacy. This is what we are left with. Perhaps you do not understand yet, but when the body dies, what remains are the stories. They never die."

"Yes, yes, I understand, and please forgive me for one additional question. The boy? What happened to him?"

Eugenio's mother cleared her throat. Her tears had dried up. "After the storm, after the *terral* dumped the Sahara Desert all over my father-in-law, questions were asked, and families were interviewed. The boy was flushed out of hiding. He eventually told the story of the murder."

"I suspect he did not want to tell it."

Eugenio's mother nodded. "He was, of course, found to be from a family on the other side. Yes, he was interrogated and gave the details."

"I see," said the new customer.

Eugenio's mother picked up on her meaning. "It was war time," she said. "The boy had to be asked. He had the information, but he did not go to the authorities. One must be punished for that."

"And the other man? The one who shot your father-in-law?"

Eugenio's mother's face darkened. "I am sorry to say he was never captured. At least as far as we know. There was blood, as I've said. He had to be a member of one of the International Brigades, foreigners who fought on our soil for a theory instead of a cause. These people could duck in and out of the country with impunity. As if the war were a game to be played."

Upstairs, Eugenio sat back from the window. He imagined his grandfather alone in the night, dying second by second with no family to bid him farewell, only strangers who wished him ill.

Although only seven, the injustice of this struck him in the middle of his little body. He ran to the shelves and pulled off one of his mother's crocks. He hoisted it over his head and slammed it to the tile floor where it smashed into a thousand angry fragments.

"Oh, my grandpa," he mourned.

"Eugenio!" his mother called from below. "What have you done?"

"No," he said, pushing open the window and hanging out of it. "What have *you* done? What has my father done?" He ducked back in but soon returned holding yet another of the crocks. "Where is the justice for my grandfather?" He dropped the crock without warning, and it fell on the small space between his mother and the new customer and was pulverized.

Chapter Five
Michael, Spokane, 1989

Once at work, Michael picked up his charts. No cancellations as yet. He poured coffee, added sugar and milk and left it to cool as he perused the file for his next appointment, an evaluation. It was a strange odyssey, cracking open a life for the first time, going over what others had to say about a person. Sometimes, it was more of a challenge to try to understand the writer. Most psychologists he knew were closet novelists. Case notes read like conversation on the moors of Scotland.

When he was younger, he had set aside paper consultation, preferring to get a feel for the client before he learned of his previous life. Now, he understood the value of fleshing out the client's life before the first visit. It followed the same neuron path that directed him to roam the house one more time at night making sure every possible entry point was locked.

At ten o'clock, the secretary, Arlene, came to his doorway, her face like ash. "Oh my God," she whispered.

"What?" Unhealthy visions of family tragedy immediately floated up in his brain.

"This is the most horrible thing."

"Come on." She was prone to kidding. "It's Eva, isn't it? Oh Christ, her plane."

"I don't want to tell you."

And looking at her more closely, Michael knew that something was about to happen that would render the rest of his life inconsequential. "Arlene," he said tentatively, "just spit it out."

"They called from court. The ambulance took Mason away. He's dead."

"Mason? He can't be...what?"

"They asked if I knew any next of kin. Do you know any next of kin, Michael?"

"This is ridiculous," he said, standing. "Don't talk this way." He began pacing around the office with no clear direction. "Who called you?"

"The clerk. I made her tell me. She said there'd been a terrible accident and does Mason have any relatives here."

"I don't think so," Michael said. "Did she actually say he was dead?"

"He fell over on the witness stand. Didn't say anything."

"This is horrible."

Michael cancelled his appointments and drove home. There, he took the still-dirty plates out of the dishwasher and soaped them up by hand. The saucers spun in his fingers. Out the window, he surveyed the junk pile the neighbors had let rot for years. He had to call up the city someday and complain. There had to be an ordinance being violated.

Finished with the dishes, he shined the toaster and bleached the grout between the counter tiles. He did the kind of necessary work that kept the Grim Reaper from taking over his thinking.

That night the phone rang, startling Michael from his doze before the television. He expected one of the kids to answer, but it kept on its demanding wail. He finally staggered to the hallway and picked it up.

"It took you long enough," Eva said.

"Where are the damn kids?"

"You're the one who's home."

"Why are you calling? Did you finish early? Do you need a ride home?"

"No," she said. There was a long pause that brought him more awake.

"I don't like the sound of that."

"I know."

"It's a horrible day," he said. "Mason died."

"What?"

He told her the shocking story, which by now played out in his head like a spot on the news.

"How awful," she said when he'd finished. "When's the service?"

"I would assume next week some time. We're going tomorrow to view the body. Want to come?"

Another pause. "I don't think I can. Besides, he wasn't really my friend."

"But you're my wife. It's how it works."

"I'm not coming home, Michael."

"Fine, so you'll wait for the funeral and see him there."

"Uh, I'm going to be here for a while."

Even though he knew better, he said, "I guess I don't understand."

"I've thought about how I would say this, but there's no other way. I'm staying in Seattle for a while. A lot of my work is taking me here, so it won't interrupt things all that much."

There was a hitch in Michael's thinking, the kind that happened when little bits of electricity tried to run down different lines and converge on one spot. "But I told you my best friend died today."

"I realize the timing is awful, but I've thought about it for quite a while now."

"How long?"

"It doesn't matter, does it?"

"Years? Months? Weeks? I'm your husband. I deserve not to be left out in the cold."

"Michael."

He wanted to lash out at her, but it wouldn't come. He was exhausted and had to admit that none of this was surprising him. If he were honest, this morning read as a foreshadow of the moment. He pictured her on the other end, sitting rigidly, speaking directly into the receiver, reading from carefully prepared notes. "Mason died while he was testifying on the stand. He just got through giving his name and address and profession, and he keeled over. No last words."

"Michael, I'm as shocked as you are. Anything we try to say to each other now pales in comparison. Could you put Carmen on the phone?"

"I don't know where she is."

"I might have known."

"She's nearly eighteen, Eva. She has friends and a life."

"I suppose Danny's gone, too."

"The house is quiet. Why don't you hop a plane and come over and we'll talk."

"I know, Michael. That'll ease your pain for tonight. But it won't solve the real problem. I think you know that."

"I'm not thinking straight. Shock, probably."

"Well, one thing I know is that I feel better over here. I don't know how to explain it. The air's clear in Seattle."

"Oh, Eva."

"We didn't go to marriage counseling like you promised. Why didn't we?"

"You know how hard it is when you're in the business and you know everybody. It's difficult to find a shrink you can trust."

"God, you've always acted like it's a curse to be in a helping profession. I just wish you would be human for a change."

"You're coming home sometime soon, aren't you? Or are we going to be in limbo forever?"

"I'll come home. Tell the kids I'm on extended leave."

"I'll tell them you don't want to come home."

"You're an asshole, Michael."

"Mason died..."

"So, go have one of your IDC nights and eulogize him. Make him a big hero for the ages, like that uncle of yours."

"He is a hero."

"I'll keep in touch," she said, signing off.

He held the phone out as if it could do more damage to him. The robot-voice told him to hang up and he did before he sat down on the floor and counted the chips in the enameled molding.

§

He was proud of the way his children looked, how they acted. They bonded together nicely at times like this. They'd gone off to town shopping and came back dressed in their new mourning clothes. Michael's son walked back and forth before the big mirror in the dining room, evaluating himself from all angles, his hands digging deep into his pockets. His daughter, so attentive and confident. Michael bit at his lip. Youth, he decided, was truly a loss to grieve.

The observance was quick. An urn of colorful glazed pottery occupied a wooden stand in the front of the room. Michael had gone two days earlier and viewed the body before the cremation. It was a ghastly scene. Mason looked huge in the confines of the simple pine coffin. Gravity was tugging his features down. Michael wanted some time alone and when it was granted, he sat tongue-tied and embarrassed, feeling the intense intimacy.

Now, in the funeral home, Michael wept. The urn had taken away that intimacy and he studied it as the service came to a close.

It took him a few minutes to get up. He fumbled in his pocket for the keys and handed them over to the kids. "I think I'll walk," he said.

Outside, he breathed deeply. He drifted away from the knot of people. The sun was behind him now and shined hot on his dark shoulders. It wasn't long before the last car took off from the curb and left the funeral home as if nothing had happened.

He walked around to the front of the place and watched traffic. He didn't hear the woman come up behind him, and when he felt the tap on his shoulder, he startled.

"Are you Michael?" she asked.

He turned, took in the vision before him. She was tall, with frighteningly elaborate curves in perfect harmony. He sucked in a wild, rapid breath. "What?"

"I said, are you Michael." The way she said it, in a honeyed, exotically low voice distracted him.

"Yes," he finally answered.

She took a step closer and enveloped him in her arms. He'd seen her before. Just as she leaned in and pressed her full, spongy lips against his, he remembered where it was. She locked him in for ten seconds before she let go.

"Compliments of Mason," she said.

"What?"

"From Mason. You know, the guy who died. Your best friend?"

As she turned to go, Michael caught her arm. "Mason picked you up a few nights ago. So, you knew him?"

"I said that kiss was from him. Yes I knew him. Do you think I would do that to just anyone on the street?"

"But why?"

"Because he made me promise I would. I don't go back on my promises. Mason thought you were his best friend." She stared into him. "Maybe even the type of guy I could count on."

She did walk away this time and Michael was trapped between wanting to watch how her body undulated beneath her dress and running after her to be caught up in whatever adventure she had to offer. The latter won out.

He ran ahead and then backpedaled as she walked along.

"What?" she asked. She carried a bright multi-colored fabric purse draped over her shoulder and she clutched the strap now with both hands. "What are you doing?"

"How do you know Mason?"

"We've been friends for a while."

Michael checked behind himself; the sidewalk was clear. "How come I don't know you then? I've known Mason for years."

She smiled. "Could be you're not the perceptive kind."

He finally stopped. He expected her to stop, as well, but she detoured around him. He waited to see if she would sneak a peek, but she walked on with a graceful command of the road until she put a key into a tiny green Karmann Ghia and drove away.

Chapter Six
Michael and Delia, Spokane, 1989

Two days later, Arlene came into his office. "I'm going home," she said.

"Are you sick?"

"I don't know if I can go on."

"Is this a permanent condition or only for today?"

"You never take me seriously," she chided. "I'm totally depressed about Mason and I don't see how you guys can go on pretending that nothing's different."

"Have you taken care of the rest of the afternoon?"

"I called the service and you guys can hang around and catch people when they come in, can't you? I just want to go home and have a glass or a bottle of red wine and lounge in the tub."

"Be careful with that."

"Who cares?" she said.

It had been quiet since Mason's death. They expected a deluge of calls from his patients wondering who they were going to see now, but only a trickle came in. Michael took in one of them. His own clients had been canceling all week so he had a lot of time on his hands. Sometime before five he was doodling on his pad, going over the pros and cons of Eva's decision, when he heard a crash in Mason's office.

When he hurried to the doorway, the tall woman from the funeral was picking at a bit of gypsum board on the wall.

"Hello," she said. She had on a pair of tight-fitting jeans and a peasant blouse. She was taking books off Mason's shelf and dropping them into a big cardboard box. The source of the crash was one of the shelves that now hung at an angle.

"What are you doing?"

"I'm cleaning up," she said. "He won't be needing these anymore. He asked me to arrange things for him." She stopped and looked at Michael. "A better question would be, Do you need some help?"

"Look," he said. "I don't do cryptic well. You've got to explain yourself."

"No, I don't."

Exasperated, he sat down in Mason's big chair and watched her. She seemed older than on the day of the funeral, tired. She handled the books with ease, though, pushing the box over with her leg, making room for another one. She wasn't looking at the titles, merely piling them in. When the shelves were clear, she turned and surveyed the room.

"He had a lot of *things*," she said. "More than I thought." Her face softened. "Funny how that works, isn't it? It doesn't seem like much while we're alive, but little things keep popping up when we're dead."

"Oh, I get it," Michael said. "You're one of those who comes in and organizes people's lives."

She put her hands on her hips. "Well, organize is probably a pleasant euphemism for what I've done to lives. Did you know Mason for long?"

"Like I said ... years."

"Hmmm. Not me. Enough time though." She swiped at her eyes and shivered a little before suddenly sitting on top of the books in one box. She wrapped her arms around her shins, bent down. "It kind of hits you when you don't expect it."

"Delayed reactions can be a shock."

"I suppose," she said. "I don't know what I was thinking. These boxes are going to be too heavy to lift."

"What's your name?"

"Delia."

"Do you have a last name?"

"It doesn't matter."

"Are you aware of this frustrating habit you have of deflecting everything I say?"

"You don't know me well enough to know if it's a habit."

"Okay, fair enough."

"I mean I've had a few last names in my life – one from marriage, some I made up. I'm tired of them. It doesn't matter what my last name is."

"Is Delia real or made up?"

She laughed. "Now you sound like my students. They keep asking questions to get away from the lesson. Is that what you're doing?"

"So, you're a professor."

"So far a teacher. I'm thinking of retiring, though. This thing with Mason, I don't know. It shakes me up." She stood and walked over to the side of Mason's desk. She picked up a cup full of pencils and turned it around. "You know, I went to see his body in the death store. It didn't faze me a bit. I've seen bodies before. But it's things like this, people's personal belongings, that get to me. It's like, where'd he get this mug, what was he doing?"

"He got it from me. It was his birthday. He drank from it before it became a home for pencils."

"I can't do this," she said. "I can't pick up after his life. Who am I to think that I deserve this? Someone else should be the one to do it." She set down the mug and wiped her hands. "I should go."

"I'm not sure you can just take these things anyway."

She walked back around the desk and stood next to him. He smelled her perfume. By reflex, he put his hand up and she grasped it. It was warm and moist, a fecund hand. "We were lovers. Doesn't that count for anything?"

"Not according to the law."

"Do you believe in rules like that? If he and I were close and not one person from his family, not one next of kin came by or called him up or wrote him a letter in three years, doesn't that make *me* more important than those people who never cared?"

"Is there something of his that you especially want?"

"Yes. I'd like his cock back. Despite what you might think, he was a remarkably agile lover."

Michael's hand slipped from hers. "I can honestly say I never actually thought about that."

"Well, it crossed my mind, plenty. It may sound harsh or cold, but it's what I'll miss. When you get to be my age, you find people have a never-ending supply of excuses as to why they can't make love. Mason never once gave me an excuse, he just gave me sex."

"Could we have dinner or something?" Michael blurted out.

She cocked her head. "What's the 'or something' part?"

"I just want to talk to you more. It amazes me Mason could have this whole other life without my knowing."

"Could you help me with the boxes?"

Michael thought how little he knew about the world in which he lived. He had heard many elaborate stories from patients over the years and had been lured inside some of them, but now he realized all these tales lived a long distance from him, were the property of others. Where was the rest of his property? Would the story of his life always be just that bumpy trip down the steps in Spain?

He followed Delia to her cottage situated between an old brick three-story apartment building and a workingman's Victorian of a color and scale he had not seen before. Her front yard resembled the garden for the other two. It was rich and colorful, the soil dark and musty. She opened the picket gate for him as he peeked around the giant box of books. His arms shook from the strain.

"You can set them down anytime!" she called as she glided up the walk and dug for her keys. "You don't have to prove anything to me."

He waited for her to push open the door and slipped past, barely making it through. He set the box down on a small table and took a deep breath.

"Don't kill yourself." She lit the gas stove and set a kettle on the burner.

"I'll get the others." He jumped down the stairs and in a few minutes was back with another carton.

She held out a cup but he shook his head. "I think I'll pass." He wiped sweat from his face.

"It's peppermint," she said. "It'll cool you off."

They sat on her front steps, admiring her yard. He and Eva had never been able to make plants grow like these. A group of burgundy hollyhocks stood tall and straight with no hint of rust. All around their base danced lobelia, Queen Anne's lace, calendula, sweet pea. "It's beautiful," he said.

"I like how busy it is. It's reflective of me on the inside."

"From my perspective, it's you on the outside as well," he said.

"It's a front." She sipped the tea and held it tightly. He thought she might be ready to say something, but she drank again and seemed in a dream.

"What do you teach?"

"High school Spanish."

"How well do you speak it?"

"Quite well, Mr. Question Man, thank you very much."

"Don't take offense, I just have known a few foreign language teachers who couldn't *hablar* their way out of a paper bag."

"Well, let's get this straight. My work is teaching Spanish to unappreciative high school students."

Although her face changed very little, Michael noticed a vein in her neck throbbed and twitched. It captured his imagination and he wondered about the course it took through the map of her body. He liked the body. He was certain he would enjoy exploring the map.

She poked him with an elbow. "Why are you here?"

"You asked me to help."

"Yes, but here you are sitting on my steps. Why?"

"I don't know. It feels like I should be."

"Won't your wife be upset?"

"No."

"I see. Is there a reason she won't be?"

Her expression told him her questions were serious. He kicked into shrink mode. "I guess I'm not used to answering direct questions from strangers."

She jumped up. "Okay, fine. Get the hell off my porch."

"Hold on a minute."

"I'm serious. Just go and that'll be the end of it."

He struggled up and faced her. "I didn't mean anything by it. I'm a private person."

She pulled a thick strand of hair away from her eyes and tucked it behind her ear. "I just haven't got the time," she said, her voice more soothing. "I just don't have the time to pretend. I was on the verge of something with Mason. Now it's over. I've lost precious time."

"I don't think you can expect something instant."

"Are we talking about two different things? I think we are. I'm not asking for your life, asshole. Don't flatter yourself. I'm just needing a little something to keep me going. I thought you guys were experts on that. I think you might be mistaken about Mason's and my relationship." She poked a finger into his chest. "I am not the least bit interested in reliving my adolescence. Anyone who is wasn't living a teenage life to begin with. Kids suffer."

"Wait!" he said as she turned to enter the house. "I'm pretty new to this. It's not what you think. Most things are secrets to me."

She hesitated and stepped in front of him. She ran a finger under his collar and leaned down to whisper in his ear. "You can't even begin to imagine the kinds of secrets there are out there."

"But I'm a psychologist."

"And you know nothing."

He wanted to defend himself but was afraid she might be right.

"And what I wouldn't tell you could fill an entire psychology text," she said. She grabbed the front of his shirt. "Come on in, let's find a place for Mason's books."

Her house was small and cozy. Michael felt, as he imagined the flowers in the yard felt, well-tended and cared for. A tiny white brick fireplace was the centerpiece of the diminutive living room. In the middle of it, just below the mantel, a sage tile painted with a black heron in the rushes was placed perfectly in a molded square. A large papier-mâché cat curled stiffly in a basket near the hearth. An old rocker and an overstuffed chair whose back was draped with an antique shawl were the only furniture in the room. Michael sat in the chair and played with the shawl's silken fringe.

They spent the afternoon scattering Mason's books around her house. As far as he could tell, there was no real rhyme or reason for the spots she found for them. The DSM-III-R, daunting and heavy, rested next to her bedside lamp. Did she waste her evenings hunting for a personal diagnosis? The Physician's Desk Reference filled with endless descriptions of prescription drugs now occupied a spot among her cookbooks on the little shelf next to the kitchen stove. The others found their own bookshelves; a few ended up stacked on the floor. It was growing dark by the time she pronounced the job done.

She cooked him a simple meal: broccoli, green beans, baby potatoes with a small side of red snapper, all steamed. She was generous with the wine as they ate off white porcelain plates perched on their laps in the living room. He wondered, briefly, what the kids were doing, whether they missed him. He also wished moments like this hadn't disappeared from his life. The wine seeped down into places long impenetrable to its effects.

"I can see why Mason liked you so much," he said.

"He talked about me?"

"No."

"Then how do you know how he felt about me?"

"I'm guessing. I don't see how he couldn't."

"Well, he better not have talked about me."

"Why not? He wasn't connected to anyone. There was no one else's heart to break."

"Because I asked him not to and he promised. What's more important than keeping your word?"

"Well, he kept it with me."

She leaned over and refilled his glass. "Would you be able to keep a promise like that?"

"I do it every day," he told her. "I took an oath of confidentiality."

"I know, but I'm talking about real life. Not some sorry invented situation. I'm asking if someone you barely knew wanted you to hold a secret, would you do it?"

"Yes."

"Even under the scrutiny of say, your wife? Or your kids? If your kids' life depended on it, could you still do it?"

"I wouldn't jeopardize my children."

"So, can we say that your kids are your weakness?"

"We could say that."

She stopped rocking. "Are you lying to me?"

"No. About what?"

"About you. I don't trust psychologists."

"I never lie and I'm always right."

She set her foot to rocking again. "That better be a joke. I can see *lie* and *wrong* written all over your face."

"Are you sure you aren't a shrink? You're so cynical and sarcastic."

"I wasn't always this way. There was a time when I was less cynical and sarcastic." She tried smiling but he could see there was intent behind it that fell short. She watched her foot keep the chair going.

"In answer to your old question," he said, "I don't know what I'm doing here. What happened to Mason bothers me a lot. I need some medicine for it."

"And I'm your medicine?"

"Possibly."

She smiled enigmatically. "I don't think I've ever been that before." She glanced at him and brought her glass up in a toast. "Are we having an IDC?"

"He told you about those, huh?"

"Yes. I think it's a terrific idea."

"It's ironic that we started IDC because of people who died. And now here's Mason newly dead."

"And you're scared."

"I'm sad. Confused. I don't like shocking things."

"Sometimes I do," she said. He could see a hint of some distant agony in her face. She held the glass gently in her lap and he watched the wine roll against the sides. The room grew quiet for a moment.

Finally, she said, "Would you start a fire for me?"

"But it's summer."

"There's some kindling on the utility porch and out back by the tree, there's a stack of Tamarack. Could you please?"

When he came back, she had not moved. The glass still sat in her cupped hands. He found an old newspaper and crumpled it up beneath the grate. He piled slivers of wood in a tent over it. It lit in a whoosh. Delia pulled on a small chain in the brick, opening the draft. In spite of that, wisps of smoke found their way into the room, leaving it with a light campfire smell.

Michael placed two perfect pieces of Tamarack on top of the kindling and the fire crackled and snapped as it penetrated the wood. He brushed off his hands and stood back.

"Thank you." She twisted her chair to the side so that now he saw her profile as she rubbed her hands together and held them flat against the flames. Her face betrayed a greater weariness around the eyes. She took a sip from her wine and set it up on the mantel. He watched her lips move and longed to know what thoughts were going through her head. Abruptly and without regard to Michael standing there, she pulled down the elastic neckline of her blouse and exposed her large and pendent breasts to the heat.

She rubbed them as the flames threw bright and dancing light on the delicate skin. She molded and caressed them. "Don't stare like that," she said without looking. "It's my house and I can do whatever I want."

"I wasn't."

"Liar. You told me you never lie."

He decided quiet was best.

"They get tired," she said. "Tired of resisting gravity. Like the rest of us."

Michael sat down and found his glass, which he held up to his face. The wine sparkled with the fire's reflection. And perhaps from the flush on his cheeks. He watched as she gathered her breasts into the crook of her elbows. She bent her head and murmured soothing, calming phrases while the fire licked them red.

When she raised her head, Michael saw a face filled briefly with bewilderment before it was quickly fired with a fierce challenge. He wanted to reach for her breasts.

But she stopped him with her voice. "I live by a creed that was taught to me by a very wise person. And I will tell it to you this once. If you ever expect to see me again, I will hold you to it."

His hands took on their own animation as they hovered in the air between him and her. He was growing aroused. The fire's heat had finally taken him over. "What is it?"

"Don't open something up you're not prepared to hang around and close."

"I think I know what you mean."

"No, I don't think you do. You're a married man, Michael."

"For the moment I am."

"You have obligations. If you think this has anything to do with sex, you're sadly mistaken. That would be the easy part."

"It'll be all right." He scooted his chair closer, wondered for a moment how she could stand so much heat and then had her breasts in his hands. They were hot to the touch as he stroked the smooth, pliant skin. He closed his eyes and envisioned the two of them together, just stroking each other, finding the delicate parts that their age had not yet found a way to diminish. A strange, nearly mystical sensation overcame him. He was being peeled. "This is amazing," he breathed.

"Shhh."

He opened his eyes to slits and saw that her own were drawn closed. Her head was tipped to one side. He watched her nostrils flare as her lips went on with erotic self-talk. His breath came quicker.

He found the knob of one nipple and rubbed it with the underside of a middle finger.

"Jesus," she said.

He did it again and explored around her large dark areola. He bent in and tried to kiss her, but her head lolled away and he couldn't tell if it was intentional. He tried again, but this time her whole body shied. He began to lower his head to brush the end of a nipple, but her hands caught him.

He thought this was her game, teasing him, denying him. She tilted her head back and he studied her eyes. Her entire history must live there. She took one of his hands and guided it to her right breast, held it flat, slightly away from the areola. She gently moved the tips of his fingers in a circular motion until he kept rubbing even when her hand slipped away. He stroked and watched her. Her tears bubbled up and spilled over the edge. He was so caught up with watching her grief that he almost missed what was happening beneath his fingertips.

There was an odd, misshapen ovoid under her skin.

"What is that?"

"A lump," she said.

He traced it. It was hard but not too hard, and when he put too much pressure on one side, it retreated from his reach. It was the size and shape of a robin's egg. "This doesn't feel right," he said.

"It isn't right." She removed his hand and returned to massaging herself in the searing heat.

Michael sat back. A heavier sweat had broken out on his forehead. "How long have you had that?"

"I don't know for sure. I've been aware of it for a few months."

"You should have it looked at."

"Maybe."

"No, you really should."

"It's probably cancer," she stated.

Michael recoiled and a wave of revulsion rose in him.

Delia didn't miss it. "It's not my fault."

"Aren't you going to do something about it?"

"Is there something that can be done?"

"Of course there is. What about chemotherapy? Radiation? Drugs, other therapies?"

She had not stopped massaging herself. "It hurts in my lymph nodes. I'm not stupid. I know what that means. Please, don't demean me like this." She began to cry again, more softly this time.

"I'm sorry."

"I've had an interesting life," she said, looking away, disconnected.

Michael thought of Eva, who lately had been considering that her life was not so rewarding. What decided whether a life was lived well or not? He watched again as Delia absently stroked at her breasts. But now it was half-hearted pawing. He wanted her to put them away, to do this when she was alone.

And, as though reading his mind, she slid back from the heat and turned her front completely away from him. "Could you do me another favor?" she said. "Could you go to the freezer and bring me one of the ice cube trays there?"

He did as she asked, glad to be away from the oppressive fire. The wood had burned quickly and now only threw up a tongue or two of blue-yellow flame.

Back, he handed her the metal tray. She opened it with a healthy pull and scooped up two of the cubes that rattled to the surface. She gently placed them on her breast, sliding them over the lump.

"My entire life has been lived from one pole to the other," she said. "I get itchy in the middle. It doesn't feel right."

"Does that help?"

"Yes, it does. And it's easier on my body than chemo. With about the same result."

"I've never been much for home remedies," he said. He now felt a stranger to her, to the house.

"What *do* you believe in?"

Nothing came because he tried too hard. Over her head on the mantel, a clock ticked away imperiously. He'd been watching the clock in his office of late. "Time."

"I'll bet you do. How much is it that you make a minute?"

"No," he said, not letting her sarcasm seep in. "I believe in the sense of time. The passage of it. After that, it gets sketchy."

She studied him, paused in the application of the ice before she consumed his thinking with a glorious soliloquy in Spanish. He was immediately swept back to Maria del Carmen's patio in 1969. He could actually smell the eucalyptus tree, hear the dogs bark behind their iron gates. She became gorgeous again, her hands the purveyors of soothing goodness as they glided across her skin. She smiled at him.

"I love that," he said.

"There's nothing like it. There's nothing like talking to someone, even if it's yourself, in another language. It wakes up the corners of your mind and I believe in using as much of your brain as you can."

He couldn't control his telling of the story of Spain and the old woman.

"I feel such an affinity with that woman," she said when he'd finished.

"Why?"

"Because she's more than you think."

"And you as well? Are you more than I think?"

"I know I am. But her... How would a village woman have a perfect command of English? Where would she learn it?"

"A lot of Europeans can speak it."

"A lot of educated Europeans can. This was not an educated woman. She was a goatherd." Delia stashed away her breasts and drew her bare feet up under her, nearly spilling herself with the excitement. "She learned it from someone." Her eyes danced again. "She knew your uncle! He was still alive!"

"I don't think so. He took a bullet and died," Michael explained again. "He was dead on the scene."

"Imagine if he wasn't, though. It's a possible explanation for this woman's knowledge."

He had to admit it was something he'd thought about before. It had kept him up late on more than one occasion.

"Haven't you been interested all these years? Haven't you tried to figure it out?"

"Well, yes," he said. "I keep coming back to it. I have his letters."

"What letters?"

"He wrote home a few times. They stopped at one point. When he got to that town, La Jolla."

"So you think because they stopped, he was killed."

"That's been what the family's always believed. Seems reasonable since we've never heard from him since. Of course, there was always hope."

She was quiet for a moment and Michael's mind returned to reading the letter on the IDC night.

"He told me I should go back to Spain," he said. "Mason said I should before it's too late."

"He usually knew what he was talking about. Will you go back?"

"I'm thinking about it. Could be the right time."

"Hmm... Did you understand what I said a few seconds ago?"

"When you were speaking Spanish? No."

"So, it's happened to you again."

"What has?"

"I just told you a secret I've kept for most of my adult life."

"Like Carmen did."

"I suppose so. The point is, are you going to go on missing out on living because you don't understand a language? Because you feel afraid?"

"I have a family to think of." He considered this, leaned his head back and dozed.

She woke him later in the night. "Come on, it's time to go."

Michael blinked at her. He stretched his leg and kicked over the empty wine bottle. He felt a strange combination of grit and heartburn roiling at the back of his throat. "But I want to stay."

She was standing before him in that same blouse and blue jeans. There was no evidence of tears, of Benedict Arnold breasts. She was alive and healthy again. "No, you have to go," she insisted. "Your time's up."

"We just ate."

"That was hours ago. Come on." She pulled him from the chair with surprising strength. Michael was only partly awake when he stood up, an erection strained at his pants. She glanced down and hesitated.

"I can't help it," he said.

"I'm not your priest or your mother, for Christ's sake. You can get hard if you want. I just want you gone." At the door, she kissed him on the cheek and gently pushed him out onto the porch. He stood in the dark quiet, hands in his pockets, fingering the tight surface of his penis, wondering how all this began.

§

Michael drove off and Delia came out on the porch to sit in the dark. Her heart was booming; she could hear it thump in her ears.

She was antsy, itchy-hot. She rubbed her thighs with flat palms, then brought her hands to her cheeks. A light flicked on in the building next to her yard. Through the gauzy curtains she saw a young woman she recognized from the street. They waved to each other occasionally. A man carrying a bottle followed the woman into the kitchen. He set the bottle on the table and grabbed the woman around the waist. They stumbled out of sight. A dog barked from another apartment.

The stars were diminished now by the neighbor's light, by Delia's own fear. She was tired of this, the not knowing, the waking up with the word **RUN** blazed across the backs of her eyes.

She had bad habits, she knew. But she never set out to learn them, they were the result of doing the opposite of what others wanted from her, a negative habit, born of turning her back on expectation. She lied with ease, as she just did with Michael about the lump on her breast. A benign cyst she'd had for years. No chemo needed, no radiation. She liked the look on men's faces when she told them that particular lie. It amused her that at first they didn't know what to say, then they couldn't stop chattering.

Lying wasn't the most of it. She was a scar on her family's reputation. Her father, her mother, various priests all had worthy intentions to change her, however limited in scope. Her parents had integrity of a sort. If integrity was defined by sticking to one's guns, they had it in spades. "You've got to believe in something," was what Dad once told her. That was the memorialized version. It was actually more in the tone of, "You can't fucking go off half-cocked like that with any longhair who says you're pretty. You've got to goddamn believe in something and that goddamn thing is yourself."

"Well, goddamn," she whispered into the night and half-giggled. She had a picture of him, of the two of them, Mom and Dad, but lost it with the last move. She lost her cat too when it scratched its way out of the cage. She missed the cat right away. In her paranoia, she wondered if she could be traced through a calico.

And that would be the worst thing, being found out at this late date. When most of the world didn't care anymore. There was a time when she felt the presence of everyone at her side, urging her on. "Get out of there, Delia," they might say. "Vamoose. What you did wasn't so bad. That guard deserved it. He was a pig. Like all the other pigs in the world who let their badges rule their thinking."

Delia could picture herself back on the road, fifteen again, full of energy fueled by hate. She reserved most of her ill feelings for her mother, who was forever unable to produce a true feeling of her own. She almost preferred her father, who never let the sun set without the whole world knowing exactly what he thought, even if it was done through his longtime companion and interpreter, her mother.

Thinking of all this, instantly, she was in a car, her bare feet perched above the glove box, the radio blaring out the open windows, something by the Byrds. "I'm okay," she said to herself. "I'm okay."

The driver, a man she didn't know, had to be at least ten years older than she was, and he bought it when she lied about her age. He drove bare-chested in cut-off jeans, his big knobby feet housed in a pair of green flip-flops. He pulled at the curly tendrils of a red-brown beard, smoked an unending number of roll-your-owns, an art that Delia was now becoming an expert at.

This was her third long-distance ride and the best one so far. The first one ended badly when the family she was hitchhiking with stopped for a rest break on the freeway and when she came back out, there wasn't a sign of their car. The second was a bust within the first few minutes. Old guy with a belly and questions about her tits. When she figured out her anxiety had a lot to do with Impala man, she took the first opportunity when the car slowed down to jump out and roll along the grass and into the ditch.

"See there," she said out loud. "I can take care of myself."

Now, Buzz. At least it's what he called himself. "Just Buzz."

She had no money, except for the few bills her mother handed over before she left the hospital. It didn't bother him, though. They both ate like birds and were comfortable sleeping in the car; he in front, Delia in back. Her wounds were healing nicely, thank you very much, and Buzz had no questions about where they came from.

But when he stopped at a hardware store and came back out with a ski mask and duct tape, it started up Delia's anxiety engine again, until he told her what they were going to do.

"Do you have a gun?" he said. "Because I don't and we're going to need to fix something up that at least looks like we have a weapon."

"Why do we need a weapon?"

"You'll find out."

She thought of her father and how fun it might be to pull even a fake weapon on him. To see his fear could be a cure for her anger. "I can't wait," she said.

"Stick with me, babe. You'll learn a lot."

And she did gain knowledge from him, plus a sense of being impermeable to any pushback.

"You've just got to take on the idea the fucking rules don't apply to you," Buzz said. "And they really don't have to. Who makes up those rules in the first place?"

"God?"

"Right."

Sometimes he drove completely naked, his body a sinewy punctuation mark in the seat, and it didn't take long until she had mastered the art of removing every stitch of clothing within seconds, a feat that attracted a lot of attention at stoplights and gas stations. How many times did she lie in wait until a family in a station wagon drew up next to them and she plastered her breasts up against the glass and flicked her tongue around her lips?

They shoplifted. They stole from empty cars and semis at rest areas. While he stood with a fake gun made out of duct tape pushed into a man's back at a convenience mart, he would say something like, "Grab some of those Payday bars, Bonnie." And she would say back, "Sure thing, Clyde."

Her first stint in jail happened somewhere in Kansas when she lifted two bottles of Boone's Farm and some Fritos from a SuperValu. The town cop picked them up not a hundred yards past the city limits. But instead of being scared, Delia lapped it up. Gave the cop so much lip at the jail he stuffed plugs in his ears and tried to read the local paper.

"Got yourself a right filthy mouth," he told her.

"You wish," she said.

When they were finally let go after paying a fine, they celebrated their release by driving north toward the Dakotas and an adventure Buzz was circumspect about. On the way, when she turned sixteen, the two began a sexual life Delia would always remember. Buzz's style was what she would later recall as gentle but firm persuasion. He was the first man to teach her about the nutritional benefits of semen; the first man to show her what could happen with a long tongue and a raspy beard. Best of all, he was playful enough to waylay her fears about what had happened with the man in the Impala.

"What is this feeling?" she asked him. "This shit-kicking, wonderful, motherfucking feeling?"

Buzz didn't hesitate. "I call it mystical ecstasy."

"Mystical ecstasy. How orgasmic."

"Never forget it, babe. It'll come in handy more than once in your life."

They made it to Sturgis where they met up with three other people, two on Harleys, the other a brooding figure in their back seat as they headed toward Minneapolis. He told her right out his name was Nigel, and if she ever heard him called a different name it would be in her best interest to forget it. She didn't know what it was yet, but there was a plan coming together. She could feel it. And the feeling was invigorating. When she asked Buzz about it, all he said was, "It's the fucking feds."

It unfolded on a sheet of butcher paper in a cramped hotel room in Rochester, Minnesota. She stood on the fringe, peeking over the shoulders of the others. A swaying light hung overhead.

"You here," Nigel said, marking an X on the carefully drawn square that represented the inside of the bank. "You there. You and you and you, here, here and here."

Delia was anxious for her X to be in the thick of it, but she was outside the bank and around the corner. Just a boxlike little drawing. "You," Nigel said. "Here." He tapped the pencil on the box. "Keep the motor running. Be ready for us."

"Got it," she said. "Running. Ready."

Nigel glanced at her and then over to Buzz. "Is this chick even old enough to drive?"

"Clean and simple is what we're looking for," one of the Harley guys said. "Right, Nige?"

He took a while to answer, his pencil tapping on the butcher paper. "Right," he finally said.

Clean it wasn't. Simple? Not by a long shot.

The explosion rocked the van. Delia jumped out as smoke billowed from the gaping hole on the ground floor of the bank. Two individuals staggered out, faces blackened, eyes turned up to the sun. Delia nearly panicked. She didn't expect an explosion. Sure, she knew about Nigel and his affinity for sparks and fire, but never once did she hear that a bomb was going to be a part of the job.

"What?" she said out loud.

The two people now stumbled toward Delia and the van; the two Harley guys. Buzz hurried after them, obviously not as hurt.

"Get in!" he shouted. "Now!"

And as expediently as they could, the Harley guys threw themselves into the back seat. Delia tried to crawl back in, but Buzz yanked her out and took over the wheel. She barely made it into the passenger seat before he sped away.

Sirens wailed all around them as he slalomed in and out of traffic. "Jesus Christ," he shouted, pounding on the dash. "Jesus fucking Christ!"

"What happened?" Delia screamed. "Where's Nigel?"

"Fucking shut up. We've got to get out of here."

One of the Harley guys leaned over to the other and picked something off his shoulder. "You got a piece of Nige on you," he said.

But the other one shook his head. "That ain't him. It's the fucking cop."

Where was Buzz now, she wondered? She'd never forget their dash to the hotel room, the cleaning out of closets and every last physical trace of them. She stole a spray bottle of Lysol off one of the maids' carts and purged the room of any hint of their fingerprints.

You make it like you never existed, Buzz had said. It's the only way you get away with it. Change your name, change your history. She knew Nigel was dead by his own hand; bomb makers needed to pay close attention. She never heard from the Harley guys again. She missed the company of them all, she thought, but was sure she also missed the Delia she used to be. Passionate Delia. Funny Delia. The Delia who made up new identities using the social security names and numbers of actual dead children from hospital documents Buzz made up for her. Never-quitting Delia. Bulletproof Delia. Guiltless Delia, for sure.

She missed it all, was tired of it all. The only thing she wanted now was to find the goddamn mystical ecstasy.

And she had run, with the rest of the young world at her side. She found safe houses, culverts, barns, the back seats of cars. She was a champion at that game.

"I am a winner," she recalled saying when she managed to escape the dark government vehicles patrolling some distant neighborhood she thought she could get lost in. "They'll never catch me." The refrain of her life. She believed she could forever hide in plain sight. But they always sniffed close, or at least her fears told her so. Then she would run again. Because they never gave up.

She pondered that she could turn herself in and finally face the consequences. So many years had passed, they might go lenient on her. Who would remember such a young, rebellious troublemaker when the world was so staid and predictable now, when people in America cared less about how they were getting screwed than about who they were going to screw? She even thought prison could be a relaxing place. She would leave people alone and they would give her peace and who knew, maybe she could actually get out in time to live her golden years as a free woman. It was a seductive thought.

But no. You couldn't be party to the killing of a cop and expect to get off lightly. That reality hadn't changed over the years, even if it was accidental. You took a policeman's life, you took the life of all policemen. Law enforcement was like an elephant with its memories.

Now in her forties, she wasn't as fleet of foot as she once was, but she was still as cagey as she ever was, and that was what had kept her out of the hands of the FBI. She remembered a maxim told her by one of the older men whose loose gang she was briefly a part of.

"Don't let the gray in my beard fool you," he had said. "Old age and treachery will always overcome youth and skill."

And now, sitting on her porch, she could tell already it was going to be an awful night. She pressed the little button on the side of her watch and the dial lit up. Midnight. The lamp blinked out in the apartment next door. The night dropped further down around her as the starlight swelled. She bit at the backs of her hands, which she curled in fists at her lips. She heard her own moaning voice as she rocked her body on the top step.

"Get it out," she told herself.

But it wasn't the FBI or the wanted posters that had her reeling. It was the other thing. It was the man who destroyed her confidence, her security, who still lived in her blood that drove her on nights like this.

She sneaked back into the house and changed into a short blue dress, skipped her underwear. She pulled the keys out of her pants pocket, and navigated the dark sidewalk to her car. She couldn't help it. She told herself it wasn't her fault.

She grabbed the old cotton purse, took a brief look in the rearview and unfolded herself from the car. She heard the steady boom-boom of the music drifting through the cinder block walls. There were cars everywhere; voices drifted from around her.

Yelling blasted from inside. At the door, she sucked in a deep breath and slipped in.

She felt every eye in the place on her. She stood for a moment, adjusted to the dim smoky light and strode quickly to the bar. She ordered a schooner, took a healthy draw from it and smiled when the jukebox picked up a country tune. Glancing down the brass-plated counter, she caught the eye of one young man who was talking earnestly to his date and immediately crossed him off. Not nearly her type. After another gulp of beer, she glanced once around the big dark room. She almost missed him and would have if he hadn't stretched his long arms high over his head.

She was so focused at times like this. Her eyes were not just shy of forty-five and in need of glasses. She could see him plainly. Mayhem bred in those deep dark orbs. A few days of stubble rode his cheeks. He had a big face, wide, square-jawed, and it might look striking on a man with some dignity. But this man was alone for a reason. He bled mean. She was instantly drawn to him.

She took another long pull from the schooner and then set it down while her tongue flicked out and cleaned the foam from her lip. Absently, she toyed with one of her breasts. The music coursed through her. She glanced at the table. He was staring at her, but was not getting up, not coming over. She grabbed the schooner and picked her way over to him. A few feet away, he scraped a chair out and she sat down.

Flipping the hair back from her face, she said, "I'm Diane."

He leaned across the table. His blunt thick finger rubbed off the new foam on her lip. "So, Diane, you buying?" He held up a shot glass and cocked his head.

She quickly fished for her wallet. She opened it to a compartment stuffed with bills.

"Nice. I want a double." He pushed over the glass and raised his hands over his head again, leaned back on two legs of his chair.

She sniffed the glass. "Scotch?"

"Ah, you're breaking my heart. Bourbon. JB."

She left and was quickly back holding a drink in each hand. She set them on the table. He'd moved the chair closer and now balanced one of his boots on a rung. She had to step over his leg to sit down. She studied him as he threw back one of the shots. About fifteen years younger than her, his features played at handsome, but were coarse. Probably the youngest in his family, or an only child. He was in solid shape, had won a few fights through sheer strength of will. A small scar near his eye stood out like victory.

"What are you looking at?" he said, balancing the other shot in his hand.

"You."

"You like?"

"I could."

This time he sipped from the drink and set it back down. "I got to be at work at seven."

"And that means what?"

"I don't have time for bullshit." He brushed a hand down the front of his jeans and she could see him in there, backing up his words.

"Yeah, well, I've got to be up early too." She finished her schooner and slammed it hard on the table.

He smiled. "I'll get a six-pack to go." Standing, he shook out one pant leg as he drained the glass. "You wait for me over by the door."

She muscled her way through the crowd and soon walked with him across the lot. He held her tight against him, his hand a claw. She tripped once on his shoes and he propped her up with his hip.

"What you driving?" he asked.

"Over there. The V-Dub."

"Uh-huh. Well, it's not going to work."

"We should meet somewhere. Your place?"

One side of his mouth shot up in a grimace. "Come on, baby, you think I can wait?"

He guided her over to the end of the lot, set down the six-pack and then planted her against the side of a '78 Ford pickup. He pressed hard against her, and she felt pressure from both sides. He ground his hips.

She captured his full lower lip with her teeth and sucked it in. He pulled it back and eyed her with a smile. With one hand, he laid a finger at her mouth. He ran it across her teeth, then pushed in. She snapped at his finger and he laughed.

He plowed deep into his pocket and pulled out keys, unlocked the pickup and crawled in. He leaned over and pulled her up to the seat. "Come on now." he said. When she was in, he fell back against the other door. His knees opened and she crawled between them. She hovered there while he unbuttoned his pants, pulled himself out. "You ready?"

In an instant her lips were on his and he gathered her hair in a knot. She bit, not hard, but he yelped, and his knees closed tight on her. He had sliced open the book of her life and the story hemorrhaged out into the cab. She caught her breath, remembered the smell of it all.

"Come on now," he hissed once more. "Come on." His voice was gruffer and she felt it ignite her own special desire. He tried to roll her over but she fought him. One leg slipped to the floor and she thought she might crouch there, but he held on with his talon fingers. He yanked her, and she feared her shoulder might pop. Now he had her back on the seat. He reached down under her dress and started poking at her with those blunt fingers.

"Ready?" he yelled. He jabbed and jammed, but she wouldn't give in, not now, not yet.

Sweat dripped from his face onto hers. Her tongue came out and licked at it. Her body was bouncing now, the pain from his fingers channeled through her. She saw the heady wash of anger and desire color his face. He peered down at her. She made a red, sticky smile with her lips.

He slipped down the front of her, ripped her dress, in another jolt of lust. She spread her legs. He slid in rough and bellowed like a bull. His stubble ground into her face, his big arms pinned her down and pressed hard and fast against her.

His body pulsed as he climaxed in large damaging waves. He flexed hard and she held him tight till he shuddered to a stop.

He lay there, his breath husky and harsh against her ear. It sent yet another current buzzing through her and she shivered.

He slipped from her. Backing out of the pickup, he stood. "Diane," he growled, as he grabbed at her legs and pulled her out, head bashing against the running board, propelling her into a starry twilight. The tiny pebbles and pieces of loose asphalt cut into her face.

She heard clearly as he buttoned up his pants and then tromped to the other side of the truck. He got in and she waited for the motor to roar to life. But in a moment, he was back out and coming around to her side. He leaned down, and she thought he might ruin it by kissing her. But he gathered in the six-pack and hurried back to the cab. He started the truck. She reasoned that this could be the weapon to kill her. But he was parked sideways and simply pulled away from her. She felt the tire whisper by her face.

Ah, the afterglow, she thought. She lay there a moment and then decided she should think about getting herself together. Tomorrow was another day designed specifically for that.

She sat up and grasped her knees. A dusty corner of her consciousness heard country music seeping out of the bar. She should stop this. This carving away of her self-worth. But what did it matter? She knew why she did it. Any dime store shrink could come up with the answer in minutes. It was inevitable and necessary. It was her fate. The positive thing was that now, unlike the embryonic moment of this particular quirk, she was the one who always walked into it, always decided who got to chop her into pathetic pieces.

She tried to stand, failed once but managed to push herself up. She still smelled the pickup's exhaust. It was pure luck when you foundamanwho gave you what you need. "*Gracias*," she sighed.

Chapter Seven
Michael, Robert and Delia, Spokane, 1989

Michael had an urge to see Delia the next morning but resisted it. Too much on his plate. A friend to grieve, self-esteem to nurture. The usual normal. No space for anything less calibrated. He rolled over on his bed, thrusting out one leg, bathing it in the cooler air. But of course he thought of her again. Those uncanny breasts. If he squeezed his eyes closed enough, he could forget about the tumor lying in there to dissuade his erection.

He kicked the sheet off, considering. He snatched the phone from the end table and checked for messages. None from Eva. None at all.

§

He arrived at work to an almost empty lot. The Karmann Ghia was there, though. Michael wondered if it wouldn't be better for everyone to get back to work to dull the shock of it all.

He went immediately to Mason's office and stood in the doorway. Delia wore the same outfit she had on the day before. Her back was to him and he stayed quiet a while, drinking her in.

She startled when she saw him, dropped a manila folder. "Jesus. Sorry, the door was unlocked so I came in. Nobody was here except for that guy down the hall."

"My colleague."

"Yes. Friendly sort, isn't he?"

"In a supra-biblical sense," Michael said.

"I shouldn't have to come back after today," she said. "He had a lot of work stuff at his house. This here is the last of it."

"Take your time," Michael said. He fumbled a little. "About last night."

"Yes. I was meaning to mention it."

"I don't know what came over me."

She rose on her tiptoes, reaching for a high shelf. "What you were talking about? Your uncle and all? It made me think." She managed to tap a notebook close to the edge and it fell into her hands. She turned and pulled her hair back and he noticed the bruising near her temple. "You do know that they were lovers, don't you?"

"My uncle and Maria del Carmen?"

"I mean it's obvious, isn't it? How would she know English so well? You said she was a villager just like everybody else. What made her so special that she had a grasp of a foreign language while Franco was in power?"

"Are you saying she learned it from him?"

She dropped the notebook into a box. "And they say you can't put two and two together."

Pertinent words milled around on Michael's tongue but did not take their proper turns. "Alive? Uncle? Goats? She did?"

"Just a thought," she said, turning back to her work.

"I love this," Michael blurted out. "Are you hungry?"

"Not now. But I'll tell you what. If you help me finish up here, I'll have lunch with you."

"Deal," Michael said. He wondered if he might follow this woman to the ends of the earth.

Now he was all clumsy feet and too many hands. Couldn't remember the name of a single restaurant in town. She suggested they pick up some fast food and go to a park, and he was giddier than a smitten teenager on a first date.

He started walking with her, remembered something and hopped back to the car. He found the letters in the glovebox.

They took their Subway fare and found an empty bench by the river in among the cottonwoods and berry vines. "Perfect," she said. "And just to be clear for the hundredth time, this is not a relationship." She took a healthy bite of her sandwich.

"I heard you," he said.

She swallowed and was about to take another bite but lay down the sandwich instead. "You're married. You've just lost a close friend so you're vulnerable, and here you are buying me lunch, trying to get a shot at my tits again."

"I'm not married," he said. He explained what had been going on and as he did, he felt, for the first time, the loss of Eva as a potential freedom.

She picked up her sandwich again. In front of them, the river flowed torpidly. Dragonflies kissed the top of the water. Bees hummed. Behind them, running shoes slapped against the asphalt, grew closer and then faded. And tears formed in Michael Virtue's eyes, ran sleek against his cheeks.

But instead of softening, Delia's face steeled up; the slightly open window closed.

"What happened to you?" he said, pointing to her temple.

"I do not move well when I've been drinking."

He nodded, took an aimless swipe at his cheek and started eating his sandwich. What was he doing? Was he so transparent that he couldn't carry on a simple conversation without coming across as a simpering fool? Willing himself strength, he said, "Your idea earlier about my uncle... I really think it could be true."

"There's an explanation for everything."

"But if he was still alive, that means he would have been there for over thirty years. Wouldn't somebody have known about him?"

"Unless he was in hiding," she said.

"I don't think it's possible for someone to hide for thirty years. He would stick out like a sore thumb."

"You've never heard of a *Topo*?"

"A what?"

"They called them moles. There were lots of people who hid out from Franco during the war. Just the other day I read where a guy came out long after Franco died. He was hidden for more than thirty years. Your uncle could have been a mole."

Michael started tabulating years in his head. He supposed it was possible his uncle could have survived and would have been, what, in his fifties, when Michael met up with the woman in Spain in '69. "Say hello to Mr. Roosevelt," he said.

"What was that?"

"Before I left, the woman said that to me."

"Makes sense." She wolfed down the last of her sandwich and crumpled up the paper. "Roosevelt was president in the Thirties."

"What's the secret you told me in Spanish last night? I mean, I don't want to make the same mistake twice, do I?"

"Not in a million years would I tell you."

"I don't have a million years."

"When a million is up, look for me. I'll tell you then." She stood.

"Where you going?" Most of his sandwich was still in the wrapper.

"You said lunch."

"But we just got here. Can't we just relax a minute?"

She frowned and sat back down, staring out at the water. Across it, the newer brick buildings of the university sprouted from the ground.

Michael dug into his pocket and pulled out the letters. He spread them out. "What you said before, about the Moles. Maybe it's true." He held one of the letters up. "My uncle wrote this. It's the last one the family ever got. What do you think?"

February 13, 1937, La Jolla
Dear Mom and Dad,

If the end were to come for you, what would you say? What would you do? Where would you go? Is there an answer to this question? It's been less than a month since I left my cozy bed in Spokane and it's not so cozy in my life anymore. I've been to hell and back and more than once. Please help me if you can. You must be wondering where I am and what I'm doing. I should have mailed the letters when I could. From now on, if I get out of this alive, I will be better at communicating. I shot a man and he died. Trouble is, he shot me too, and, pardon the expression,

Mom, but it hurts like hell. It's on my left side and I can't find a bullet in there, so it must have gone all the way through. They say that's good, but you couldn't tell it by me. He was some kind of officer, for the so-called enemy judging by his uniform. My dear parents, I have gotten myself into a bit of a pickle, but for now, it looks like I might be safe. When I get the chance, I'll mail these to you. Do they have medicine for gunshot wounds here? I wonder.

Help me, please.
Your loving son,
Robert

Delia brought the letter down to her lap, looked up to the sky. "It's all there, just like I said." She handed the letter back to him. "Let me see the others."

They traded and she quickly started reading. Once in a while, she murmured a phrase. "The train trip was scary in the snow. The Atlantic crossing was horrible. Kissed the soil of France when he got off the ship." When she was finished, she handed them back and stood again.

"You're leaving?" he said.

"I don't know how I can be more clear than I have been. There's nothing here, Michael. Nothing. No chance."

"It's just that Mason was my best friend and I knew nothing about you. To me that means you just came on the scene, or you and he were damn excellent at hiding."

"Do you think you can find a better way to trivialize the relationship I had with your so-called best friend than calling it a cat and mouse game?"

"What are you so angry about?"

She threw the Subway wrapping at him and it bounced off his forehead before he had a chance to flinch. "You're not my therapist," she said. "This is so typical. Just another man who can't take no for an answer. Wow, how unique."

He figured it was the suddenness of Mason's death that was creating this roller coaster ride and for that he forgave her.

She stared at him and he could feel something razor-like cutting at him as she spoke. "I always leave, Michael. I always know I'm going to leave. I always have to leave."

"So, if Mason hadn't died, you would have left him?"

"You don't understand. I don't leave specific people. I just leave. Why is that so hard to fathom?"

"But you're a teacher. How can you just pick up and go?"

She examined him for a moment. "I am absolutely convinced you were born in some other century. Are you for real with this naïve game you try to play?"

"I'm beginning to think what you don't know about people is a lot..."

"I don't *care* about people. They're fucked up. They're not worth putting any time into. Even the reasonable ones, sooner or later, will let you down. Me included. Remember this: I will disappoint you one day. Speaking of which." She came toward the bench. "Thanks and all for everything and have a nice life."

He tried to grab her but missed.

Delia noticed and squatted down. "Come on, man. Give me a break. Can't you just let me go?"

"I had the best time last night, and it didn't have a lot to do with your breasts. I felt something and it's why I'm this way now. It's been a long time since I felt something. And what I'd like to know is how do you stay alive for your whole life without feeling anything?"

She rose up again. "Well, now you're talking. I don't know how to answer that. I guess you have to have something to look forward to, some change."

He glanced at the bruise. "You have a good life, too."

She touched him on the shoulder. "You don't know me and you don't want to."

"Another place, another time?"

"No. It's never that. It's always the same place. The same time." She started to walk away, turned. "Those letters. They're a whole life. Get after it."

§

Delia once again sat on her front steps, a glass of red wine in her hand. Night fell a half hour before, but there remained a faint glow on the horizon. She had decided to leave. Three years was long enough. Sure, the world was falling apart in general, but the powers that be always seemed to have a little extra left over to hunt down the inconsequential ones. Like Delia.

The tiff with Michael bothered her. It made her think of younger times, even younger than the trip with Buzz.

After graduation from middle school, on one of her nights roaming the streets, a guy in a red Impala began to follow her. She was not afraid, had never been one to run and hide. She turned once, then a second time to get a look at whoever it was. After two blocks, the car sped ahead and pulled over to the curb. A man leaned across the seat and rolled down the passenger window. When she got close, he said: "Want a ride?"

"No," she said without looking.

"Why not?"

"Beat it." But she stopped right there. She'd heard of these moments. Mere asides to a normally-lived life, but important nonetheless. "Where would we go?" she said.

"Wherever you like."

"Are you a sex fiend?"

"Do I look like a sex fiend?"

She got a good look at him and was surprised to see he was older than most of the males who ogled her. Not that handsome, but not plain either. He wore a white, pocketed t-shirt and his hair was sheared in a buzz cut.

She walked over to the car and stood on the parking strip. Her heart picked up its beat. The car shined under the streetlamp. It was spotless on the inside, an exquisite red and white tuck and roll. The fragrance of cologne drifted up to her, something like driftwood at the ocean.

"I'm not going to hurt you." He leaned even further and opened the door, shoving it wider with a gentle push.

Now the inside of the car lit up and Delia could hear acoustic guitar music, a love ballad maybe. "All right then." Once she made up her mind, she wasted no time sliding in and closing the door.

He stared at her, smiling. "I'm glad you decided to come along."

She brushed at the bucket seat, soft and cushiony. "I'm trying to get my dad to buy one of these."

He put the car in gear and pulled slowly from the curb.

"He's pretty ancient though. He won't listen."

"Yeah, I got an old man like that." From the dash, he snatched up a pack of cigarettes. "You want one?" He shook it until a few of them poked out.

She took one but held it in her lap. It felt awkward. A light flickered and she glanced over to see a Zippo flame waiting for her. She held out the cigarette and he laughed, taking it from her. He lit it, sucked in a deep breath and then handed it back. "My dad will kill me," she said.

"Pretend you're facing a firing squad. One smoke before you die."

But she still just held it in her hand. "So where are we going?"

"We could drive around if you want. You got something better to do?"

She shivered and tried bringing the cigarette to her lips, just left it there.

"You can roll up that window if you want."

"It's okay." Resting her elbow on the frame, she wished she had dressed for fun instead of for exercise. She finally inhaled the smoke and held it as it fought to get out, a grueling tickle finally forcing her to cough.

"Yeah, I thought so," he said.

"This is nasty."

He swiped it from her. "Now you know. Experience is the best teacher."

She leaned back in the seat and closed her eyes. Oh, if her father could see her now. She'd be in a whole mess of trouble. But who cared? Served him right for keeping her prisoner.

"You got a boyfriend?"

"Me? Ha. What a laugh."

"Really? Why not? Pretty little woman like you. I'd think all the boys would be out for you. I know I would."

"It's not how it works," she said. "And besides, I'm very particular."

"So, I must have passed your test, beings you're here in the car with me."

"Well, yeah. So far you have." She hoped her thrill was not showing. She didn't want to give the impression she was new to this. And to be honest, she wasn't new to it, at least in her fantasies she wasn't. "Where are we going?" she said again.

"You thirsty?"

"What do you mean?"

"I mean, are you thirsty?"

"Kind of."

"All right then." By now they were on the outskirts of town and he pulled over to the side of the road. He got out and Delia watched him go to the trunk and unlatch it. He rummaged around and came back with a paper sack. "Here you go."

When she took it, bottles clinked together. She peered down inside. "Is this beer?"

"Sure thing. Is that a problem?"

"No, course not."

He pulled back on the road. "We're going to have to find a spot to drink it, though," he said. "If it's all right with you."

"The cemetery," she said. "We could go there."

"All right," he said, and sped up.

Now on the porch, she stopped herself and took a drink of wine. Get rid of that thought for a while. Instead, how about she was mid-life and still unconnected. How much longer can I keep it up, she wondered. Especially with guys like Michael lurking around. They always lurked around. Too many close calls in the last twenty years; the kind only a younger woman could squeeze herself out of. And she felt them closing in again. After so many years, you developed a special sense about it. She smiled. Some might call it paranoia.

But where could she go? Where had others gone? Some Spanish-speaking country would be best. The Philippines? Why did the government have such a long memory?

Mason was gone. In a way, he had kept her alive and aware. And Michael was no Mason to keep her focused. Things were changing again. She smelled it in the air, sensed it in her bones, heard it in every backfire. When there were visitors in her classroom, she wondered who would show up outside the door and would he be plainclothes or in uniform. They were still looking, there was no question about that. And she was still hiding. The ones who had been caught, well, they were careless. Delia would stay on point and fight it out till they quit looking.

Chapter Eight
Robert, France, 1937

The first thing Robert Martin did was push past the other passengers on the gangplank, jump to the ground and kiss the stable soil of Le Havre, France. He'd never been there, never thought of it as a place he might visit, but he instantly fell in love with the country after the long and perilous ride on a very unstable ocean liner.

He was still kissing France when his friend, Max, hoisted him up by the collar and pulled him from the rest of the milling volunteers.

"You're going to get some disease," Max said. "Don't act crazy."

"I'm not crazy," said Robert. He pulled out the waistband of his trousers. "I bet I lost ten pounds on that boat. I didn't think a fellow could puke that much."

Max took off his round wire glasses and rubbed them on his shirt. "I thought the Spaniards would be here to meet us. I don't see anybody." He refit the glasses on his wide nose. "You see anybody official-looking, Bob?"

Robert glanced around. A group of men stood hunched over cigarettes, chatting in a language Robert had never heard. He soaked up the surreal nature, not sure he was comfortable with it. But Max strode over, insinuated himself in among those towering men and soon they all were stepping back, using their hands to communicate.

Robert crept up and heard Max say, "We've got to elect a leader or we're getting nowhere." And, like a small ocean wave, the group moved in, fell back, moved in again and back as they pounded out the politics of their dilemma.

Eventually, one of the big-faced men was chosen. He held up his hands and his thick fingers called for quiet. "I am Enos," he said. "We are all here for the same cause. We are all here to fight for freedom."

Some of the other men, who spoke the same language, clapped, but those who didn't, understood the meaning, nonetheless. Robert looked back at the ship. For an instant, seasickness be damned, he wanted to jump back on it and sail home.

§

Robert thought this: Never ride in the back of an unheated and poorly ventilated lorry in the middle of winter as a means to get to Paris. His legs started cramping not five miles out of Le Havre, and progressively grew worse. His attempts to stretch them out were met with angry resistance.

He closed his eyes and dreamed of Spokane, formulated what his next letter to his parents would say. He mailed the ones he'd written onboard, uncertain that the Frenchman wearing the official postman garb would follow through. Robert wondered how long his dollars would last and checked the coins through the fabric of his pants. He made a vow to keep his family informed every step of the way.

Eventually he drifted off into a fitful sleep. Pangs of hunger and the jostling of the truck lost their power to wake him. When he finally did rouse again, it was because of the cacophony tuning up outside.

A gendarme unsnapped the back of the truck and secured the canvas to the side. He spoke a rapid French: "Come on now, you must get out. Scramble. You're blocking traffic."

Robert could barely move, but as each future soldier exited from the truck, he could finally push out his legs. He heard them snap and pop back into place and he gingerly stepped down from the lorry into an even more different world.

The group moved inside of what looked to be a huge public market. Heads of pigs glared at Robert, flocks of tiny dead birds hung from rafters. The place smelled like drying blood; the language flew through his brain. He kept track of Max directly ahead of him as he glanced at shopping women and their children. His group congregated behind a wood partition where animal parts lay discarded, crowded by flies.

Finally, what looked to be someone in charge was speaking loudly with Enos, who nodded enthusiastically. Robert bumped shoulders with Max and Max bumped him back, smiling. "This is it, buddy," Max said. He removed his glasses, rubbed at his face. A new growth of beard pushed through his skin.

"Do you understand any of this?" Robert said.

"A little. I heard the word hotel. Maybe we'll get a bath."

They were led out the back of the market by yet another man, this one dressed more simply. His hat sported two holes and Robert wondered if they were from bullets. The man spoke Spanish and Max hurried to catch up so he could hear better.

"What's he saying?" said Robert.

"You should have listened closer in Spanish class," Max said. He grabbed Robert's arm and pulled them along faster.

The group ended up at an old hotel whose façade had seen better days. The window trim could use a coat of paint.

The Spanish man rushed the front desk and spoke earnestly. "These are the men we talked about earlier. They are spending only one night. I pray you have the space for them." Max whispered all of this as Robert listened intently.

They were assigned three to a room, but it was simple to trade with others who were friends, and so Max and Robert found themselves sleeping in one wider bed while one of the other Americans was consigned to a cot in the corner. The facilities were meager. One bathroom down the hall served fifteen men.

They went out as one group, found a noisy bar, drank their fill of French wine and French ladies, then retreated back to the hotel. Eventually, the noise dampened down. The American in the corner snored quietly and Robert listened to Max's even breathing next to him.

He was slightly drunk, although not the room-spinning kind. But his inner voice was sober. While there was certainly adventure in the wind and he loved Paris, he couldn't stop thinking about tomorrow and the day after. He was glad to be here with his friend, glad to be of help in changing the world, but what if the world wouldn't change? What if he was unable to pick up a rifle and kill another person?

He whispered softly to himself, "I am here for a cause. I am here to help Max. I am here to stop the fascists." Over and over he repeated this. As if he needed convincing.

Chapter Nine
Eugenio II, Andalusia, 1989

Eugenio Robles grew up to be a man of great spirit, loyalty and perseverance. His parents, after the incident when he threw the clay pot down on the street, treated him cautiously and decided it would be best if they didn't discuss history until he was better able to hear it. That day never came.

Whenever his family went to their country home in La Jolla, it was a struggle to find someone to play with. Eugenio wasn't particularly happy there, but he was a boy after all and longed to be a part of the games village boys played; *pistoleros*, hunting hares with long sticks as rifles, loping along goat paths. At first, he generally tagged along behind them, mimicking their moves until he was discovered.

"You," one boy once said. "What do you think you're doing?"

"Playing," he said quietly. He picked at the strips of bark on his stick.

The boy walked back to Eugenio with a kind of swagger. He pulled at Eugenio's shirt, unraveled a bit of cotton. "Who said you could play?"

"Nobody. But I want to."

"Play with your brother, dickhead."

The boy popped Eugenio on the forehead, but when he turned to go, Eugenio slid his leg out and tripped the boy. He sucked in a breath and held it.

They came all at once. The first one bounded off his stomach, the next and those after slugged him repeatedly in the face and chest until Eugenio could bear it no longer and vomited.

The boys jumped back, yelling, hitting him with sticks. One last kick and they were back down the goat path and Eugenio was left to examine himself; the blood that trickled from his nose, the aches like heavy stones in his gut, and the feeling of having nowhere to go where he would be let in.

It happened every year, this ritual. Eugenio would stalk the village boys out of their sight, waiting and hoping for some sign that would allow him to enter this hallowed fraternity. The day never happened and Eugenio was destined to become a lonely boy.

He was a good student of history and spent many hours alone up in his room in the city studying the great internal conflict of his country. His parents were proud of his knowledge and imagined him one day as a professor at a university in Madrid or Salamanca. But if they had been in that room with him while he was studying, they would have discovered that he had conflated much of his life between his youth and 1930s Spain. Sometimes he would confuse them, wonder if he had actually been a part of the army of the right, or that army had been a part of his summers in La Jolla. He moved from a good to an excellent student, a man with promise who could take over the reins of a new Spain once Franco had passed.

But, instead of throwing his lot into education or politics, when he turned eighteen, Eugenio dug his claws into law enforcement. He was selected for Civil Guard training and impressed his superiors with his dedication and thoroughness. He had grown into a tall, broad-shouldered young man. He worked out almost every evening so that his biceps, when flexed, resembled the working hindquarters of a galloping thoroughbred. He was admired by some, envied by most. He left the other men to fight for second shrift amongst themselves and graduated at the top of his class.

As a result, he was able to choose where he wanted to be stationed, and, because of his well-known misfortune with the kids of La Jolla, it came as a surprise to those who did not know him well that he chose to stay put in his own province. Not Madrid, not Barcelona or Seville, but Málaga. There was a reason for this choice as all would soon find out.

§

One day, early in his assignment, he drove his Land Rover up to La Jolla. It had not changed much since his boyhood days. The one-lane road still meandered about ten kilometers up from the sea, winding back on itself like an escaping rattlesnake. The town still sat nestled among the ravines dug out over years of flash floods so that now the surrounding hillsides looked like the pocked and weathered faces of old men. All along these hills were planted Muscat grapes whose small ancient stumps were gnarled fists thrust from the ground. It was arid terrain. The only plants that thrived there required little water – olives, almonds, and lemons, with an occasional sour orange.

The streets were cobblestone; a good many of the houses lay in partial ruin. Eugenio parked his Land Rover in front of the *Boquete de José* which stood on the edge of the town square. He emerged from the vehicle stretching his back. Outside the store, a canary lived in a small cage made of eucalyptus dowels. The bird jammed itself against the side of the cage as Eugenio entered.

The place smelled of the sweet/sour frontier of aging meat. A cured pig leg hung from a hook in one corner. Behind the counter, Pepe, a man of sixty-five, stood with a jar of *vino terreno* already poised over a small glass. He blinked once and the large mole on his left eyelid kept it closed for a moment longer than the right one.

"Yes, yes," said Eugenio as he removed his leather tricorne hat and laid it on the counter. He slicked back his black hair with one smooth motion of his hand. He watched the last drop of wine drip into the glass and then raised it and downed it in one noisy gulp. It was refilled before he could wipe his mouth.

"A beautiful day," Pepe said, expectant. "Warm, but not too warm. You should be comfortable in your uniform."

"Huh," Eugenio grunted. "I am always too hot in this blessed thing." The second drink was quickly gone.

"The young, they sweat." Hopefully, Pepe watched Eugenio's eyes as they glanced along the shelves behind the counter. Sometimes the guards did buy, and at Málaga prices.

"Do you remember me?" Eugenio asked.

"What? Should I?" He squinted and studied the young Guardia closer. To help him, Eugenio removed his sunglasses.

"Aha," said Pepe. "I do remember you. Robles, no?"

Eugenio set his sunglasses on the bridge of his nose. "Yes, that's right. I came here as a child. I wasn't liked."

Pepe nodded. "The boys here were like animals. As men, they aren't much better, but thankfully most have moved away. Welcome back." Pepe held out his hand, felt the Guardia's firm grip. "*Pipas*, I have."

"No. I've got sunflower husks all over the floor of my truck. I'm looking for something else."

"Perhaps some ice cream. I have new in yesterday. Vanilla?"

"It's people I'm looking for," Eugenio said.

"Ah, people."

"I'm looking for people to help me."

"Well, here you certainly have one."

"Oh, yes?" Eugenio studied the man. Was that sweat starting to trickle from his temples?

"From most there was no help," Pepe went on to say. "But not all families here were unsympathetic."

"This is true. Can I assume your family is one of those that was not loyal to the left?"

Pepe straightened up. "You may assume that, sir."

"And yet, here in a liberal village you have a successful business."

"Even those on the wrong side must eat," Pepe said.

At that moment, Pepe's wife, Maria del Mar, poked her head through the curtain that separated their living quarters from the store itself. "It's time," she said before she noticed Eugenio. "Pardon," she added.

"Time for what?" Pepe said rather gruffly.

"The pain is worse," she said. "Pardon," she added again to Eugenio.

"No need. Sir, you should be kinder to your wife. She needs your help. Perhaps I should..."

"No, no. It is not proper for her to ask me this." He turned to Maria del Mar. "Get one of your friends. I am quite busy out here."

"I know you," Maria del Mar said as she limped into the room. She was dressed in mourning even though it had been twenty years since the death of her mother. It was a much simpler life to slip on black day after day. "You resemble the Robles family who always came here on the weekends."

"Ay, Maria," said Pepe. "Must you?"

"You know she's right. I am a Robles. You have an excellent eye, Madam."

"One would think you wouldn't return to a village like this," Maria del Mar said. "The children were not good to you. I am sorry for that. "

Pepe walked over and pulled aside the curtain for her. "I believe you need to find your friend for the injection."

"A pleasure," Maria del Mar said to Eugenio as she was leaving the room. "Forgive the children."

"Women," said Pepe. "My apologies. Now, you were saying?"

"I've brought a name for you. I would like it if you would keep your eyes on this person for a while. And I would like to keep it between you and me."

"I am here to serve," Pepe said. "Who is it?"

"Maria del Carmen Escobar."

Pepe didn't flinch even though he was surprised to hear the name. "I'll keep an eye out."

Eugenio picked up his hat and placed it square on his head. "Good day then. I will be back. Perhaps the next time you will have some Bollycao that I can buy."

"Ah," said Pepe. "The children love it so, it is hard to keep it on my shelves. But I will save one just for you."

"Thank you." Eugenio left the store, the canary flapping once more as he passed.

§

Maria del Carmen Escobar was up in the hills when she saw the Guardia's Land Rover motoring toward the village. From her vantage point with her goats, it resembled a toy her grandchild might play with if she had a grandchild. But she didn't and that was fate.

She had heard there was to be a replacement for the Guardia who had recently retired. An unnecessary pain. That man still had several good years left in him and he liked the drink more than anything else. Couldn't he have stayed on? All her problems might have been settled if he had only waited a few years. These new Civil Guards were so young and seemingly so unknowledgeable about the history of the country they served. That fact might translate into an easier time for Carmen Escobar, but she wouldn't know until she met this one.

She picked up a stone and tossed it toward a trio of goats who were standing dangerously close to loose gravel above a ravine. They bounced away when she clucked her palate and warned them.

She continued to watch the Guardia make his way to the village and was not surprised to see the vehicle park in front of Pepe's store. It was at the center of town, a natural place to introduce oneself to the locals. A young man climbed out of the Land Rover. She noticed the way his uniform clung to his body, the tightness of his shirt, the surge of muscle as he bent to lower his pant legs to the top of his boots. She might be nearing seventy but the longing was still there, the remembrance of youth.

She reached down and picked up her bag. Inside was a hunk of *queso de las Alpujarras*, fine and tasty, cheese made from her own goats' milk, and a Vienna of day-old bread. It was a natural lunch. Not in the least suspicious. People were used to seeing Carmen tackle the inclines.

From her early youth, she romped through the rolling, gaunt but gallant hills surrounding La Jolla, where she did, in fact, once fall in love and give her heart to a man. But oh, how war changed things. People, circumstances, hopes and dreams, and the contours of a beautiful face.

Below her, the young Guardia emerged from Pepe's store and slid into his Land Rover. He backed up and headed out toward the other end of town. Goodbye, she thought. And stay away for a long time.

Later, she penned in her goats and walked to the store. There, in the back, she found her friend, Maria del Mar, lying on her bed, writhing in agony. Carmen doubled her fists.

"Your Pepe has not come in to help you?" she said. From a drawer on the side of the room, she removed a large syringe and a small, corked glass bottle.

"I have a husband?" Maria del Mar said between gritted teeth.

Carmen pulled up her friend's dress, yanked down her panties and jabbed the loaded syringe into one rather lumpy and ample cheek. She pushed the cylinder against the drug and imagined it to be Pepe's head she was filling, not with painkillers but goat piss.

"Ah, you are a blessed woman," said Maria del Mar when the medicine began to do its work. "The best woman."

Carmen set the empty syringe aside and sat down. She picked up a clammy hand. "When will you get your surgery?"

"When I can no longer walk."

"I'm afraid that time has come." She patted the hand, noticed the dirt beneath the nails. "You must have others do the work for you."

"Would *you*? When you give up your goats, I give up the soil."

"Fair enough," said Carmen. "And who was this young man who paid Pepe a visit this morning?"

"You know very well who it was. Yet another boy who does not understand his limits."

"And since when do boys have any limits at all? They would walk over the top of us if they didn't need to eat."

"His thoughts and his pants are too tight. So secretive. One man talks to another and who knows?"

"And what secrets was he interested in?" Carmen said.

"Oh, something very very important. I heard your name mentioned."

"Me?"

Carmen waited, but her friend faded into the bliss of the drug. She believed it was the drug that led her friend to say what the young Guardia was looking for. He would not talk to Pepe about women, nor money for that matter. No, he would just introduce himself and let Pepe know that he was the new cock in town, test out how his crow worked. She assured herself there was nothing to be concerned about. The Guardia visited La Jolla about once every two weeks.

No, not to worry.

Chapter Ten
Michael and Delia II, Spokane, 1989

Michael Virtue was lonelier now than he could ever have imagined. He'd uncovered the truth of his friendship with Mason; their mutual appreciation and shared love of the absurd. And now, at the height of one of life's absurdities – no Mason.

He missed his wife, forgave his kids for wanting to move to Seattle. He felt it would be a long time coming, this forgiving thing for Eva and him. Who was this Eva? Where had she been during their marriage? His sense of wellbeing was nearly gone. In front of the TV at night, he watched programs he didn't follow well nor care about. Yet, he sat with the remote in his hand, changing stations every few seconds, eating popcorn and drinking blended scotch.

He felt an anxiety ready to explode. To deal with it, he did what he'd done lately, went to the chest in his room and pulled out one of his uncle's letters.

January 20, 1937, Middle of the Atlantic

Dear Mom and Dad,

Max is my best friend. I know that now. He's one of those guys you can be years away from and when you see him, you pick right up where you left off. I think people around us got tired of our catching up. He's sleeping now in the bunk across the room and I'm writing to you while the ship gently sways under my pen. We've been lucky so far; the weather has held. But I just heard the forecast and I'm preparing my stomach for the bad news. Do you know why Max's family moved back to New York? They woke up one morning with a Star of David burned into their front yard on Bernard. Have you heard of that happening in Spokane? I thought it was only going on in Germany, but Max set me straight. "In Brooklyn, I can be around more of my own kind," he said. "We're safer if we stand together." It sounded like war talk and when I said it to Max, he reminded me that it was war we were sailing to. Out on the deck with a glass of wine under the stars, he filled me in on the history of his family and of his people in general. Once in a while, I could see a sparkle in his eyes as he talked about moving from one place to another, trying to find a home. "It's our destiny," he said. And when I gave him my apologies, he said, "I don't need them because I strongly believe that the more you move, the more you're likely to end up finding the perfect place." I hugged him. It was spontaneous and a first for me. Max felt strong and steady as he hugged me back. "Are you ready?" he said. I nodded. "No," he said. "Are you really ready?" I had to think for a few moments. "Yes, I am," I finally said. But Max saw something in me and he smiled. "You're a good friend." And now, as I write this, I think he knows that I'm here because of him and for no other reason. Maybe that makes me a good friend, or it makes me a fool. Either way, I'm sitting in a room on a ship heading to somewhere I've never been and I have no real idea about. But it's the definition of adventure, isn't it? Don't misunderstand me, but sometimes I think that my upbringing was too safe, too normal. Not that you ever did anything at all wrong, it's only that the more I see and hear about the rest of the world, the more unprepared for life I am. I hope that will change now. I'm looking forward to it. I will keep you informed of all my movements. And don't worry. According to Max, we have all the gods who ever lived on our side. What could go wrong with that kind of protection?

Your loving son, Robert

§

Michael set the letter aside. Here was a man who followed his best friend to the ends of the earth to help him right a wrong. He admired his uncle once more. Could he ever do that? Maybe.

But he settled in, expecting to wake up in front of the TV sometime in the middle of the night and trundle off to bed. His new normal.

But the phone rang and changed it all.

§

Delia was panicking. It could have been anyone who followed her home from the bar. But it was *that* car, the black one with the tinted windows. The one everyone recognized, exposed like an undercover narc at an outdoor concert. She didn't even bother to turn her car off when she pulled to the curb, grabbed her bag and sprinted for the front door of her house. The Karmann Ghia kept rolling until it bumped into another car ten feet ahead of it.

"My God, my God, my God," she muttered breathlessly, fear eating her up as she burst into the bathroom and started scooping items out of her drawers and stuffing them into her bag. How much time did she have?

She slammed out of the bathroom, her bag heavy on her shoulder. In the bedroom, she stopped only for a moment and scanned the room.

"Fuck," she breathed. "Not now."

She turned and ran back to the living room. Out the window, she saw the car pull up to the curb. Dropping to a crouch, she hurried through the kitchen and out the back door.

She fled down the alley, looking over her shoulder for the dark figures who could step out, guns raised, and end her time on Earth. But they weren't there, not yet, and she skittered like an agile spider, squeezing through the small spaces between outbuildings and fences, some of them wire, slicing and biting her hands and arms.

Any street she encountered, she ran across and hid in bushes, under trees, swing sets, Big Toys, whatever gave her a moment of invisibility.

Eventually, she had to stop behind a large green dumpster where she crouched, panting. What to do? It wasn't the first time they'd come for her, but she'd always had warning. She could be wrong, the blood pumping in her veins was older now, could deliver incorrect information.

Delia rubbed the viscous blood into her skin. She was safe for the time being, but she had to move quickly. They needed to regroup and that would buy her time.

§

Michael was tearing into a new bag of caramel popcorn when he picked up the phone. He took a mouthful.

The voice on the other end said: "You've got to go back. You've got to."

He recognized the voice immediately, of course, but as he tried to answer her he spit out a sticky wad of corn. "What's going on?"

"Tell me where you live."

"What..."

"Now!" Delia screamed. He thought he heard traffic in the background. He gave her the address and the line fell silent.

He jumped up and pulled on his sweats, picked up the lump of popcorn settling into the carpet. He sniffed his armpits, ran to the bathroom and slathered on deodorant. It was a full two minutes before he stopped to think about her call. The shrill desperation in her voice, the incoherence of her message. Adrenaline chewed at his heart, not unlike when his motorcycle bumped down the stairs in Spain.

She knocked on his back window, once, then twice. Loud, banging, urgent sounds. He ran to the door and out on the mat. She stood for a moment, looking like a beggar, scabs already forming on her arms.

"Turn the light off," she whispered, and when he had, she hurried past him. "Turn them all off." She flew around the house, switching off lamps and overheads so that only the wavy light from the TV filled the room. She picked up the remote and stabbed at the red button. When it was completely dark, she dropped to the sofa.

"Hello to you too," Michael said.

"Shut the fuck up."

An irritated current coursed through him. "What's going on?" He grabbed for her, fought her resistance, and dragged her into the bathroom, slamming the door. He booted away the wet towel from the morning and held her wrist up to the mirror. The drying blood made a swirling pattern against her skin. He slid open a drawer and took out a brown plastic bottle of hydrogen peroxide. Opening it with his teeth, he poured it over her wounds.

She winced, but no longer struggled. "Listen," she said. "I didn't want to involve you, but I already have so you've got to do what I say or you could be in trouble."

"Slow down," Michael said, as he might to a highly anxious client. The rest of the bottle ran pink over her skin and down into the drain. He tossed the empty in the trash. Then he examined her arms, finally looking up into the mirror. She looked haggard and scared.

"No, I can't slow down. Listen, Mike, I know we've had our differences, but I want you to hear me out and make whatever you want out of it. I need your help and if Mason were alive it would be his couch I'd be sitting on and asking this."

Michael let go of her. "Okay."

"It's not safe. And I'm sorry for that, but it can't be helped. Remember when I said I'm always moving? Well, this is one of those times. I think I avoided them for a while, but I can't go home."

"Avoided who?"

"It doesn't matter. Trust is what I need from you." She paused and cocked her head, flashed her eyes to the side. "Did you hear that?"

"I didn't hear anything."

She flipped off the light and tiptoed out of the bathroom and over to one of the windows, peeking out. She was there for a full minute before she sat down on the sofa.

Michael stood in the darkness. "What is it you want me to do?"

"You're split up with your wife, right? Aren't your kids over with her? It's summer. You could get away for a while, couldn't you?"

"Away to where?"

"I want you to help me get out. I want you to go with me. I want you to be my partner."

"I'm married..."

"And now's not the time to act stupid. Just say yes or no and that will be that."

"Can I think about it?"

This time she turned to him, eyes wide. "Does it look like we have any time for you to think about it?"

"No," he said. His wife and children flashed through his mind as he struggled to answer her. "Yes," he said, and that's all it took.

She nodded quickly, ran across the room. Michael stood slack-jawed and watched as she grabbed his phone and made a travel agency out of it. He heard:

"Barry? Yes. Yes. Call in... I'd say half an hour. Yes. Then what? Okay. Yes, they were. East, so head them West. Thanks. As always."

She wiped off the handset with a handkerchief. When she looked up, he was still gawking.

"You'd better get ready. We have to go. Like right now."

He cobbled together a shaving kit and backpack, stuffed his little life into them and hurried out to her, stopped, wondered what he was doing. "I don't even know you," he said.

But, within minutes, he swept himself out of the house and, functionally, out of his world.

Chapter Eleven
Maria del Carmen, Andalusia, 1989

It had been a long time since Carmen Escobar led an anxious life. Since she was twelve or thirteen was the last she could remember. Not that she didn't have good reason to, it was just her nature. Only in one period did she feel the pinpricks of nervous demons, but even then she kept her head clear enough so she was capable of accomplishing the task she was destined to perform.

And she had performed it well for fifty years, through sickness and earthquakes and prying eyes and the brain of an irascible and skeptical man. Thanks to God who showed her the way at age twelve, she was able to live the most meaningful life possible.

Now, very early in the morning, she crossed herself as she normally did while she stood in her goat pen behind the mud rock walls she built entirely on her own, and pondered her future. Of all the near misses and guilt-ridden moments of almost disclosure, why did this particular moment create an anxiety that had not visited her in years? She may have known why, but didn't want to say it, didn't want to disclose the truth to the world at large, not quite yet, not until permission was granted by the only one who could give it, and that is why she sidelined her dilemma and gathered her goats for the trip up the hill.

They were *Malagueñan*, of course, these goats with their big bugged steel blue eyes and fanciful beards; they were red and brown and black and white, and smelly, like any good goat must be, and noisy like a flock of children taking to the street on the last day of school. And, they could read her like that flock of children waiting for direction from their mother. They jockeyed and jabbered at her gate until she slid the heavy wood crossbar aside. They filed out, honoring the hierarchy that had been fought over on a daily basis, and continued up the hill while Maria del Carmen paused, looked over to the church, crossed herself backwards and then spit on the ground. "Blas Alvarez," she muttered. "You will pay someday."

Meanwhile, her goats milled on the cobblestones rooted in the *martirio*, the place for the martyred, high above her house.

When she arrived there, she stopped, shading her eyes. The sun rose out of the Mediterranean like a blood orange spilling its juice in a fiery fan over the surface of the sea. The younger ones took this for granted, the beginning of a new day, but Carmen knew better. The gift of a day was so much more than *motos* and autos and electronic machines. To draw breath, yes, that was the precious thing.

She sucked in a deep one as she led her charges off the *martirio* and into the thick thorny deep-rooted bushes along her chosen path. On the way, she thought about how easy it was to fool the foolish. Every single person, after all, had his own focus, and rarely strayed from it. Not that they didn't notice other things around them. They ticked off the normal and usual; that woman washed her clothes at the *pila* every Thursday; this woman took the smoky school bus down to the coast on a Tuesday to visit her sister and to drop off and pick up the sewing she performed late at night during the rest of the week; the other woman tended her herd of goats from dawn till dusk, and smelled like her charges most of the time. She was a sad case, that woman, with never a man at her side to keep her in line.

So, if say on this morning of summer, Carmen Escobar took off into the countryside, the residents marked off in their heads that yes, this day is like any other. I do not have to worry about this pitiful woman, she is doing her job, living her life, until the day when I will attend her funeral and tick her off my charts for good.

But Carmen Escobar was not just a goatherd. She was so much more. Some didn't know this, but most folks did and, out of habit, kept it to themselves. They knew instinctively that she was special and different. That she disappeared with her animals for a lot longer than was necessary. They knew her routine included a secret and this secret belonged to the entire town; and most of the town, like a good friend, kept it close to its chest. No, Carmen Escobar was so much more than just another spinster waiting to die. She held the faith of La Jolla in her hands.

Her trip was always, by necessity, circuitous. If a resident of the rugged hills should see her leave the *martirio*, he might think, *Oh, there she goes to Pepe Camion's family land where her goats love to pick their way through the thorns and rocks to drink from Pepe's spring that bubbles out of nowhere in the middle of nothing.* That spring watered the oasis of canary grass with its storm of yellow flower heads her goats would see as a sumptuous dessert.

But that particular person would be wrong. For, before she got to Pepe's land, Carmen took a hard jog left and up into the dense grove of spindly cane that formed a kind of curtain all the way up the slope, hiding her from the village. Then, if someone on the other side of the cane, say, Jorge Villalobos with his fat belly and no lung power to speak of, happened to see Carmen, he might think, *Oh there goes that poor wretch on up to the crest. Perhaps she wants to get a look at Ventura, the lost village she is rumored to have once lived in as a young child until the water turned bitter and the family had to move closer to the sea.*

But he would be wrong as well. For it was far below the crest that Carmen made another hard turn, back through the floppy cane, through a forest of flowering pink oleander to where she was now hidden from the village on this side by the rounded hump called La Loma. It was up and through that hump that she got her first look at Ventura. No, she never lived there as a child, never lived there as an adult, but she had visited this ghost town almost every day of her life since she was twelve.

On the lee flank of La Loma, Carmen stopped a moment while her goats grazed on the few blades of grass lucky enough to be kissed by shade. But it was not just for her animals she rested. Her side was rioting again, sending spurts of pain in jagged waves. She placed her hand on it and pressed lightly. She could feel something there, like the baby she never conceived perhaps. Was that its head, were those its tiny kicking legs? She must go to the doctor, find out what this torture was, and then, most likely, ignore it. Who, at her age, needed to worry about simple physical deficiencies? There, see now? Her warm hand did the trick, and she could move up further.

The carcass of a small house sat on the prominent brow of the dead village. From a distance, it still sparkled white, but close up, it was a leper, with open sores of mud showing through its decaying hide. A tumbledown pergola made of cane lived at a slant in front of the house, and on it were draped the dried vines and leaves of a grape that thought it had a chance every early spring, only to live out its inevitable truth come mid-summer.

But below this house, yes just under the old tilting wall that has held it up for years, a rhizome of hope resided. A generous sweep of low growing iris, fanned out for a good ten meters, adding perhaps a half meter of new blades per year. "How is this possible?" Carmen asked yet again as she approached it. These flowers were long gone with the season, but the robust little swords shot up from everywhere; a Roman army buried in shallow graves. Her goats would love to get their teeth on these plants, but she didn't linger and neither did they.

It was the steepest part of the rise right by the house, and Carmen labored as she climbed. She was careful to take a slightly different route, a meter or two to the left of yesterday's path, so her movements appeared to obey the whims of her goats and not of a silly woman with an even sillier task.

And finally, she was there at Ventura's main road. The first level spot of the climb. The goats flooded the narrow street and stood, admonishing her. Now she felt like the ruins that surrounded her: neglected, decaying, hurting, darting in and out of people's recollections, but not quite making a permanent dent.

I knew that village, that Ventura. I lived there.

My grandmother took the wash every day to the Moorish well.

I turned one last time to wave goodbye to my childhood.

Franco's minions had my uncle killed there.

I can still smell the exquisite fragrance of the first press of the year.

But had they been back since? Not really. Had they sworn their allegiance to return to it someday and restore it to its greatness? No. And this was what made it the perfect place for Carmen's task.

There were sometimes visitors who came to gawk, but the deep ruts and exposed rocks of the road stopped them before they got too far. Carmen never knew them, nor they her. They might snap pictures. She could be a timeless relic from their vacation.

Leafing through the snapshots one day, they could say, *Oh look. There's the old lady with the goats. God, I wish my life had been that simple.*

Beyond where the street ended was another that turned upwards toward the top of the village. Carmen took this one. As a younger woman, she feared the high walls lining it might one day tumble over her, but now, who cared? If it happened, it happened. Did she really feel that way? No. She must admit she still had hope, much like the iris below.

There once was an olive oil factory at the tip-top of the village. It was abandoned years ago, before the war had barely begun. Bombed, is what happened to it. Sabotaged. The first thing the enemy tried to do was poison the oil that came from the stone presses. Failing this, someone planted a bomb beneath the largest press creating an explosion that so lit up the night sky that sailors down on the Med thought it could have been a celebration of the Blessed Virgin. The blast that tore apart the whole factory and the bodies of the workers was a masterpiece of espionage. Ventura was neutral in its sentiments toward the war, and after the eruption of flames and flesh, it officially remained that way.

Whichever side did it, when the people still didn't leave the town, the perpetrators returned and poisoned the old Moorish well. Babies cried and retched and died until the wagons were finally drawn up and the exodus from Ventura was finalized.

Now Carmen picked her way through the more than fifty-year-old rubble of the blast. Dried grasses poked through it, in some spots, the delicate pink-throated blossoms of capers dwarfed it. One partial wall of the old factory remained and it was to that point she walked. Her goats, after generations of practice, waited for her on the steep street.

A miracle of the bombing was that a single oil storage jar, plunged deep into the ground and topped by a wide clay circular lid was left unscathed. But few realized it. The jar itself had been covered by the detritus from the explosion and it was not until later, when the place was left to die that she discovered it. A twelve-year-old girl with an unsatisfied curiosity could accomplish much in 1937, a year filled with paralyzing fear and caution. The jar was three meters deep and four in diameter at its widest point, rounded at the belly and flat on the bottom. It had once held uncountable liters of olive oil, and still smelled of it even though more than a year had passed since it contained its last first press. On her hands and knees and peering into it on that day in 1937 was like peeking into her own uncertain future; dark, oily and nearly impenetrable as it was.

She found the right-sized limb to touch the bottom of the jar, then sought out another to match and set to work building a ladder out of sticks with pieces of heavy cloth to tie the rungs. The place became her hideout, her sanctuary from the hellish internecine battles that orbited around her.

Now, it was hidden much as it was fifty years ago. She set down her canvas bag and got to work. Her goats wandered, bleating their impatience. Despite the pain in her side, the process took very little time. She had covered it with spare limbs from local windfall from almond and olive trees, with parts of the old walls strewn in and out to leave it as natural as it once was when the horror had settled over the town. At the top of the jar, she scraped the lid aside. As usual, there arose from below a mixture of oil and human waste. But she poked her head in.

"Roberto? *Soy yo*. Are you breathing?"

And, as was usually the case, she heard back in a guttural, grainy voice, "Not quite so loud, please."

"Ah, all right," she said with relief. "So, you are yet alive."

Chapter Twelve
Robert, Ventura, 1989

He was his own mayor, police chief, priest and occasional lover. And had been for fifty plus years. His calendar told him such, but he hasn't much paid attention to it in he can't remember how long. He only gauged life by what was brought to him and, to his way of thinking, the view could be narrow.

He was seventy-four years old, suffered a crushing pain in both of his knees, perhaps from spending so much time on them. His whole life was cramped, in spite of the remodels he had done in his home over the years. With enormous effort, he had expanded his three by four meter cell into a home now maybe three by seven or so, by excavating tiny spoonsful of dirt and stone, one scrape at a time, each one stored in a small cloth bag to be removed and dumped unceremoniously by his friend and benefactor. He imagined that all around the perimeter of Ventura stood monuments to his work, like miniature termite mounds. To secure his home, he had installed thick olive branches tight against the ceiling. Crude wood shelves were shoved into clefts dug into the walls and he carved out small recesses as well to hold candles he could light on days when he yearned to read news of the world or when the darkness was simply too much to bear.

He liked routine. He slept on a pad filled with goat hair and old clothing. He woke up precisely nine hours after he lay himself down at night. He relieved himself in the far corner of the room in a jar that had always served that purpose. He ate whatever was left in the bag that Carmen brought the day before. He threw the blanket over the pad, lay down again upon it and began a series of exercises he learned from Mr. Pratt at Lewis and Clark High School. He didn't get as far as he did when he was younger, but it was always his intent to make it further.

After his workout, he went to the pile of papers arranged on a shelf in the opposite corner of the room. Here he had saved his own letters to his parents, copies of the International Herald Tribune, articles in magazines about the end of the war, the death of Franco, the atomic bomb, a cure for polio, the sad end of a king and the ascension of a queen. He read it all over and over until it became senseless chatter on the fringes of his thinking. He napped after, began again after his nap.

There was a newer development. In the past four years, he had enjoyed conversations with others who may or may not have been present in his room. He was not sure what he wanted the truth to be. If they were real, then he could be in trouble. If they were not, then he could be in trouble. Nevertheless, these conversations had become a part of his routine.

Late afternoon and evening were spent in anticipation of the arrival of the one woman in his life who had ever made his blood roil. But lately, he had grown concerned about Carmen, mainly because his brain misfired when he tried too hard to think about her and himself and their life together.

He still believed he could trust her. But she was also the one who brought him everything he knew about the outside world, so was it possible she brought the wrong news? Did the fox always bring you the truth about the goings on in the henhouse? He wanted to believe in her. It was at one time so easy to do. She saved his life and who couldn't trust that kind of person? But, as the years had jelled into a whole scheme with a memory, having been rescued may not have been the preferred outcome.

He retrieved the ladder from one corner and set it up against the lip of the jar, pushing it into a sturdy position. He stood back and watched as she carefully descended, balancing a cloth bag over her shoulder.

"Have you made sure?" he said.

"Ah, Robertito. Your questions weigh on me. Can you not hear? Can you not see?"

When her feet hit the uneven floor, he grabbed for her shoulders and kissed both of her cheeks.

"And to you as well," she said. She pulled the contents from the bag, a chunk of cheese, half a Vienna, a ripe tomato, and water. "I will bring lemons tomorrow so you will not suffer scurvy, and beans, I think." She stopped because she heard nothing back from him. "Is it hurting you?" she said.

"A little."

"Come on then, let me see."

She carefully unbuttoned the shirt she gave him on The Day of the Kings, when was it, in 1974? He tilted his head toward the sun, as a small child might, enduring the ministrations of his mother. He shouldered one sleeve off and allowed her expert hands to probe at the old scar on his side where the bullet entered.

"I can feel the slug today," he said.

Using the middle three fingers of both hands, she began to massage the spot that had grown looser over time.

"Ay," he whispered.

"Too much?"

"Are you staying for breakfast?"

"I can't. I have an appointment."

His interest pricked up his ears. "You have what?"

"Don't worry. Everyone has an appointment at one time or another. It took all last night to find my identity card so I can go." She stopped massaging him. "There now. Is that better?"

Before she could remove her hands, he grabbed a wrist and pulled it in close. "Mari Carmen, he was here again."

"Now, Roberto."

"He was. He sits in your chair without asking permission and talks to me about what I've done."

"There, there, you must know it's just your imagination. A member of that family would never sit without permission." She twisted her wrist and escaped his clutches. "And now I must go."

"Tell me again," he said.

"I have told you too many times." She paused, saw the earnestness of his expectation, and said, "He is dead. Fourteen years now. It is not possible for him to rise after all this time."

"You have proof?"

She bit her lip to cool her exasperation. "Your corner over there is stacked with the proof of his death."

He took a step toward her. "But, *mi vida*, you forget about *la limpieza*, don't you?"

"The betrayal? He was alive then, Robertito. Now I really must go."

She turned abruptly, realized she had forgotten, and gathered in two of his offerings; a plastic bag and a clay jar. She brought him enough to sustain life, and in return she got his shit.

He watched her climb. There had been a time when he hoped for a glimpse under her skirts, and he had to admit the longing was still there, however diminished. When she'd reached the top, he waited for her to step off the ladder and then he pulled it back in. He stood a moment longer in the sun that slanted across his face, before she pushed the lid back on, and he was awash in darkness once more.

In the very beginning, she did not visit him every day. She was not able to. Walking at night was a danger in itself, especially after he shot the lieutenant. Every Nationalist in Malaga province was looking for the hated foreigner who had murdered a patriot. They roamed the local villages like wild dogs, plundering what they wanted, taking by force what was resisted. For this reason, Carmen Escobar stayed home many evenings, worrying, she told him, that when she finally braved the outside, she would find him dead from starvation and rotting in his oily grave.

Robert sat on one of the rush chairs. Already he anticipated her visit tomorrow. He sliced bits of cheese on the table he built from wood Carmen scavenged from the dead houses surrounding him. Planks of pine nailed to sawhorses spaced a meter apart.

"You're not expecting to entertain a crowd, are you?" she had said when she questioned the projected size of the table.

Now a chunk of bread from the Vienna. At the holiday, she would bring *jamon serrano* and his mouth watered at the prospect. He bit into the sandwich and winced. The cheese was not thoroughly ripe, he thought. Did he have enough time left for it to age?

The lieutenant came when Robert was chewing the day-old bread. He occupied the other chair, usually reserved for Carmen. The man smoked black tobacco, sat with a hunch. When he moved, only from the waist up, his face transformed into a gape of pain.

"Edify me," said Francisco Robles de Casares. "How is it that you, an unknown foreigner and bad shot, could draw breath for so much longer than me, when it's not even your own air to draw?"

"Easy," Robert said. "You need blood to live and all of yours sank in the grass where you died. I still have most of mine."

"Did it hurt when I shot you?" Francisco said. "Did you feel much pain?"

"As I've already told you many times, a great deal of pain. Yes."

Francisco took a long pull on his cigarette and expelled it into the room, tilting back his head in satisfaction. "At least I have that, and possibly more." He inhaled another, shorter puff, and held the cigarette out. "Tell me something I've always wondered. Where did you come from? How could you be in this village? There were no foreign fighters who were republicans. And yet, there you were, hiding in the brush off some piffling road in the hills. An American in an international uniform. Were you a deserter? A man scared of his own pale shadow?"

"Stop that talk. You're an idiot. You know nothing."

"Did you join the Loyalist bandits? Did you come of your own accord and get lost? Oh yes, what a mistake that would have been. Tell me, Roberto. How did you come to La Jolla?"

"I had orders."

"From whom? The pitiful farmers? The teachers poisoning the minds of our children? There was never anyone strong enough to give orders. Oh, I know. Maybe you stopped believing in anarchy?"

"I am not an anarchist."

"So sorry. I meant to say did you stop believing in communism?"

"I am not a communist."

"Socialism?"

"Shut up."

Francisco laughed out loud. "Perhaps a syndicalist you were. Please say yes, I am running out of isms for you to be a part of. The Left. What a queer group of disorganized human debris."

"I have my own brand of belief," Robert said.

"Don't tell me. You were a conscientious objector?"

"I volunteered. How could I be if I volunteered?"

"Come now, Roberto. We both know what you did. It's just that I wish I had been a better shot."

"You said earlier, 'And maybe more.' What does that mean?"

Francisco smiled, the big toothy grin that haunted Robert. "Carmen is right, you know. There are immense changes in the world out there. But they are not what she thinks they are."

"I knew it," said Roberto. "Another *limpieza* is on the way."

The lieutenant slapped at his chest. "Ay. Yes, the cleaning. Our finest hour, no? Come one, come all, you are forgiven. Come back and join the stream of us headed for a brighter future. You Loyalists were all alike. Your belief in the impossible was always your doom."

"And compared to your unbearable betrayal? Give me the naïve any day."

"Bold words for such a man with a low tolerance for pain." He dropped the last bit of cigarette to the floor and rubbed it out with his boot.

"Tell me then," Robert said. "Tell me what the plan is for men like me."

Francisco leaned forward, a grimace painted his face. "I want my bullet back!" he shouted. "Give me the slug that hides in your flesh and I will tell you what is in store for you. That is the deal we made."

Unconsciously, Robert's fingers strayed to his belly. "I'm afraid I can't. By shooting me, you gave up your right to the bullet."

"If I could, I would carve it out myself. But as you can see, I have lost most of my function. For which you are to blame."

"If you had not gotten down from your horse that night, neither of us would be here today."

"A tantalizing thought. Are you meaning to say I could have gone home to the loving arms of my wife? I could have ridden to my house instead of stopping to help a small child who had no business being a part of the war? That deep in the dark of my own bedroom I could have lifted my nightshirt and sunk my enormously engorged member into the soft and resplendent sex of my sweet and ejected my seed into the history of my entire line while she whispered in my ear, 'My love, my heart, yes, my love. Feed me more.'? Is this what you are saying?"

"Yes."

Francisco began to cry. "*Dios mio*. You are so smug because you still have life. But look around you. This is not a life. Breathing is easy. You do that and call it life." He sucked the tears back and glared at Robert. "Give me my bullet back. I must have it. It's my only hope."

"What is the plan?" Robert repeated. But he stood, balancing himself against the table. "What am I saying? I can't trust you. I could give your bullet back and you could turn me in."

Francisco leaned back and dug in his pocket for another cigarette. He pulled out an empty pack, crumpled it and threw it on the floor as well. "We are at an impasse," he said. "You have a bad life and I have a wretched death."

"An impasse."

"But I have one thing you can never have and it's important to me and everyone I've ever known. Do you know what that is, *Don Roberto*?"

"What is it?"

"Revenge," Francisco said, as he faded away, his last words an echo. "And for that, I can wait forever."

Chapter Thirteen
Michael and Delia III, Andalusia, 1989

Michael Virtue sat on TWA flying high over the Atlantic. Beside him sat his new lover, Antoinette Parks, formerly Delia. Toni is what she has asked him to call her. And she wanted him to practice because they couldn't afford to make any mistakes. He needed to commit to them having been together for years so her new name would roll off his tongue.

He wondered what had finally pushed him to say yes. Was it Eva's calm and assured manner as she disassembled his life? Mason's death? Or was it really the thought of adventure, of making a broad turn and heading in a different direction to solve a mystery?

Delia wanted to fly straight to Madrid and get lost in its immense scope, which she believed would make it easier for her. If they lived on their tourist visas, all they would have to do would be to leave the country once every six months and they could stay on indefinitely. Six months? What happened to the short trip to wrap up loose ends with his uncle? This diversion they'd agreed on was growing into a lifelong change. This perhaps was not for him after all. In the end, she had relented about going to Málaga. She just had wanted to be gone and now they were.

"Won't the school report that you're missing if they can't get hold of you?" he said for the third time since takeoff hours ago.

She pulled down her sunglasses to reveal a set of dark, sleepy eyes. "It's summer. Don't let your nerves get the best of you," she said. "I have to use the restroom." The man on the aisle stood to let her out. To Michael, he appeared cut and strong, and his hair was clipped too short to be a casual traveler. Government worker? Was Michael inheriting Delia's paranoia? When Delia was gone, the man sat back down, smiled at Michael.

"Women," he said. "Big hearts, small bladders."

"Ain't that the truth?"

Waiting for more, the man eventually picked up a book and Michael spent the time before Delia's return, trying to make out the title on the cover.

The PA system crackled in the Málaga airport, but Michael couldn't understand a word. He recognized nothing from twenty years ago. Unlike before, now he was hyper-vigilant. There was the man who sat next to him on the plane. He didn't look as large amongst the debarking crowd, but still, there he was, and he noticed Michael and smiled again.

"Good luck," he said before he melted away forever.

"You're drawing attention to yourself," Delia said. She pulled a small-wheeled bag as they headed for the carousels. She was a different person here; her stride more contained, her hips performed a less exaggerated sway. Michael just wanted to sit for a moment and collect himself, come up with a plan for the next couple of days, but Delia was on her own mission.

When they stepped out of the building, it was the sun he remembered, blinding white and hot. He blinked with the pain.

"Where are we staying?" he said.

"I don't know." They each had two larger bags and they caught the attention of the hovering *taxistas.*

"The city or where?" Michael said.

But Delia was busy negotiating with one of the drivers and he waited, dutifully. "La Jolla," he said, but not loud enough for anyone else to hear.

"Listen," Delia said. "I think we should lay low for a couple of days somewhere near here. This driver knows a small hotel that tourists never go to."

Before he could answer, she pointed to the bags and directed the man to help them.

So many cars, Michael thought as they wove their way through the traffic. What a difference a score of years could make.

"You've come to the right place," the driver said. "*Andalucia* is the place for lovers."

"We're partners," Delia said.

"Married then?" said the man.

She turned to the back seat and looked right at Michael. Watch and learn, she seemed to say. "No. Not yet. We're on our annual junket. It's a promise we made when we got together."

"*Andalucia* is for partners," the driver said.

He dropped them at the Hotel Ecuador, a series of *casitas* nestled among drying date palms, earnest plumbago and a Bird of Paradise, the only plant on the property getting any real attention.

They chose two rooms situated next to each other, although Michael briefly entertained a fantasy of the money-saving decision to room together. But, in spite of the name change, Delia remained the same private person, and the clerk didn't ask. So, Michael stacked his bags on the bench at the end of a bed with a dip in the middle that promised discomfort. He sat for a moment on the edge of it, imagined himself on the lip of a precipice. He didn't want to fall off and ruin everything he'd gained in his life, but he also felt compelled by the possibilities of this adventure. He nodded his head and fell back on the bed, slept the sleep of the prodigiously jet-lagged.

The following morning, they rented a car and drove up the coast through a tangle of old fishing villages now with restaurants, bars, hotels and apartments thrown in amongst the old dories. On their right, the sea was a sparkling blue. With the windows open, they could smell a hint of Africa perhaps, a few miles across the water. Also, bits of something frying, of garlic, of wet salt. At the La Jolla sign, they turned up the hill. Nine kilometers to get there. Michael could feel his skin bump up, his heart tending to its business. He remembered this. The narrow road snaking through spiky agave plants and olive trees, with their rugged and wide-lined trunks. The grass hadn't seen water in months. Even though they were on asphalt, dust flew up from the wheels of the car. He wondered about his motorcycle.

Halfway up, they passed a smoking waste dump where the land fell steeply from the road. Near it, a small herd of goats stood bleating.

"Now, we're talking," Michael said. He felt a tie to something, a rejoining of an umbilicus.

But the blind curves were making Delia grumbly and she clutched the wheel tighter. "Talking about what? The landfill or the fucking maniac drivers?"

He ignored her. He was back on his motorcycle again and the twenty years had stripped away. When they reached the top of their climb, he sucked in a breath. He had stopped here once. In the distance, a wide cut in the Sierras was shaped like a U. Miles and miles of patterned farms and hills squared the landscape, parceled out over centuries.

"Pull over," he said.

She found a slightly wider spot on the slender shoulder and stopped the car. Michael got out. The breeze tousled his hair. It was warm, too hot to start running like a child, which is what he wanted to do. It was overpowering, this desire, and it felt delivered by the wind.

"What?" said Delia.

"It's magnificent."

"You really need to get hold of yourself." But she got out too and leaned against the front of the car. She pointed below. "Is that it?"

Michael recognized the old church. It had a new coat of gold paint. The rest of the village spilled down the hill in a bright white light of houses, limned in red along the rooftops.

"Yes." He searched one side of the village but couldn't make out the house where he once visited an old woman.

"This place is deserted," she said.

"You haven't even seen it yet." He came back to the car. "Come on. At least give it a look."

They drove down the extra kilometer and a half to a round gravel parking lot surrounded by pepper trees. Another car was parked there, so they pulled up next to it. They got out and started walking down toward the center of town. Soon, a light brown Land Rover with a Guardia logo glided past them. The two followed the vehicle's path.

"How are we doing?" Michael said as they descended into the middle of the village.

"How condescending," Delia said. "The royal 'we'."

Her face had grown harder than it was just a few minutes ago. He was beginning to understand her better. As they passed people in the street and they greeted the two, she seemed troubled and did not answer back.

"And if you keep staring at me, I may haul off and punch you."

They came upon the small cobblestone square, to one side of which sat *Boquete de José*. On the other side, was a hole-in-the-wall bar marked only by a sign advertising Victoria beer. Two small rickety tables and three woven cane chairs sat outside it. An older man wearing a felt hat sat at one. His suspenders were frayed at the edges and his belly poked through them.

Michael carefully pulled out the two empty chairs and placed them in front of one of the tables. All the while searching around the square, Delia finally sat.

"What do you want?" Michael said. He had exchanged money at the airport and *pesetas* now clumped in a wad in his pocket.

"One of those Victorias," she said.

While she waited, she noticed the Land Rover that passed them on the hill, now parked in front of the *Boquete de José*. It gleamed fresh and new even though dust seemed crammed into every nook in the plaza. She was about to go in and see if Michael needed help with his Spanish, when a young man in uniform came out of the store. He stopped and stretched his back. He walked to the passenger side of the Land Rover and Delia could hear every creak of the leather he wore. He was strapping, robust.

She felt a stir, which vanished when Michael stumbled out of the bar.

He placed two short bottles on the table. She touched one of them. "These aren't even cold."

"I don't think the fridge is working. But they're not that warm." To prove it, he put one up to his lips and burbled a drink. When he set it down, he said, "That guy is staring at you."

She saw the young man, now leaning against the Land Rover, arms crossed. He was looking in her direction, but his sunglasses kept her from knowing for sure if it was her he was studying. She knew he was a *Guardia* because of the hat that sat like a perched bird of prey on his head. Two older women in black scurried by him. When they'd passed, the young man pushed away and walked toward Delia and Michael.

He stopped a few feet away, his belt at eye level to Delia. "Do you have identification?" he said.

"No," said Delia. "I left it at the hotel."

"You know, you're supposed to have it on your person at all times."

"I know the number if that helps."

The young man glanced over to Michael. "And you?"

"What?"

"He doesn't speak Spanish," said Delia. "But he's with me. Next time, we'll remember to bring ID."

"You plan on returning then?"

She pointed toward Michael. "He knows someone here."

"Really? Who?"

"Michael, what's the name of the woman you talked to when you were here last?"

He shrugged. "Maria something."

"Does he know how many women are named Maria here?" the young man asked.

"Every woman?"

The young man took a step closer and removed his sunglasses as he peered at her. "How is it that you know Spanish so well?"

"I teach it," Delia quickly said. She could not tell if she was breathless because of the proximity of this man, or because she was anxious around any man wearing a uniform of authority. His face was unblemished, his mouth a straight line. His hair curled around his ears. He didn't belong in this get-up, she thought.

Abruptly, he replaced his sunglasses. "Next time then," he said.

Delia watched him walk away.

"What was that about?" Michael said. He finished his beer and set it on the table. It barely made a dent in his implacable thirst.

"He wonders what we're doing here," she said, still looking after the man until he ducked back in the store. Not now, she thought. Stay calm. "I feel the same."

"This Maria could be dead. If so, we can go on our way and figure something else out. I just, you know, I'd like to know how it played out."

She picked up her bottle, examined it, and set it back down. "Well, we're here. Let's get it over with."

§

La Jolla indeed rambled along an incline. Walking down through the village was easier than walking back up. For now, they headed down. The main street was narrow and shaded by two-story white stucco buildings shooting up on the sides. Their surfaces were uneven, evidence of heavy repair over the years. Women and old men stood or sat in their doorways. Younger men were absent.

At the first three doors, Delia's questions were heard, but ignored. No one knew which Maria she was asking about. At the fourth door, a memory tickled at Michael.

"Goats," he blurted out. "She had *cabras*."

"Ah, yes, that Maria," said an old woman with a mole crowding the vision in one eye. She stepped out into the street and pointed. "To the right and then to the left and then straight on. That is where Carmen lives."

"Fucking A," said Michael as they walked away. "I knew it."

"Don't say that. It doesn't fit you. Nothing worse than a guy trying to be someone he isn't."

"Sorry, ma'am." Michael was practically bouncing.

They smelled goats before they got to Carmen's house. There were no windows on the street side; the rest plunged away below. They walked down a series of flat stones to a wooden gate. To the side, a bell hung with a strong twine attached to the clapper.

Delia slammed the clapper over and over. She paused and then gave it three more good swings. They waited and this time Michael rang it, but to no effect.

"Let's leave a note," he said.

Delia rummaged through her bag, found a pen, but nothing more. So, Michael pulled out a one hundred *peseta* bill from his pocket.

"Give it here," said Delia.

But he shook his head and stole the pen from her. "I know just what to put." He placed the note against the smoothest part of the gate and wrote a short message. When he finished, he found a bit of wire, shoved one end into a rift in the gate and then perforated the note so it would stay on the other end.

"The wind is too strong; it will probably blow away," Delia said.

"If it does, it does, but I think it's meant to stay."

She squinted and read the message. She won't remember that."

"She'll know," he said.

Then he shaded his eyes and scanned the hillside. "I wish I could remember where I crashed my bike."

§

It was some time after Delia and Michael left the village that Carmen returned with her goats. Starting at the *martirio*, women greeted her and said, "There were foreigners asking after you today." Just like that, six different women positioned at intervals down through the town with the same message.

"Foreigners from where? From Madrid? Barcelona?"

"No, real foreigners. Maybe *Alemanes*."

"Germans? For me? Are you sure?"

"I showed them the path to your house. Yes, I'm sure."

When she reached her gate, the *peseta* note still hung from the wire. She removed it, read the words, and quickly let herself in. While her goats streamed in around her, she re-read the note. It touched her memory, begged for an interpretation, and finally it came.

"Ah, yes," she said.

She turned her head up to the sky. "I would say *Gracias a Dios*, God, if you were up there. But as you are not, I will say nothing."

She wondered, briefly, if Pepe or Carlos, or any other storeowner would accept this bill with "Say Hello to Mr. Roosevelt" now written across it.

§

The day transposed into a star-swept night and Carmen felt the cold even through her wool sweater. She sat on a rock across the ravine from her home. Her goats were tucked in, but she still could hear them snort and struggle for a better position in the pen. It was unlike her to be up after dark, but she couldn't sleep, couldn't eat, and couldn't figure out what would be the significance of the money attached to her gate today.

Of course, she remembered the young man and his motorcycle. and who he was looking for. Who could forget that? He was naïve then; would he still be now? And her friends had said he was accompanied by a beautiful woman. His wife?

How she had wanted to share her life in a different way with someone. At first, someone special, then later, someone who would love her back, and then, much later, someone who would simply make noise so she could know she was not alone. Would that not be a blessing as she approached death?

But there were no blessings for Carmen Escobar. Duty, yes, plenty of that in her years. Observance of all that was holy? Perhaps she could use a little more attention to this. Loyalty? Unequivocally.

She thought, once, that her faithfulness might pay off handsomely, especially when Franco took his last breath. Her eagerness for the next step was palpable; it showed all over her.

"Oh, Maria," her friends had said. "Finally, has love come to you? Will you at last experience the best that a man has to offer?"

"Shut up," she had told them, but was secretly pleased to be the subject of so many whispers and so much romantic conjecture.

She had nearly given herself away in her flight to Ventura to tell Robert. "He is dead," she urgently said through cupped hands in the dirt. "He is finally gone."

But, as she now knew and may have known then, a man sentenced to a decades-long life underground could no longer hear of changes in his fortune. He could only understand, as Robert Martin did in 1975, "If I continue to steer the course, I will live on."

"I can't believe you," he had said to her. "And I'm sorry that I can't."

And now, sitting under the Andalusian stars, Carmen Escobar said to herself, "Why do I keep on with this man? Am I not in my own prison all these years as well?"

She thought of when she was a girl of twelve and how she often brought her mother grief. "Mari Carmen, why can't you just stay indoors with the rest of us? Why do you risk your life in these times? The factory has been bombed. There is no reason for you to go exploring up there. The wrong people hide in that place."

But she soon learned who the real wrong people were. They didn't hide in abandoned villages. Sometimes they lived right next door. And they seldom, if ever, hid.

The rest of the night was lost for her. She didn't move from the spot as her thoughts drifted. The physical pain from 1937 was sealed over long ago but it was the psychological that ground at her still.

In one moment, to be twelve and a virgin. In the next to still be twelve, but now a humiliated woman, no, a barren cypher of womanhood. Oh, that special pain. The pain that made you cry forever.

"No," she said aloud. "I will not visit there again."

But she did, of course. Just like the night she was dragged out of her house, kicking and shouting, passed along the street among men she didn't know and some she did. There were foreigners who spoke a language she had never heard. Finally dumped in front of the barber who, against his own will as well, shaved her head down to the very nubbin. Then an entire jar of castor oil forced down her throat before she was made to march, oh that horrible march up and down the streets under the lights of torches held by slobbering intoxicated men.

"Why?" she recalled asking every one of these men.

"Whore," each and every one of them answered back.

And she hadn't even known what that meant.

She soiled herself, could never control it after the castor oil. She thought then the humiliation was complete. But she was wrong. One of those men with the torches seized her and slung her over his shoulder. He carried her into an alley where right before they disappeared, she saw the priest, Blas Alvarez, leaning against a wall, his finger curled under his nose, eyes closed, mumbling a prayer. She thought, open your eyes, Father, save me.

But another man was waiting in the alley with a bucket of cold water. The two ripped off her nightgown and dashed her private parts with the water, then scrubbed her until she bled with a stiff brush meant for horses.

"Mama!" she cried. "Papa! God!"

But these men with the blank eyes held her down and shoved things inside her, not flesh, but objects, stone and wood and whatever else they could grab. She screamed and screamed for friends and neighbors to rescue her. Soon, blood was flowing brightly in concert with the pain that flamed through her.

"Whore," they spat as they unbuttoned their trousers and urinated upon her. Then they left her there to bleed out and to die. Later, she awoke under the spell of shock. She could not feel the lower half of her body. It was dark in the alley. Wet with urine and blood, she reached out a hand and felt the whitewash chipping on the wall her head was lodged against.

"Mama," she tried, but her voice was not hers; instead, it was deep and guttural, like a snuffling dog picking through the entrails of a slaughtered pig. And she felt like that as she grew weak and colder. A girl of twelve, once warm and grateful in her bed, now shivering and dying on the cobblestones of her very own village.

Chapter Fourteen
Robert, France, 1937

The day dawned cold and dry. They had been driving all night. Robert caught glimpses of the Mediterranean whenever the truck stopped to let the men stretch their legs. Most stood on the side of the road and smoked, staring out to the water, but also keeping a tennis match going with their eyes. At Valencia they turned inland, and slowly rose in altitude as the land became flatter, more arid. The road was dotted with chuckholes and the men bounced around the back of the truck, giving up on holding on and bumping into each other in a kind of military dance.

On February 5th, they arrived at Albacete where the republican training camp was located. The tailgate dropped and, one by one, the men jumped out on shaky legs. Once out, Robert scanned the area. Suspiciously, on the side of one low building, he thought he saw splatters of blood, as if a gruesome execution had taken place there. He shaded his eyes against the glaring sun, and shivered.

Four men stood in front of the group, each shouting out orders in a different language. One was American, and he invited Robert and Max to form a line far to the right of the truck. Six or seven others lined up with them.

"I'm Peters," said the man. "Welcome to hell. Who wants to see the devil?"

Max laughed.

"First things first," said Peters. "You guys smell like shit. Over there where that truck's parked, you'll find a fire hose and a little bar of soap. Strip down and lather yourselves up. It may be a while before you get clean again. Move."

And they did. Hardly a well-oiled machine, they trotted, ran, walked to the truck. Having taken the lead, Max quickly found the chunks of soap, handed one to Robert, and had his clothes off in seconds. He stood under the spray, shouted to the sky at how cold it was, then proceeded to cover his body with lather.

"We're finally here, buddy," he said to Robert as the two worked to rid their bodies of grime.

"Thank God there's sun. I'm about to freeze my nuts off," Robert said.

"You could use a little toughening up." Max nudged him, nearly knocking him over.

Robert couldn't help the trembling as he stood beneath the hose once more and rinsed off every speck of soap. "Now what?" he said, but he saw his friend already at a long table where uniforms lay in rows.

He shook the water off and walked over. "You'll need a small," a man was saying to Max. "Since these are French, look for *petit*."

It was all there, underwear, blouse and pants, boots. All used. Different styles. All from the Great War.

When they secured their uniforms, the man said, "Let's go." He led them to one of the buildings. As Robert trotted by, he saw the stains up close and indeed they were blood, now caked, with flies trying to find any remnants. He gulped, feeling exposed in his nakedness.

Inside the barracks, a long affair populated with cots, some already used, they were allowed to dry off before donning their uniforms. A French medium was not quite the same as in the U.S., but Robert made do. When he was laced up, he stood and faced Max.

"How do I look?" he said.

"Like a mean son-of-a-bitch."

Robert thought that was actually what Max looked like. As if he were crouched like an animal, ready to spring.

Later, they were instructed to line up outside the barracks where they would receive their necessities. When Robert got to the front, he was handed a pack containing a tiny pick and shovel, and a long stick. He looked around.

"Do I get a gun?"

"They'll be here. For now, just pretend."

And later, they did. They formed a unit of twenty-five, bonded by their language. Quickly, they were led to march. Robert spent a good deal of time trying to match his steps to those around him, but Max, in the front row, set the pace, and within minutes, the unit moved as one. Max seemed to ignore the fact it was a piece of cane that rested on his shoulder.

By nightfall, Robert was exhausted. And his feet hurt. They were stuffed into his boots already formed from the size of the previous owner. He wondered if the man was dead and if so, how did he die.

Chow was bread and soup from yet another line. He sat out on a pile of stones next to Max. "Not exactly a top-notch unit," he said.

"Quiet," said Max. "It is what it is. Think of what you'll learn."

"Those sticks aren't going to be much protection when the rebels find us."

Max sighed and used the last of his bread to scoop out the soup. "The more you suffer, the more you learn."

"Then I'm learning a lot. Where are the girls?"

Max stood. The light was so low, he could only see a few feet away. "Let's go." He started walking away from the barracks.

"Hey, where you headed?" said Robert.

"Follow me."

At another block of barracks, men had built a fire in the middle of the grounds. They crowded around it, some laughing, some singing.

"Why come halfway around the world just to hang out with Americans?" Max said.

They stood for a while inside the shadow of the fire. Stories were being told. There was laughter, to be sure, but the tales were punctuated by moments of deep silence. Robert didn't understand a word. What strange language was this?

After a few minutes, Max joined the group. He stood closer to the fire, rubbed his hands together. "Must be in the thirties." He wrapped his coat tighter around himself.

The other men stopped talking, adjusted the caps on their heads, chewed on what was left of their bread.

"We don't mean to stop you," Max said. "Can we stay?"

One man nodded, thrust out his hand. "Roman," he said.

Robert stepped closer. The firelight flickered on his face.

"Max." He shook Roman's hand. "And this is my friend, Robert. We're Americans. Where you from?"

"Hello, Robert. I am from Poland. This man is from Czechoslovakia. Over there, Prussia. All of us are from Europe."

"Thank you for being here," said Max. "It's important."

The Czech man spoke in his own language.

"Excuse me, but he is finishing his story," Roman said. "We are telling of how we came to be here."

Robert watched the faces of all the men as they listened. On them, he saw fear, sorrow, surprise, understanding. Carefully, he sat down on the cold earth. Soon, he realized he didn't have to understand the words to get the meaning. When the man finished his story, the group applauded.

"He's a Jew," Roman said to Max. "And I think you are too. So you can appreciate what he tells us. He says his family was in Poland and were captured by the Nazis. They did not understand why. They were imprisoned. Starved. Beaten. He was sure all would die. The family elected him to be the one to get help. Instead of food, he fortified himself with passion. One night, he found a way to escape. How he grieves that he left his parents behind. But he escaped. He walked, ran away from Poland, back to Czechoslovakia. But no one would have him. And the Nazis, they wanted Czechoslovakia too. So, he learned about this war in

Spain against the fascists. He thinks he can defeat the fascists here and that will make a path back to find his parents."

Max clapped his hands, smiled at the man. "You're right. I am a Jew. And I've come for the same reason. To defeat the fascists and claim the power for the real people."

"Welcome, comrade," Roman said. "We all say welcome. And what about your friend?"

All eyes traveled to Robert. "I'm not Jewish," Robert said. "But I'm here to fight for the cause."

"And how did you both get here?"

Max glanced back, caught Robert's eye. "Nothing like your Czech friend. We heard the call, could not ignore it. You know how that is."

Roman nodded. "We all heard it." He stopped and looked up to the sky. Very softly, he began to sing *The Internationale*. One by one, the men stood up. The voices grew louder. Robert felt a tingle on his flesh. Finally, he thought. Finally, I'm a part of this.

In Polish, the entire group sang: *...orgarnic ludzki rod.* Max laughed and clapped, tried to pick out and shout the Polish words, but ended up singing his own version: *The Internationale unites the human race.*

Robert noticed a man holding a rifle now stood about ten yards away. He tipped back his beret and walked toward the group. About halfway there, he yelled:

"No, no. If you are to fight in Spain, you must learn it in Spanish."

"And who are you?" Roman said, standing.

The man stepped closer, straightened his rifle and pointed it at Roman. "I am Andre Marty, the base commander. You are very close, young man. Salute me or die."

Robert's stomach knotted up. He looked quickly to Max, who was simply staring at Marty.

Slowly, reluctantly, Roman's hand came up in a close-fisted salute.

Marty lowered his rifle. "If we are to win this war, we must have discipline. All of you. Go to your barracks for the night."

When the group hesitated, once again Marty raised his rifle. He watched them intently as they jumped up and hurried to their beds.

§

"They are upon us," Marty said the next day to the entire group standing at loose attention. "The Falangists have struck."

The news hit Robert square in the gut. I'm not ready, he thought. But Max, of course, was one of those pumping air.

"The lorries have arrived with your weapons," Marty continued. "Spend time getting to know them. Your weapon is your friend. Your God. Your lover. Act like you love it back."

In line at one of the lorries, Robert stood with his head down and his hands in his pockets.

"You should be happy," Max said. "Now your stick can be firewood."

"Do you know how to shoot? Have you even held a gun before?" He knew the answer was no for himself. Since he'd heard about the impending battle, he could only visualize his rifle exploding in his hands.

"I've held a gun. Never shot it. But how hard can it be? And think of the thrill you're going to feel. One by one, you get rid of the enemy."

Robert reached up when he got to the head of the line. He was handed down a rifle from the Great War. "Careful the cosmoline," said the man handing it to him. "Got to clean it off before you use it. And here's your hundred." He was passed a box of bullets.

"What the hell's cosmoline?" Robert said as he and Max walked away.

"Some kind of wax to keep the weapon from rusting and locking up. And, hey, point that thing the other way."

Robert noticed how more seasoned men were carrying their weapons and slid his over his shoulder by the strap.

"We're leaving in ten minutes," shouted the battalion commander. "Everything you own in the world. Either take it or leave it."

"Now?" said Robert.

Another American bumped his shoulder. "Talk about on-the-job training, eh?"

It was a bomb of disorganization. Robert was not the only one still wet behind the ears, but there were others who had a look of determination on their faces that Robert seemed not to possess. He filled his pack with the pick and shovel, with chunks of bread going stale. Outside, he found Max looking calm in the midst of chaos, and the two jogged to a waiting truck. They jumped on, leaned against one of the weak sides and took off, they were told, toward Madrid.

§

Robert and Max sat in a trench dug out by someone else. Drying dung was scattered along the bottom. Robert used a communal cloth to wipe his weapon clean of the cosmoline. Further up the line, a weapons expert tested each soldier about his knowledge of the gun. In the distance, the sound of bombs crept into their hearing. Robert scanned the horizon, but could see nothing beyond a ridge.

"It's okay," Max said. "My dad says you get used to it quick enough. You don't even think about the fact that you might die."

Robert nodded. "My dad, too. I know it'll be okay. But it's all coming so fast."

"These guys are good. We're all here for the same purpose. Think about it like it's a baseball team, or football maybe. Think about relying on each other to win."

"How is it you know so much about this?" Robert said.

Max grabbed the cloth back from Robert and polished the stock of his gun. "Because it's all I could think about in the last six months. It lit a fire when Franco invaded the country. It made me mad... made me, I don't know, more radical, I guess."

"Are you a Communist then?"

"I'm the opposite of a Fascist. If that makes me a Communist, so be it."

"I don't know what I am," Robert said.

"It's really okay. Do you see anybody drilling you about it? You have a right to be here as much as anyone else. Just do your best."

The weapons expert was older, had lines of worry around his eyes. He said he became an expert during the Great War. He showed both Max and Robert about the use of their Russian rifles.

"You load like this. And you re-load like this." He pulled back the bolt. "Only don't re-load 'cause you missed. You got exactly a hundred of these babies. Shoot to kill every time." He handed the rifle back to Robert. "Good luck, son." And he was instantly further down the line.

Robert stared at his weapon, hoping it might talk to him, tell him the intricacies of warfare. Max scrambled out of the trench and started practicing.

Later, the commander of the Abraham Lincoln Battalion called everyone forward. He read off names from a list. There would be three units of infantrymen, one unit of machine gunners.

"Dammit," Max said, when his name didn't show up on the machine gunners' list. "You can get more Nazis with one of those."

Both Robert and Max were assigned to the infantry, each given a time for sentry duty.

"What does a sentry do here?" asked Robert.

"He's on the lookout," whispered Max. "You warn the others if you see anything out of the ordinary. You see anybody sneaking around from the other side, you report it."

Night dropped over the barren land. Under the stars, sentries of ancient olive trees created the landscape. Robert was due for his turn at midnight, and he waited patiently, his gun over his legs. Beside him, Max slept. How can anybody sleep at a time like this, Robert wondered. He looked down on his friend and hoped he could come through for him.

At midnight, Robert followed one of the commanders to a spot on the very edge of the precipice. Down below, the Jarama River flowed peacefully through a valley.

"It's quiet now," the man said. "But it was hell today. Don't take anything for granted. It might be the last time you do. The rebels have some crafty gents doing their dirty work."

"I'll do my best, sir," Robert said.

The man slapped him on the back. "Don't call me that. Think of all of us as the same." Then he disappeared.

For a few minutes it was quiet. Then he heard voices. He lifted his gun, had it at the ready. His heart hammered. He wished he were braver.

The voices rang across the valley. They sounded familiar. It was the way his fellow soldiers talked to each other. And he knew what his fellow soldiers talked about. Women. Bars. How all the enemy were *maricones*. He wished he knew Spanish better. Then he could pick apart the sounds. But this didn't really sound like the Spanish he heard around his own barracks. In fact, it might not be Spanish at all. He tightened his grip around the rifle.

It grew colder as he waited, listening. Next time he'd bring a blanket to hide under. Something wiggled along the seam of his trousers. An insect gift from the previous owner? He scratched absently, thought of his mother and father. He'd write them again soon. He hoped to be able to send the letters he'd accumulated, but that might be difficult. He imagined his mother, sitting in their kitchen nook at night, worrying about her son. Why did he agree to do this?

The voices appeared again. Did they seem closer? Were they closer? He bit at his lip, tasted copper. For an unknown reason, he stood, trying to hear better perhaps. It was clearer this way. And the voices were closer. But they laughed. If they were the Falangists, why would they raise their voices to alert their enemy? It had to be voices coming from behind him, his fellow soldiers, those that couldn't sleep in the makeshift trenches. Those who couldn't abide the cold weather and needed to jump up and wave their arms to get heat into their bodies.

Robert's thoughts died down. His heart slowed. He felt warmer now, more secure. In another hour his replacement tapped on his shoulder. When he turned, it was Max, ready to relieve him.

"We're in it now," Max said.

§

Robert awoke to frantic voices. At first, he thought he was back out at sentry, but he was asleep in the trenches, covered by his coat. When the shouting started, he grabbed for his rifle and sat upright. A light came toward him, and he pointed his rifle at it, but it was his comrades and he climbed out of the trench to get orders on what he must do.

When he got to the group of soldiers, he could see that one of them lay on the ground. He pushed through and found Max, pale and lifeless on the crunchy grass. His throat was slashed, ear to ear, but no blood ran from the wound.

"Oh, fuck," he said. "Fuck, fuck, fuck." He dropped to his knees and took one of Max's hands. He felt for a pulse, but the hand was cold, no life pumped through him. A cloud fell over his thinking. He couldn't register this shock. He felt hands on his back, a pat here and there.

"Who did this?" he finally said. "Franco?"

"Yes, but not who we thought. It's the Africans, the Moors. Silent killers, those boys."

A hundred thoughts flew through Robert's head. Should he have warned Max about the voices when he took over the watch? Should he have stayed with his friend? Could he have fought off the killers?

"Nothing we can do," said their commander. "Who wants burial detail?"

No one, of course, relished the idea, but Robert's hand shot up as he started to cry. "I'll do it."

"You'll need help. You there, O'Neill, Rutherford... you give him a hand. Bury him deep, boys. Tell us when you're ready and we'll give him a proper send-off."

Daytime heat kept the ground from freezing, so the picks and shovels served well to dig a hole deep and wide enough to suit the needs of Max. Sometime later, it was ready and they carefully laid his body, now wrapped in a shroud, in the center of the grave. When they had filled it half full, one of them walked back to the battalion and invited the others.

"We need a cross," Rutherford said.

But Robert was quick to say, "No, we don't. It wouldn't matter to him. He was a Jew." He filled in the last of the grave and stood back. "What do Jews do anyway?"

They looked from one to the other, before one of them stepped out. "I'm am Jewish," he said. "I'll do it." He asked Robert to stand next to him. "I know you were this man's friend." He reached out and quickly tore a part of Robert's uniform. "This is a sample of our grief, the tearing away of this man from us. Blessed are You, Truthful Judge. God has given, God has taken away, blessed be the name of God."

Robert felt the cool air penetrate the hole in his shirt.

"We need to say a few words," said the man. "And it makes sense that it would be you. Please?"

Robert sucked in a heavy breath and raised his head to the sky. "Max was my best friend. Always was. He was a guy who believed strongly in the rightness of things. He didn't have an easy life, and he didn't die well. But he did die fighting for a cause he strongly believed in and for that we should all be grateful that he was in our lives, even if for a short time. He was a kind and generous man. He is the reason I am here now. May he rest in peace."

A murmur flowed through the group of them.

The man then said, "He is now sheltered beneath the wings of God's presence."

"Amen," they all said in unison.

"I don't know of anything else to say," said the man, and he disappeared back into the group.

The commander said, "Let's all get back to our posts. We'll need to double up. The Moors are out there, we know that now. So look out for each other. Max here didn't have a chance. I should have said something. They move like whispers. Watch out."

The group slipped away, but Robert stayed. The commander looked back, shook his head. "You're going to have to get over this fast," he said. "You can't let it drag you down. Spend a few minutes, but then hightail it back here. We don't know where those assholes are."

Robert dropped to his knees. From the time they brought Max into their midst only three hours had passed. It was still deep night, but morning would come within a few more hours. He placed his hand on the fresh dirt, thought about Max's smile and positive talk, his love for life and what was right. He hoped he could transfer a bit of his friend to himself, but so far it wasn't working. The shock was still fresh, disabling. His brain wouldn't let him think the way he should be thinking.

After a few more minutes, he stood and walked back toward the trenches. His courage had taken flight. I can't do this now, he thought. Where am I going? What can I do? He dropped down in the trench again. The men around him were fitful, but mostly sleeping. He gathered his pack, stuffed in his pick and shovel, some bread, a bit of cheese. He picked up his rifle and hefted it on his shoulder.

"You're not going on duty so soon?" one of the guys said.

"Yes. Yes, I am."

"Good luck then."

"Thanks."

Robert crawled out of the trench and slowly made his way back to Max's grave. The further he got from the trenches, the lonelier he felt. He squatted and once again caressed the dirt with his hand.

"See you, buddy," he said. "I'm going off to fight the war."

And then he stood and turned, walking in the opposite direction from the rest of the troops.

Chapter Fifteen
Eugenio III, Andalusia, 1989

He had little time for beauty. It could throw him off the trail. He had seen it happen with his colleagues. One look and they were caught up in carnal tension. But not Eugenio. Not usually. But he had to peek out the window at the American woman sitting on the other side of the square. He was mad and aroused at the same time. He could swear she was zeroing in on him, and, maybe for the first time, he felt stripped down, nearly helpless. Was it because she was American?

Grow up, Eugenio, he thought. Remember why you're here. But he had to get one more peek. The woman was gorgeous and spoke his language well.

Eventually, he dropped his gaze and turned to Pepe.

"Do you get many foreign visitors this far up in the hills?" he said.

"A few," said Pepe, dabbling with some spare coins sitting on the counter. "But not many. The drive up is tiresome."

"It's that garbage dump," Eugenio said. "But when they do come, these foreigners, why do they come?"

"Perhaps for the Murillo in the church. Or for the architecture. We are more modern here now. Not like before the war. Maybe you'd like to tour the church with our priest."

"That won't be necessary." He scanned the shelves. Still no Bollycao.

Anticipating the *Guardia's* disappointment, Pepe said, "Juanito is dropping off a shipment of chocolate sandwiches today. Will you wait for it?"

"What else do they come for?" Eugenio said.

"The foreigners?" Pepe sighed. "I don't know why they come. Sometimes I think they just take the wrong road."

"Do you think that some come because they've heard of the legend?"

"The legend, *señor*?"

"Don't pretend you don't know what I'm talking about. The war. The story of the foreigner and the saint."

Now Pepe was truly searching. He felt sweat gather under his arms. "The saint? From the war?"

"Of course, the war. What else is there to talk about?"

"But the foreigners, they wouldn't know of that story, would they?"

Eugenio leaned over the counter, cutting the sun off from Pepe's face.

"Francisco Robles de Casares was a saint. Never forget that."

"I won't," said Pepe. "I never will."

"You really have no idea what it means, do you?" Here Eugenio stopped and took note of himself. He stood straighter again and pulled on the waistcoat of his uniform. "In any event, the legend is very important to me. I need to understand it better. I might be willing to help out a dedicated entrepreneur such as you, if I, too, get help."

"How could you help?"

"I'll say no more. But I hope I've found the eyes and ears of La Jolla de Málaga."

Pepe pointed at one of his eyes. Then at an ear. Then nodded solemnly.

"So, you do understand what I'm saying?"

"Yes, sir, I do."

Eugenio placed his hands on his hips. Through the cluttered window, he saw the woman still sitting at the bar across the square. "I have a test for you," he said. "To see how well you can uncover news for me."

"Anything."

"Find out what those foreigners are here for."

"Which?" Pepe said, straining to see past the flowers crowding the glass.

"You see them? The beautiful woman and the simple man?"

"I see them."

"I want to know about them."

"But they could just finish their drinks and be gone forever."

"I guess we'll find out," Eugenio said. "Next time then."

"At your service," said Pepe.

§

Michael Virtue sat up in his bed at the Hotel Ecuador. His sleep was off, his wakefulness as well. Earlier he tried to call his kids, but to no avail. The connection was raw, kept dropping. He heard Eva's voice, then nothing, then a great sad static. Three times with the same result.

He rolled out of bed and pulled on his jeans. In his bag, he found a shirt and uncurled it over his head. He needed a walk.

Outside, the air was warm and dry. The lights were still on at the front desk. He padded by in his deck shoes.

He found a bar, crowded and noisy. The clientele spilled out to a patio with its arrangement of metal tables. His bare Spanish was completely lost in the great hubbub of voices. He spied a couple getting up from one table and hurried to it. The group next to it stole one of his chairs, but he just smiled and sat.

It took a few minutes for a waiter to walk by. Michael held up a finger. "*Una caña*," he said. The waiter scribbled it down and was soon lost in the bodies.

Wide awake now, Michael tried to listen to the conversations around him, but understanding was nearly impossible. He leaned back and waited for his beer. Glancing through the window, he saw her, sitting toward the end of the giant semi-circle of a bar, a cigarette in her hand, hovering above the counter.

There was a man next to her, a smile pasted on his grizzled face. His hair was crafted in dreadlocks, and he was constantly running his hand underneath and flipping them away. The last time he did this, Delia broke into deep and natural laughter. And, as she laughed, her fingers brushed against the back of the man's hand.

So provocative, Michael thought. In front of the fireplace at her home and now this, in plain sight. What's she after, the psychologist in him wondered. He stopped staring at her, just in time for the waiter to drop off his beer. He pulled a wad of bills from his pocket and the waiter sifted through them, removed what he needed, hesitated, and then captured another note. When Michael glanced up, he grinned and dashed off to another table.

Michael took a long drink. Through the glass, he could see that Delia had now left the bar. Dreadlock man was gone as well. He felt a strange sense of loss. He stood up and peered further inside, catching a glimpse of the man, hair flopping against his back.

Michael quickly scraped the change into his pocket, downed the rest of his beer, and took off once more through the crowd. He caught up with them on the other side of the building. But he ducked back behind the corner when he spied them kissing on the sidewalk. Then, something odd happened. Delia flattened out the man's hand and held it against her cheek. She pulled it back and guided it hard at her cheek again. Then again. He could hear the slap from where he hid. She let go, but the man seemed to get the drift. He slapped her, gently, but firmly on his own now. One more, and she left him, walking quickly down the sidewalk. When the man followed, Michael broke from his hiding place and moved in behind them.

They turned at the opposite corner of the building and headed down the steps toward the hotel. He lost them for a moment in front of the Bird of Paradise, but picked them up again as they walked past Michael's own cottage and into Delia's.

Now would be the time to go into his room and try to go back to sleep, but he couldn't talk himself into leaving.

As he sneaked around to the back, he thought about Mason for a moment. How many times did the two of them talk about guys who would do the very same thing that Michael was now doing? But the light was on inside the cottage and he ducked behind the branches of a hibiscus and watched.

The lamp near the side of the bed shone low, but it didn't keep him from seeing what was happening. The man kept wanting to kiss her again, but Delia pushed him away, actually shoved him so that he stumbled backward. She, meanwhile, took this time to yank off her clothes, so that by the time the man had recovered, she lay topless on the bed.

Seeing her, Michael now felt awkward. It was as if a light shined directly over him, revealing the kind of person he actually was. Sick, he thought. What am I doing? He escaped the hibiscus and quickly walked away.

He ended up at the main office, where the night manager sat on a high stool, reading the newspaper. In a mime of what Delia did with the man, Michael slapped one of his own cheeks, shaking his head. He had to stop doing this with her, this chasing, this stalking. This wasn't what he came for.

Michael approached the man. "Can I ask you a question?"

"If you speak slowly. My English is not so perfect."

"What do you know about the Civil War here in Malaga?"

The manager reacted as if struck. "This is not a subject we talk easily about."

"I had an uncle," Michael said. "He disappeared in one of the local villages back at the start of the war. My partner says he could be one of the people who hid out. Is that even possible?"

The manager set down the newspaper, then picked it up again and folded it in smaller and smaller squares. "I am not very old… I remember Franco but little else."

"I just need to know if it's a possibility."

"Please. Let's talk football. Or tourist spots you can visit. Anything else."

Michael stayed only a moment longer. Through the window, he could see the manager as he unfolded the newspaper.

Back in his room, Michael heard noises coming from Delia's cottage. He turned on the TV to cover the noises and lay down on his bed.

Michael had thought about his uncle since he was five years old. Back then he was lectured by his father about the foolhardiness of war, of youth. "A wicked combination," his father had said. "Young guys think they're bulletproof, and before you know it, they walk right into the bullets."

Michael hadn't really understood this at the time, but whenever his uncle popped into his thinking, it was in a different context than simple youthful ignorance. Instead, as the years past, Robert took on a mythic quality – like that of an adventurer, like Odysseus. Someone who had taken his life and made something of it, challenged himself. Regardless of what others thought, he chose his route and followed through. These qualities became heroic for Michael, most likely were the basis for his earlier trip to Spain.

"There's a reason I'm here," said Michael aloud to himself. "And it's got nothing to do with Delia's needs. It has to do with Robert."

He clicked off the TV, slid further down in the sheets and covered his head with one of the pillows, hoping to drown out the sounds from next door. Soon he was dreaming of sailing on the bright Mediterranean in the midst of a great adventure.

A few hours later, he awakened. It was quieter, although he could still hear the pounding of a bass coming from the bar. He tried again to call his family. After failing to connect on the first two attempts, on the third, Danny picked up.

"Hey, Dad," Danny said. "You sound far away."

"Well, I am. What are you doing?"

"Hanging out at Mom's condo."

"And Carmen?"

"Don't know. I think she's still asleep."

"It's afternoon there, isn't it?"

"Like I said, I don't know what she's doing. Mom's taking us to a game tonight."

"Good for her. Is she there?"

"Hold on."

There was a shuffle in the background and soon Eva came on the line.

"Where's Carmen?" Michael said.

"Wow. You sound so far away. I can barely hear you."

"Do you even know where your daughter is?"

"Ah, what a relief," she said. "For a minute there I thought you'd changed."

"Very funny. I made it to Spain."

The pause went on too long.

"Eva?"

"Good, Michael. It'll be good for you. How long are you planning to be there?"

"Not sure. You should see it, though. It's beautiful here."

"I'm sure it is. But you haven't answered my question. How long are you going to be there?"

"Couple weeks."

"You do have a return ticket, don't you?"

"Of course. I'm not running away."

"Well, I hope you aren't. Come on, I know it's late there. Get some sleep." The phone clicked and buzzed.

He held it in his hand for a while. That was a bad idea, he thought. Eva was mad at him for making the trip. He'd never been much of an impulsive man before.

He finally hung up. He knew the night would be consumed with memories of Eva in their early days. That was the problem with leaving a life behind. Too much blank space to fill in with new desires.

§

The next morning before he dressed, Michael packed his bags. The sun had yet to rise. He stripped and slid into the shower, which was, at best, lukewarm. He leaned his head against the wall and let the water pound down his back. But the water went cold so he rinsed off and stepped out into the room. He dressed in the same clothes he'd worn the day before.

The bar opened just as the sun came over the mountain, and they served breakfast. He ordered eggs and toast and as it arrived, Delia walked in.

She sat down without a word. He could smell perfume and noticed her hair was wet at her neck and ears. After she gave her order, she said, "I hope you slept better than I did last night."

"I'm surprised you slept at all," he said. He tested his cup of Nescafe. "We have to leave today."

"Why?"

"I guess I should say I have to leave. You can stay if you want. I've got things to investigate."

"I assume you mean your uncle."

"Yes."

"I don't know. It's a little town. I wonder what that *Guardia's* after."

Her breakfast arrived, a potato and onion omelet, and she started in on it. When Michael finished, he watched her. "Don't let me hold you back," he said.

She picked at her food, thinking.

"I called the fam last night," he said.

"And they were just hopping to get you back home."

"Not really."

She cut into her omelet and a bit of it dribbled on the plate. "I can come with, I guess. My calendar's not exactly full these days."

"There could be a hostel there, or something like that we can stay in."

"I'm not convinced that town is the place we should be. But, I'm game so far. Unless you decide to take up chasing me again."

"Not going to happen. I'm over you."

She took her last bite of omelet and sat, fork in hand, staring at him. "What a thing for a partner to say," she said. She waited a moment and smiled before she pushed her plate away.

After breakfast, they drove off from the hotel. This time they did not slow for pedestrians or animals. Soon they were up the hill to the village, only now, they didn't stop at the *martirio*, rather they drove down the right-hand street toward Carmen's house.

The note was gone from the nail. He pounded and pounded on the gate but got no answer. Behind him, Delia grabbed hold of his hand. "She's out working," she said.

They got back in the car and sat for a moment.

"What's next?" Delia asked.

"I want to find my motorcycle."

"Do I have to remind you that it was twenty years ago? Do you know what can happen in that amount of time?"

"As a matter of fact, I do. Every time I look in a mirror."

She opened her door. "You drive then."

Michael muttered as he slid behind the wheel. They bounced further down the hill. "I know it was on this side of the village."

They made a wide turn and the lowland behind La Jolla spread out below them.

"Yes," he said. "Only those new trees over there weren't here before."

At the bottom, a sign said, *Prohibido la Caza* and *Lo Puerto*, with an arrow pointing down a road torn up by weather and overuse. Michael stopped the car.

"Does that say it's illegal to get married here?"

She shook her head. "You really need me, you know that? It says, NO HUNTING."

It was a carnival ride to the next village – up the exposed rocks, and down the dry hollows. Once, the undercarriage of the car made an ominous scraping sound and Michael kept checking the rearview to see if they were leaving a trail of oil.

When they reached the next town, he again stopped the car. A group of women stood at the top of a curve. "Ask them," he said. "I remember concrete stairs. Ask them if they know where some are."

Delia got out and stretched, then walked toward the women. She chatted with them for a minute or two and then came back.

"You're in luck," she said. "The stairs are in the village on the road straight ahead. But if we walk down the riverbed, we will see them. Or, we can take this middle path and cut across to hit the bottom of them. Only we have to walk from here."

Michael pulled the car farther over to the side of the track and got out. "We need the exercise, don't we?"

The women above watched as the two of them sought out the head of the middle trail, and nodded their heads in unison when they'd found it. The path was wide enough for a goat and covered with loose gravel and sand. It led, in a double-back pattern, down to the riverbed, the bottom of which was coated with swirled deposits of heavy grained sand. They picked their way along it, keeping the village in sight above them. Soon, Michael was sweating.

Ahead, a grove of tall and narrow bamboo cane shot up on both sides. It blocked their view of the village for a moment. Michael stopped in the middle, took his bearings. Stunted oleander threw out a few pink flowers. He was beginning to feel it, perhaps a sense memory, but something reminded him.

"What?" Delia said.

"The smell."

She inhaled deeply, cocked her head. "I'd say goats in rut, manure and garlic."

"You're so cynical," he said as he took off again.

"Look around you. There's nothing here."

"Then that should make it paradise for you."

She picked up her pace and left him behind, but he didn't try to catch up. Maybe he was naïve. But it could have been that the smells were bringing his memory back. He knew he could make romance out of tragedy. Wasn't IDC his idea to begin with?

The cane thinned out and Delia stopped and waited for him. When he got close, she pointed toward the hill. He could see it now, a set of steps, dried lichen coloring them a dull green. He counted them, but lost track at thirty. Ahead, the sides of the riverbed grew slowly higher. They decided to walk out of it where the going was easier.

The group of women had moved to the top of the stairs. "They're a curious lot," he said.

"Too curious, if you ask me."

They soon arrived at the bottom of the stairway. Delia traced small indentations in the cement.

"Old footsteps," she said. She glanced at them as they rose. "Look how the balls of their feet made deeper impressions. People were in a hurry when this was laid."

But Michael had closed his eyes so he could see himself hitting this bottom and spinning out of control towards the river. He walked back, staring down, and there it was, or a descendent of it, a thick broom jutting out just at the point where the ground dropped off into the arroyo. He pointed down.

"Right here," he said. "Right here is where I saved my own life."

She stood firm and leaned over the edge. "You're shitting me."

"What?" Michael scrambled over as well, but slipped and had to grab the branch for the second time in twenty years.

"See that? Down there. The rust and chrome? I think we may have found your bike."

To realize a part of him had never left this place filled Michael with excitement and a kind of awe. "This is great."

"It's a heap of junk."

"I'm going down there." Already, he was searching for an opening that would allow it. Finding none, he started trotting back the way they came.

"I'll be right here," she yelled after him.

He was glad she didn't come. This was his history, not hers. At the spot they turned up, he jumped down into the riverbed again. His feet slid in the thick sand, but he hopped from stone to stone. In another minute he came across the wreckage.

Of course, there wasn't much left of it. The forked frame that once held the wheel in place now resembled the tusks of a small elephant. The handlebars had no covers at the ends. No rear wheel either, no motor even. No seat, except for errant leather strands attached to metal; the goats had a field day over the years. Half of it was buried in the sand and he imagined the river ebbing and flowing with the seasons, drowning the remains every year.

He sat down next to it. In one of his fantasies, he thought some enterprising young man had dragged it out and taken it home, where he added parts here and there when he was flush, until he had re-fashioned the bike into a machine that even those original Italian artisans would be proud of. So much for fantasy. He touched it and felt the warmth. Holding onto the rusting metal, he closed his eyes again. Now he heard it, not just smelled it. A bell.

He opened his eyes in time to see the first goat round the corner up ahead. Then one behind, then two, then the whole herd hobbled along in back of the be-belled leader. Ten yards away, the animal stopped and bleated. Michael stood just as a small stone kicked up the dust near his foot. On the other side of the riverbed, he saw her, dressed in black, her white hair wrapped severely in a bun. She tossed another rock in his direction.

He waved, and she raised her walking stick in the air.

She walked between two tall canes and stepped down into the riverbed. Her goats charted her progress, but were not moving. Michael finally unpinned himself from his spot.

"I left you a note," he said, extending his hand.

Before she could answer, a voice shouted down from above, "Michael, I'm going back to the car. Looks like you have your hands full."

He waved her off.

"They've been talking about this woman in town," Carmen said. "Is she your wife?"

"No."

"Your mistress?"

"On second thought, let's call her my wife. It's so good to see you."

"Why have you returned?" Looking down at the motorcycle, she added "You won't get much for this now."

"I came back for different reasons."

"And they don't include the woman?"

"Less so than I thought. I know one thing though. I'm happy to be here with you."

"But we must keep moving." She clucked her tongue and the goats began spreading out like fresh water across the riverbed.

He glanced at her as they walked along. The lines on her face might be a bit deeper, her hair more yellow than before, but nothing much had changed about her.

"Why did you write the note you wrote? And on money... How American of you."

"Because it's what you said before I left last time. And it's always made me wonder, why would you say that? Nixon was president then, not Roosevelt. It just seemed odd is all."

"I knew it had to be you." She added, "I've said that to no one else."

"My partner thinks you had a secret you were keeping. She said the war here was during the time Roosevelt was president and you knew more about my uncle than you told me."

"She is a curious type, no?"

"She thinks Uncle Robert might still have been alive when you and I were talking back in sixty-nine."

"I see. But most of the time, guesses are not reality." She stopped and tossed another stone. "You have children, do you?"

"Yes."

"Where are they?"

"Back home."

"In Spokane still?"

"No, actually they're in Seattle now."

"And do you like this Seattle better?"

"Well, I'm not living there. I'm still in Spokane."

He was reminded of when they walked to her house after his accident. Protected by the cane, he could be there again, blathering away, trying to clear his addled brain from the recent changes in his life.

"We're taking a break from each other," he said.

"You said yes to a break from your children?"

"I think I'd better tell you something. But you can't tell anyone else. This woman I'm with, she's not my partner."

"I see. She's a friend."

"It's my wife who needs a break from me. I didn't have much choice. She was gone when she told me."

"I remember you well... So young and excited about your life. Taking chances with the *moto* and now, after only twenty years, you're defeated."

"Only twenty years? It's a long time."

"Is it?" She stopped. "You close your eyes and go to sleep and when you wake up, twenty years have passed. It's seconds in a whole life."

They started walking again, slower this time so that the goats caught up and passed them.

In another forty-five minutes, they arrived at her gate with the goats crowding around. When she pushed the door through, they leapt in, two or three of them stepping on Michael's feet.

"You can count, no?" said Carmen.

"Well, yes, of course."

"Good. I will make coffee while you count the goats. I have thirty-two."

Michael faced the mob of animals. How was this possible? It was like counting barn cats. He started over and over again but couldn't get beyond ten. He sat down and rubbed at his chin.

§

Delia was bored. She drove back along the rutted road toward La Jolla. She parked near the square and got out, walked up the street to *Boquete de José*. She stopped and put a finger through the slats in the birdcage, sending the canary into fluttering madness.

Pepe waited for her at the counter. His hair was slicked back; he wore a clean shirt, still stiff from the clothesline. "Good morning," he said.

"Cigarettes?"

He showed her the wall. "I have *Celta, Ducado, Fortuna,* perhaps *Diamante*?"

"Black tobacco makes me ill," she said. "I'll take *Fortuna*." She dug in her purse for change and threw it on the counter.

Pepe moved it around with one fat finger until he'd corralled nearly 200 *pesetas*.

"Expensive," she said, already opening the pack.

"This brand more than the others." He watched her pull one out and put it to her lips. He licked his own. He picked up a lighter and flicked it on, held it beneath the cigarette and delighted in her drawing in the smoke.

"I had to stop," he said. "Otherwise I would join you." He patted his chest.

"Too bad. A cigarette can come in handy." She rolled this one in her fingers, studied it a moment.

"Where have you learned Spanish so well?" he said.

"I don't speak it well, but thank you. I teach it."

"Ah, in America?"

She almost answered, but half-nodded instead. When she blew the smoke out, she said, "That policeman who was in here yesterday?"

"Yes? Eugenio?"

"Is he here much?"

"The *Guardia* usually come by once a week on their survey of the villages. But Eugenio, he likes to come more often."

"Will he be here tomorrow then?"

"No. But the next day, most likely he will come then."

"Do you know why he comes so frequently?"

"Who knows? He is learning the ropes. He's a man from the capital who chose to work close to home. Maybe his family keeps him here."

"So he has family in La Jolla?"

"Not now. They had a weekend house here once, but no longer. He visited as a child. Why do you want to know so much about him?"

"No reason." She took another puff.

"He is young and he is good looking, much like you. I can see why you might want to know."

She laughed, but said nothing. Instead, she turned and stood in the doorway. The smoke now drifted in front of her, even filtered up and through the slats in the birdcage. This is the problem, she thought. I would prefer to be in Madrid. You can get lost in a city like Madrid, but here, everyone is after everyone else's business. It's how it works. She took one last long drag off the cigarette and tossed it on the cobblestones where it burned for another minute before putting itself out.

§

Michael sat at Carmen's table. He had drunk half of the thick coffee she set before him. An hour ago, they finished counting the goats, which was simple after all.

"You run them through the chute, one by one, and count them that way," she said, and the task was accomplished in minutes.

"So, was he?" Michael now said. He felt the tingle from the coffee. "Was my uncle still alive in sixty-nine?"

She studied him for quite some time, until she caught a resemblance between him and Robert. But who was this young, impulsive man? Did he always get excited so easily? Would he take the news and ruin decades of work and love by running out in the streets and shouting, "Roberto still lives?" Could she trust him with the rest of her life?

"Would you do me the favor of not asking such a question, or at least of not expecting an answer?"

"But..."

"This whole story of your uncle and the war, it would be so harmful to so many to bring it up again. It's a wound that never closed."

"But, with all due respect, it's been fifty years now. Time heals, doesn't it?"

"It's not always time that does the healing. There are other things as well."

"Like?"

"Like revenge? Is that the word, *venganza*? There is much of that over the years." She quickly gulped her coffee and set it down on the table. "Come with me. I want to show you something."

He followed her out of the gate and up to the street. She greeted people as they traversed the village on their way down to a small barrio.

"Through here," she said, as they turned into a narrow alley near the community sink. It was busy with women talking, laughing, scrubbing. But they grew quiet as Carmen led Michael past. They ended up at a small room attached to a larger house. The room had old wood shutters now partly closed. The door was open, except for strings of long beads, each an inch apart from the other. The beads were made of dried grains and actual pieces of ceramic.

Carmen stood outside and said, "Victoria! Victorita! Are you in there?"

There was movement on the inside, a shuffling sound and a short woman in black appeared behind the beads. She lacked two front teeth. "I am," she said.

Her history was etched on her face; Michael imagined it was not a good one. An old scar lingered menacingly on her left cheek. She glanced at Michael.

"Victoria," Carmen said. "How do we know each other?"

"We are longtime friends. Why?"

"May I tell this man your story?"

"Why does he want to know?"

"His uncle was in the war."

Victoria's eyes widened, and her hands came up to her stomach.

"He was Roberto."

Michael noticed a change stream cross the woman's face. The scar got brighter somehow, fiery. "I don't know, Carmen."

"Please."

And, after a moment, the woman parted the curtains and allowed them into her room. It was one long dark space with only a bit of sunlight straining in from the half-shuttered window. A metal brazier hooked to a propane tank sat on one side; a pair of chairs, one with a blanket draped over it lined the opposite wall. An old sepia-toned photograph rested on a shelf above them. In it, a boy stood with his hands behind his back. The paws of a dead rabbit hung behind his legs. Michael stared at it as he was offered one of the chairs.

"Yes, it's him," Carmen said.

"Not my uncle."

"No, of course not. Robert was much older than this child. No, this is Vicente, Victoria's brother."

"The boy who...?"

"No. Efrain was *my* brother. But Vicente was taken..." She cleared her throat and turned to Victoria. "I am sorry, but I must go outside for a moment with this gentleman."

Victoria smiled for the first time, but it quickly faded. She walked over to the picture and caressed it with shaking fingers. "Just a boy," she said.

Outside, Carmen and Michael leaned against the side of the house. "I have to explain this in English and I'm afraid Victoria doesn't know I speak it." She patted the stucco wall. "After more than fifty years, nothing changes. Vicente was made to run like a rabbit in the picture while the men, the rebel soldiers took shots at him. He was so agile, so brave. They missed, time after time."

"How horrible."

"So, after a minute, one of them gave the gun to Victoria."

"No."

"Oh yes. And they made her, well, I do not have to finish the sentence."

"Just to be clear, this is not the kid Robert took the bullet for?"

"No."

"The one he took the bullet for was your brother?"

"You know the story. I thought I told you when you were here before."

"Not all of it," he said. "The part about him being your brother you left out."

"Back then, once they knew who you were, there was no place to hide."

"The Nationalists?"

"The rebels, yes. They took over Málaga and it was a wave of fire and thunder, rolling through every village. They didn't care whether you were a woman or a child. They only wanted to know your allegiance."

"I'm sorry," Michael said.

"Even children who could not speak yet were slaughtered."

"And your brother? He was shot too?"

"Not in the usual way," she said. "It was worse for him."

"Oh God. I'm so sorry for bringing it up again."

"I think for that you are forgiven. We live with it day to day. You haven't opened up anything new." She started walking up the hill, but stopped and motioned for him. "Come, I have another thing to show you." But as they got closer to the church, Maria del Carmen hesitated and Michael noticed.

"Is something wrong?" he said.

"I'm not sure if our priest is in today."

"Are we not allowed in if he is?"

Carmen huffed noisily and took his elbow. "We will do it regardless."

They walked through the tall and wide double doors. To the left was the original confessional, once polished, but now dulled by hands and anxiety. Above them, a silvered dome was orbited by small murals of a celestial blue. Across the nave, in a rectangular recess, a painting hung. Michael was reminded of Velasquez, but it was not painted by that master.

"Murillo," said Carmen. "A *Sevillano*. He painted this."

It was a beautiful work in reds and yellows with a black background. A young man posed, dressed in finery reminiscent of the 1600s, but there was something wrong. Michael walked ahead of her. A deep wound slashed across the middle of the painting and someone had made a poor attempt at repairing it.

"The war," said Carmen. "Some were not happy with the church. With our priest."

Her answer only created more questions, but something about the way she answered caused him to retreat. He stepped back as a priest emerged from the chancel.

"Come," she said. "I must help my friend and you must find yours."

But Michael lingered, observed the priest. He must have been over eighty years old, his fingers hooked by arthritis.

"Come," urged Carmen.

"Hello," said Michael. He walked up to Blas Alvarez and shook his hand. "...a beautiful church."

"Yes, we are most proud of it." He looked beyond a confused Michael. "Did you wish to confess?" he said to Carmen.

"I have nothing to confess."

"As you wish," said Blas Alvarez. "When you are ready, I will be here."

Carmen turned and headed quickly to the front of the church. She stood for a moment, made the sign of the cross, then spit on the floor and stomped outside.

They stayed close to the walls of the houses they passed. All the while, Michael wondered what Carmen's problem with the priest was. But it was not his battle. He thought about his uncle and how out of place he must have felt fighting for a cause that was not his own. And he thought about what it might take to leave your own home to fight in a foreign land for an idea you might not fully understand.

They reached the square, where Michael saw the rental car. Delia sat in it, a cigarette smoking in her hand. When he said his goodbye to Carmen, he walked over to the car.

"Did you get your fill of goat herding?" she said.

"Was I supposed to know you'd end up here?"

She opened the door, dropped the butt to the ground and let him put it out with his heel. "I can feel something here," she said. "And it's not good."

"What exactly?"

"I don't know. I have a sixth sense about trouble and it's spinning pretty damn radar-fast."

"I don't want to go."

"From the country? From here?"

"I feel something too. Part of my family was here. I just saw a woman crying over something my uncle was involved in over fifty years ago. Things die hard."

"Well, from what I've been able to gather about your life, I can see where that might be true for you."

"Oh God."

"You've had a nice, privileged life. Wife and kids, decent job. Hope for the future. Anything less than that would be intriguing, if not downright romantic."

"Where does this need to denigrate me come from?"

"Look, Mikey, there are people right in your hometown who struggle every day and who hold grudges and hold bad memories for their whole lives. And you should know this, given the job you have. It's not their fault you can't bring yourself to identify with them or romanticize about their problems."

"You mean like people who have men in black suits and cars following them around?"

"Funny. But, yeah, maybe."

"All I know is I want to spend some time here. I feel something opening up inside me. And believe me, that's a new feeling."

"Your wife leaving you isn't enough change?"

He slapped the side of the car. "Well, I can see you're never going to get it. I'm staying. You can take the car and do whatever it is you need to do. Good luck."

He started walking away. "Michael," she called. "I don't think I can stay here. It's too little. It's too close."

"But that's exactly why I like it." He headed toward *Boquete de José*.

"Michael," she called again. His shoulders dropped as he turned once more.

"Good luck to you, too." Then she started up the car and drove away.

Chapter Sixteen
Robert, On The Road, Spain, 1937

Dear Mom and Dad:

I have the worst news. My best friend Max is dead. The enemy slit his throat and it feels like it's my fault. I'll never get over this so when I get back home, please don't bring it up. Oh, the world, the world. It's so awful. I wish I'd never left Spokane. If I'd only tried harder to find a job. Oh, Pop. I've met fellas from everywhere. And they could be my friends only not now because I couldn't do it. I couldn't wait another minute to get out of there. It'd be different if these damn people would have attacked us first, but they didn't. I'm on the road now, trying to find a town called Malaga where I can catch a boat and get back home. But I have to be careful. I ran into a Czech guy whose radiator had overheated and when I stopped to help him, I saw he had official papers in his panel truck. It's hard to tell who's on what side when. The same as your war. My war, well it doesn't seem like my war. I'm scared. I wet my pants more than once just trying to stay alive. I got a ride with some girls who were on their way to a wedding. They were happy and flirty like there wasn't even a war going on. They let me off in a place called Valencia and wished me luck. Now I'm on a road so close to the sea that I can smell clamshells when the wind is right. But I can also smell fuel from the planes that fly over from out of nowhere and force me into the ditch so I don't get caught in the strafe they lay down in the middle of the road. I hold my hands over my face and cry and cry in those ditches. I got one ride with a man driving a truck full of chickens. He took me to Almeria but he was the first one to give me a warning. Watch out for the Camisas Negras, he said. The Italian Black Shirts are marching methodically from Málaga in my direction, picking off any refugees they find along the way. It took a minute to realize that I'm a refugee. I need to be careful but I have my assignment. I have to get to Málaga to save my life.

Your lonely son,
Robert

Chapter Seventeen
Delia, Andalusia, 1989

Men are like this, she thought, as she drove down the hill toward the coast. It was why she kept her distance. If you got too close, they took advantage because they could sense emotional weakness and jumped on it. Why would she think Michael Virtue would be different than any other man?

But instead of feeling calmer, as she generally did when she had left one behind, she was as jumpy as the car going over the ruts in this pitiful road. She needed to find someone who didn't care so much, if not just for a night, just for an hour or two. Minutes? She knew she needed something to break the anxiety.

Why was she so nervous? She imagined the authorities had been to her place back home, ransacked it. What would they find? Not much. Student work. Old contracts from schools who hired her to teach Spanish. No evidence of a past life. Maybe they were tracking down her family. Her father would be more than eager to help the feds hunt her down.

She thought about him as she passed the dumpsite. Before, he might have been the type of father who would work hard to arrange a marriage for her. He would find a man like himself, because his view of himself was of a man who did right, thought right, believed right. And what father wouldn't want the same for his only daughter?

But she was never quite satisfactory enough for him. "You're like a cow who gives milk and then kicks over the bucket," he once said, completely oblivious that choosing to compare her to a bovine might not have been the kindest thing to say.

Constant battles. Nights in her bedroom. Days in the drudgery of a school where she never fit in, even with other kids who never fit in. But a glorious peace just walking the neighborhood streets at night. A kind of Hallelujah Chorus she hummed with every step. In high school she wasn't sneaking out her window to meet up with some boy. All the girls she knew who had boyfriends were slaves to them. No, she snuck out to breathe in freedom, to be rid of the shackles she'd always felt within her family. The sex came later.

§

Now on the coast of Spain, Delia came to the bottom of the hill. Traffic was heavy on the beach highway and she waited for a break in it. She felt itchy again, but slightly less paranoid than before. She tilted her sunglasses up, then down, until they were practically bouncing on the bridge of her nose. She saw a dump truck holding up the traffic and when the last car passed it by, she pulled out, barely missing its front fender, hearing horns and yelling, but safe on the highway. She gave a little wave to the driver and he honked again. She kept glancing in the mirror. There looked to be someone in the passenger seat, but she couldn't be sure. She slowed down and the truck came right up to her bumper, then backed off a few feet. Up and back again.

Delia put her hand out the window and moved it in a serpentine motion, gliding on the air. This was her favorite place to be. Gaming. Carefully, she put up her hand and gave the driver the finger. Then she pulled it in, pushed it back out. In and out. She checked the mirror. The driver was leaning over his wheel, smiling big through the dirty windshield. She flicked her fingers at him in the rearview.

After another quarter mile, she put on her blinker and pulled over to the side of the road but the driver did not do the same. Instead, he honked his horn and flew by her. She sat for a moment while cars and trucks whizzed by. She hated to lose. Thought for a moment of all the times she had won.

She let go then. Lay her head back. Loosened her brain. Connected with everything inside her, floated. She whispered to no one: *Take me. Take me there. Wreck me. Pull me apart.* And now she was gliding through the woods late at night. She heard the crashing of brush and whipping of branches. She was nude, the forest floor bit at the soles of her feet, but she could not feel any pain. She was beyond that. The evidence congealed on the front seat of the Impala.

He would catch up with her, but it was the anticipation, the expectation, the longing for him to take his time that caused the explosions all around and inside of her. She was on the edge of it, this precipice of fear and desire, she bled it, nursed from it. He wants me, she thought in a mind gone dotty from terror.

Now there came a light, a bright white light that struck her from behind, throwing a running shadow ahead of her in the woods. He was gaining. He will win, and she will lie alone, a rotting mess on the forest floor. Solid, liquid, gas. The way things worked. The way love worked.

§

She rented a room in a hostel in downtown Malaga and now tried to sleep on the single cot with the wafer-thin pad. She felt more alive than she had earlier in the day. The thrumming had not stopped. She wanted it to last through the night and into the next day, maybe the day after. It nourished her, threw everything else into the back seat of this sputtering mobile life of hers.

A flashing pink light pierced the thin curtain in the tiny room. It announced the hostel's presence on the busy street. *Pension.* It distracted her.

"No, don't go," she said as the humming in her body started to fade. If it had substance, she would hold it tight. "Stay. You have to." But it was melancholy now. In spite of the flashing light, a little gloomy.

She sat up and threw her hands above her head, stretching. She stroked herself, tried to put the need to sleep, but failed.

§

The other came hurtling back. The lights in the forest, the running, the falling, the retching. The battering with the long thick flashlight, the almost death. The saving of her life. This all rushed at once and forced her to watch the pink flashing light outside the window in Málaga as it counted her heartbeats, saying, "He loves me. He loves me not."

And, as always, the aftermath crept in. Saved by strong arms lifting her up in the cool darkness of Coeur d'Alene, Idaho.

"You came," she remembered herself saying. But she didn't know this man, only could feel the slight bump of his badge against her arm as he carried her out of the forested park and to a waiting ambulance.

She liked the whirling sound of the siren and the cataclysmic lights reflecting off the buildings as they sped to the hospital.

She recalled an examination; pinching, probing, but with apologies this time, not like when the Impala man was doing the same thing just hours before.

"Where's my mom?" she whispered.

"Honey, she's on her way. The roads are clogged, but she'll be here."

Then many men in badges. One woman. She did the talking.

"Are you sure he's over six feet tall? Was his hair definitely blonde? You said before he made you get on your hands and knees?"

"Yeah, yeah," she said. "To all of them. Yes. Where's my mom? I need her."

The nice woman whispered to her assistant. "Try to get her on the phone again, will you?"

She couldn't see out the window in the room, but it was still a night of stars thanks to the drugs they'd pumped into her. They worried about giving painkillers to a minor, but nobody was showing up to claim her and the pain was chewing her alive. Did they overlook something? They checked every opening, every crevice, every possible place the Impala man could have wrought his awful work.

It wasn't until the next day her mother showed up. She stood in the doorway, her hair done up like every Friday, her patent leather purse hanging dark from her elbow. She adjusted her glasses whose rhinestone wings just wanted to fly off her face.

"Oh, my darling," she said, holding out her arms as she walked through the room. "Oh, what happened?"

But Delia peered around her. "Where's Dad?"

Her mom stopped and pushed the purse back up her arm. "Daddy says to tell you he loves you." She pulled a plastic chair up close and sat. "I don't need to know the details, honey, but how are you?"

And Delia told her what she could, which was fast fading from her memory.

"That happens," the doctor said to her. "Your brain tries to protect you. You may not recall everything."

After the requisite talk about the assault, her mother now leaned in even closer. "Daddy wants to know what you were doing out so late by yourself and so far from home."

"It wasn't that late, and I wasn't that far," Delia said.

"Daddy says he's trying to be fair, he's trying to understand, but he absolutely has to know the answers to his questions."

"Why?"

"You know him, sugar."

"But can't I just go home? Can't I just get in my own bed and pull the covers up? Didn't you always say that? Home is the best medicine there is?"

"Oh yes, of course, my darling, I have always said that and it's true." She smiled through gritted teeth. "How long are they going to keep you here?"

"Aren't you here to take me home?" Delia said.

"Oh, my little sweetheart, if only you hadn't been out so late by yourself and so far away."

"Mom?"

She stared at the floor. "My lamb, Daddy says you can't come home."

§

And now entranced by the flashing pink light, Delia felt the oddest sensation. Was that a tear breaking loose and swimming down her face? How strange. A tool she abhorred with that prehensile mind of hers. Was this a signal? How come the thrum in her vagina hadn't lasted this time?

"No," she said out loud. "This is not happening."

It was the worst when the hunter lost her weapon.

Chapter Eighteen
Carmen, Andalusia 1989

Carmen stood on the inside of her gate with her hands pressed hard against it. Why had Michael come now? Why was his presence loosening the chains around her recollections? She might as well have led him to every single place in the village that reminded her of the reality of her life.

And most specifically, she would call him inside the church to the polished wood of the confessional she had crawled to just days after the village first fell. She pulled on the cabinet door, slid herself in on painful limbs and knelt patiently, clutching her rosary.

It seemed like hours before the priest stumbled into the confessional. She listened as he adjusted his vestments around him. He pulled aside the screen.

"Bless me father, for I have sinned," she said.

"Indeed, you have."

She could smell him through the screen. Liquor, sweat, something else acrid like dried blood.

"Tell me, child."

"I have been punished," said Maria del Carmen. "For something I didn't do. But I must have done it. Am I right?"

"God knows everything."

"Yes."

"And because of God, so do I."

"You do?"

"Yes, my daughter. That is why you've come. God has directed you to confess to me. What then have you to confess?"

She thought of all the things she must divulge in order to feel clean again. To wash away the blood and the urine resting on her soul. Everything? She couldn't possibly. But is that why they came for her?

"Tell me," Blas Alvarez said. "Do you want eternal damnation?"

"No, sir, of course not."

"Do you want more punishment?"

"More? I saw you in the street, Your Grace... You saw me. Must I confess for the sins of others?"

The confessional rattled as the priest moved closer to the screen. She could see his heavy lips mashed against it. "In God's world, no one suffers without deserving it. Now confess."

But Maria del Carmen rose to her wobbly feet, pushed open the door and escaped. She hobbled across the marble floor, her scuffles resonating up through the dome. Behind her, Blas Alvarez stepped out.

"I know things," he called after her. "And you'll never escape."

§

Or would Maria del Carmen tell Michael this? "Come here," she could say. "See this spot? This is the place the truck came loaded with men from Almachar, all in their work clothes, all wide-eyed, terrified."

"Come dance with us," said the leader of the Black Shirts stationed in La Jolla. He beckoned over and over. "Come down here now. Don't be afraid. We will celebrate."

And the men, one by one and with great trepidation, climbed out of the truck and stood, hands crossed in front of them, looked around with shivering stares.

"But there are no women," one of them said.

"I'll show you," said the leader. He turned to the houses surrounding them. "Come out now, and we will watch these fine fellows dance."

But they weren't women. They weren't even Spaniards. Italians, a whole company of them, held rifles, took positions around the square. The terror returned to the eyes of the men from Almachar.

The leader raised his arm high. "Now," he said loudly. "We will dance."

And Maria del Carmen Escobar remembered this: The sound of weapons all going off at the same time, the puffs of smoke that followed. The men from the neighboring village jerking from side to side and around in circles like marionettes on dancing strings. The color of the cobblestones in the square as they turned from grey to pink to a deep foreboding crimson. And soon, not one of the men from Almachar was dancing. The men of La Jolla rushed out and dragged away the bodies, leaving swathes of raw red serpentine in their wake. In a few minutes came the women, some of them happily, others with reluctant steps.

The Italians with the rifles waded through the gore to them while the men of La Jolla were instructed to start clapping a flamenco rhythm. First one man clapped, but too slowly and he was shot, then the group clapped, three beats, two beats, three beats. Carmen watched in horror as the women of her town were made to dance with foreigners in the fresh blood of honest and loyal men.

From out of the rectory flew Father Blas Alvarez. At last, Carmen thought. Surely the priest would put a stop to the madness. He waved his arms wildly until the clapping slowed and then stopped. His eyes roved the square as he shook his head sadly and said, "Look at this. You should be ashamed of yourselves. How can you let this happen?" His eyes waded through the timid crowd and finally latched onto Maria del Carmen's. Gently, she pulled up her scarf to where it covered most of her head. She admonished him with her stare as he stood in his cassock that trailed around him with every slight movement. He picked up the heavy cross hanging between the open buttons of his pellegrina and kissed it, adjusted his skull cap. He thinks he's a bishop, thought Maria del Carmen.

The leader of the Black Shirts walked up to him and planted himself deep in the gore. "This is an order from *El Caudillo* himself," he said.

"No, no," said Father Blas. "Forgive me. It is not the executions. It is not the blood. It is not the repression. This I understand. This there is room for in God's direction. But, kind sir, it is the dancing. Here so near to the house of glory. How can we have dancing?"

Now, in her mind, Carmen says to Michael, Shall I show you more examples? There are more, you know. Many more.

Many.

Chapter Nineteen
Michael and Carmen, Andalusia, 1989

It was as if Michael Virtue had awakened once more in 1969. He felt a nibbling at his cheek, inhaled an odor that might never leave his nose again. He fluttered open his eyes and through a fisheye lens saw the extended warped snout of one of Carmen's goats.

"Get," he said to no effect.

He was sleeping in a room just off the pen, on a thin foam pad that covered a platform of whitewashed brick. The goat moved from Michael's face to his wool blanket.

But he hadn't rattled down the steps on his doomed motorcycle this time. He was billeted here in this room because he realized too late that darkness was finally falling and he had no other place to stay.

"Then you'll stay here," Carmen had said. And she seemed joyful at the prospect. She had carefully taken an expertly folded blanket from the old armoire, which she later told him had been made by her father in anticipation of her future wedding. The blanket itself had been a gift for the same purpose.

"There is no electricity out here, but I think you'll not need it. The goats never do and they get along fine."

She had a sense of the absurd that sneaked up on him, leaving him hopelessly befuddled, yet charmed.

Now, he reached out and flicked the goat's snout; it turned and ran off. Through the open door, he saw others as they gathered.

He rolled out of bed and stepped into his pants, carefully avoiding the animal's fresh leavings.

He washed his face in the watering trough, slapped water under his arms and then nosed his way into his shirt. The goats treated him as their leader today. They kicked and butted at him before he could slip through the gate and lock it behind himself.

He climbed the stairs to the main level and there found Carmen working around the stove. Water threw off steam in a saucepan rattling over a flame.

"Ah," she said. "The rich man awakens."

"Sorry. What time is it?"

"I don't know. But it's later than you think. Coffee?" Without waiting for an answer, she pulled down a cup from the one shelf, retrieved a half-full jar of Nescafe. "The chickens are on a break so I only have one egg for you."

"One's enough," he said.

He looked around the unfinished kitchen. The concrete walls were almost bare. He could see space between the windows and the wall. But through the window, he could also see a slice of the Mediterranean whose distant waters now glittered.

"Nice view," he said.

"There are better." She cracked the egg and dropped it in a pan sizzling with three cloves of garlic. The room quickly suffused with the fragrance. "It's a day-old Vienna," she said. "Too early for the drunken bread man."

His hunger emerged as soon as he took his first bite, and he wished her chickens were not on break. He wolfed down the breakfast in seconds.

Carmen watched him with interest.

"Aren't you going to eat?" he said.

"I ate much earlier. As did most of the world, I suspect."

"You want me to take your goats out?"

"Do you know how?"

"I met one this morning."

"You think that herding is nothing more than following the animals around the hills?"

"I just want to pay you back for the bed and for the breakfast."

She pondered this a moment and said, "It would give me pleasure to see you herd my goats."

"Okay then, it's settled."

Michael once had a dog which, if he called it, would turn and run in the opposite direction. He bought a whistle, which no one could hear, including, apparently, the animal itself. One day it took off and never returned.

Carmen's goats used a similar tactic when he unlatched the gate and set them free. While he wanted them to feed along the bank of the ravine, they instead made a dash for the road, which led up to the *martirio*. Michael tried to run ahead and turn them around, but hearing him pick up his pace created a sense of stampede and their hooves clacked against the cobblestones as they worked to satisfy their new boss.

He was sweating by the time he reached the top where the goats obediently gathered, bleating at him. Behind all this, Carmen was certain she had not had such fine entertainment in years. She came up to Michael and pointed to his mouth.

"Open it," she said. "You see there? You see your palate? Use your tongue to click against it. Try it."

But Michael's tongue was like a recalcitrant slug. It rolled around and merely tapped the roof of his mouth when he commanded it to. It made no sound whatsoever.

"No, click it," Carmen said. And she demonstrated, sending off a noise that perked up the goats' ears and rang down along the ravine. "They must understand you are their leader, in spite of what the one with the bell thinks."

Meanwhile, behind them three people had congregated. One of them, a young woman, held an umbrella for shade from the sun. They didn't say a word, merely watched the lessons.

"I'm not very good at this," said Michael.

"You have no practice. Practice now."

And he did. His tongue strengthened with the exercise. It lodged against the roof of his mouth and when he snapped it away, produced a facsimile of what he hoped for. But the goats simply cocked their heads, stupefied. Their tails twitched. When Michael checked back with Carmen, there were now six villagers watching.

"I guess I'm not meant to be a goatherd," he said.

"And I'm not meant to be a teacher, but look at us here, me teaching you to be a goatherd." She turned to the crowd. *"Por favor!* This is not a show."

The group started to break up. Michael kept practicing and did get better, although the muscles in the floor of his mouth started to ache.

"We'll go now," Carmen said, and she passed by him, clicking her more professional tongue and tossing pebbles. Her crew trotted across the *martirio* and disappeared down the other side in a cloud of dust.

"Thanks," said Michael. "That was getting a little awkward."

"You're just not a goatherd yet."

They walked the edge of the ravine as the goats balanced and ate along the slope. They moved, he thought, like a swarm of locusts, mowing down every edible thing in their way. He was surprised the landscape was not complete dust after centuries of grazing.

After a few hundred yards, Carmen took them down a more level path. Michael noticed her shoes bulged as did her ankles. She soon picked up a stick and used it for balance. After every few feet, she placed her hand on her torso and held it there a moment. Perhaps the years of this job were taking their toll. She said something, but he couldn't hear her.

"Qué?"

She turned. "I am wanting to know why you've really come back."

"I've thought a lot about this town lately."

"That is mostly a lie. You want something else and this woman, this friend of yours, she is running from something. I can see it in her eyes. There is a dram of fear in them although she hides it well." Carmen took off then, leaving Michael to consider her words.

He caught up in a few minutes and wanted to adjust his previous observation of her decline. She was strong both in leg and in lung, while he struggled with the up and down of the hills. Too much time behind a desk, he thought. Too much time in his mind and in the minds of others. He was puffing by the time Carmen found a flat rock to sit on. She held her stick like a lance as she waited for Michael to find his own place.

"I think you're here because of your uncle," she said.

"Well, yeah, I think I said that."

"Your friend, the one with only a little fear in her eyes has told you Roberto was alive when you came to see me before. That is her belief based on what you told her about your visit?"

"Yes. She mentioned it as a theory."

"And do you believe her?"

"I don't know. But you would be the one who could tell me the truth."

On the ground, a line of black ants was negotiating the gravelly terrain. "The truth," she murmured. Looking back up, she added, "You realize it's a large task to find the truth in anything? Even though we humans invented the word, we also make it difficult to tell it."

"Okay. But it's yes or no, isn't it? Was my uncle still alive when I came to visit you in 1969?"

Carmen wished she could see herself. She was certain her face would register that she didn't want to answer his question, but she might be answering it by her latency in saying anything. "I will tell you, but I also beg a favor."

"And the favor is...?"

"That you not tell anyone else. Especially not this friend of yours."

"I doubt I'll see her again," he said. "But I agree. I won't tell. Who would care?"

"It might surprise you to know there remain a good many people who could be interested in the answer I am about to give you. Our civil war was much like yours, like most wars; good lives were lost, entire families were destroyed. And for what? For the pleasure of declaring yourself the winner of a conflict and getting to rule the people of your country for over thirty years? Who cares about the glee of a narcissist like Franco? And now most of these humble people are dead. So, in the end it means nothing to the world but a blip on the record. But war means everything to those who have lost."

"I don't like war," he said.

"Yes." It took Michael a moment to realize she had answered his question.

"Are you saying my uncle was alive?"

"He was, yes. And I didn't tell you."

"But what difference would it have made?"

"It would have made all the difference. I promised I would not tell anyone. Roberto was still living."

"But where? Where was he?"

"Hidden. They call them *Topos*. Moles. Your uncle was on the losing side and was sure to be murdered. He had to hide."

"My friend told me about the Moles," Michael said. But he was stunned and couldn't keep his thinking straight. He kept rubbing the top of his head. "But 1969 was thirty years after the war ended. He was still in hiding after thirty years?"

"That's a short time for those wanting to keep breathing. You, for example, have been living for longer than that. Why wouldn't your uncle want to stay alive as well?" Carmen cast her eyes up to the hills. The Land Rover had just crossed from the other side of the crest and now was snaking down the narrow road. She watched it with disgust, then absently dropped her hand down to her side and rubbed at it again.

"So, is there a grave I can visit to pay my respects?"

Already the guilt was backing up in Carmen, but time was breaking down along with her body. She saw the future and it was not complete or satisfying. The ache in her side could be longing, if she were a romantic. It could be she was now becoming that. "Yes, there is a grave you can visit."

"I want to go there," he said. "As soon as possible."

Above them, the Land Rover raced by, sending the weeds on the verge into a frenzy.

"It may not be so easy," she said.

"I don't care how hard it is. I think it's the reason I came here twenty years ago and, as you say, it's why I'm here now. So, if you could help me out, it would be greatly appreciated."

"Call that goat over there," Carmen said, pointing.

Michael tried his tongue out again and this time it worked. A perfect click echoed across to where the goats grazed. A few looked up, awaiting further instructions.

"Good. You're learning."

§

Robert Martin sat in the dark. He was counting; the numbers buzzed in his head. At number 25, he abruptly stood, took two steps forward, turned, two more, another left-hand turn, and two additional. Before making his final turn, he saw the other chair was now occupied.

"Ah, you," he said.

It was a young boy, dressed in tatters. Blood crusted at the edge of his mouth and at the opening to one ear. There was something Dickensian about him, Robert thought.

"Hello, Don Roberto," the boy said.

"Tell me, Efrain, have they broken you yet? Have they dug out the truth?"

"That will never happen."

"Good boy. It's best to be brave in the long run. We must win. Are you hungry?" Robert checked the table for the bag of food, but when he picked it up its lightness told him it had been a while since Carmen visited.

"No," Efrain said. "And like you taught me, never let them know what your sore spot is. They'll take advantage of your weakness and we can't let them have that."

"I had a coach once back in Spokane – those were actually his words. It helped me on the basketball court. Ah, we were a powerhouse back then, Lewis and Clark was. Have you heard of them?"

Efrain shook his head, set loose the crust at his mouth. A fresh trickle of blood snaked down his dirty chin.

"Yes, well they were famous American explorers. Trekked into uncharted territory under orders of their president. We should be proud of them, shouldn't we? They made it possible for the United States to stretch from coast to coast. I am happy to say I am an alumnus of their high school."

"Yes, you are," Efrain said.

"Did I tell you already?" Robert looked up to the lid of his home. "Have I told you about Maggie?"

"Your dance partner? Yes."

"The bunion derby?"

"Yes."

"The corn carnival?"

"All those things."

Robert lifted his arms and started waltzing around the small space. "God, we were a pair. Dear Maggie with blossoms on her cheeks and ribbons in her hair. And the stamina of a goddamn ox. She held me up, she did. We won once, you know. Almost twice. It was August that year and if not for that one couple, those fame-hungry Ohioans who decided to get married during the contest, I know we would have won again. It threw us off our game, the wedding did. Never recovered after that. You see, Efrain, the secret is to keep going. The rest periods are what kill you off. If you can be busy, even with those ten-minute breaks, then you are guaranteed to be one of the last couples standing. You could win a lot of money."

He stopped dancing when he nearly tumbled over his chair.

"Have you danced, Efrain?"

"The Flamenco, but only once, with my sister. I was dragged off the floor because there was a man who wanted to dance with her."

"Mari Carmen?"

"Yes."

"For the life of me, I can't imagine her dancing."

"She was twelve. I was eight. Children dance."

Now Robert noticed the blood dripping from Efrain's chin. He walked over closer and, hands on knees, studied it. "You've had an accident."

"He would have missed, you know."

"Who would have?"

"The lieutenant. It was dark. I could have dodged the bullet and ran. If I had, I could have danced again with my sister. Instead of…"

"What?"

"You know."

Robert bowed his head. "Yes, Carmen told me."

"Then you know. The truth of what happened after you fired the shot is not good for me."

"Are you telling me you didn't get away?"

The boy touched the blood, smeared it on his chin. "They tried to get it out of me, but I told them I didn't know. That was the truth. I didn't know. Carmen told me to go home and hide myself. She was the one who found your nest."

"So, will you tell them?"

His lip quivered. "Oh, Don Roberto, us poor babies."

"Tell me."

"I can't." The boy's hands flew to his face and, through splayed fingers, he said, "Like broken flowerpots on the wall. Swinging like pendulums."

"Efrain, I have to know. Why won't you tell me? Did you break down and give me up?"

Efrain's hands fell. "How could I? I've told you, I never knew where you were hidden."

"You didn't talk to Carmen?"

"Oh no. I had to hide myself. Even from my family. When they caught up with me, I hadn't spoken to my sister. Have you seen her?"

"Yes, I have. Beautiful young girl. Reminds me of my Maggie. Have I told you about her?"

"No one else knows what they did," the boy said. "Only I know."

"Will you tell me?"

"No. Why tell the criminal what he already knows?"

"Me? But I'm not the criminal. I saved your life. I took the bullet. Here. Look." Robert pulled up his shirt and located the scar. "There's your proof." He jabbed at the wound.

"You want to see mine?" the boy said, standing.

"No."

"I'll show you anyway." He grabbed the tails of his shirt and pulled them up and over his head. The shirt was streaked with fresh blood. His little concave chest was dotted with tiny leaking holes, festering burns.

Robert turned away.

"There is more." The boy unsnapped his pants and let them fall to the floor. "Look. You have to look."

But Robert chose instead to take up his dance once more, his arms extended, his legs waltzing. "Oh, my Maggie," he said. He hummed a tune; *The Blue Danube*. "I am entranced," he said. "Deeply affected."

He did this while Carmen's baby brother stood before him, naked, unhealed wounds of torture on his chest, only a jagged weeping stub where a penis once bounced, the bone from a compound fracture thrust through the skin on his left leg.

"Witness," the boy said. "Give testimony to what was supervised by Blas Alvarez, the blessed priest of La Jolla de Malaga."

"I can't," said Robert. "I must dance now. One, two, three. One, two, three. Won't you join me?"

But the boy had gone, transfigured into a seraph before disappearing into the ceiling of Robert's tiny home.

Chapter Twenty
Eugenio IV, Andalusia, 1989

"What do you have for me?" Eugenio asked of Pepe as he stood at the counter. He had just torn the cellophane wrapper off a *Bollycao* and bitten into the gummy bread stuffed with a thick blob of chocolate in the center.

"Good, no?"

"It's stale." He took another clamping bite and talked around a chocolate tongue. "Tell me. I'm counting on you."

"She keeps working. She still gives my wife her shots. But if you ask me, she is making an addict out of my Maria del Mar."

"Does this matter to me?"

"No. To me either. She takes out her goats. She spends the days in the hills." He stopped, held up his palms in supplication. "What more can I say?"

"She is the sister of Efrain, the boy the American saved."

A cloud passed over Pepe's face. He grimaced, expelled a tight breath. "Yes, she is his sister. Bad business, that."

"Are you suggesting what the boy did was right?"

"Of course not. He should not have run. He should have made himself available. He should have told the men where the American had gone. It's just that…"

"That what?"

"The techniques may have been severe for a boy child of that age."

"Do you know how many rebels were murdered by children? I do." Eugenio downed the last of the sandwich and wiped his hands by rubbing them on Pepe's counter. "Thousands were killed. Priests, empire builders, loyal soldiers." Eugenio's face grew red, a tear let loose and traveled partway down his cheek until he swiped it away.

Pepe took the opportunity to lean his elbow on the glass. He felt as fluttery as the canary in its prison. He had never seen this from a *Guardia*. "It was all bad business," he said.

Eugenio looked up, sniffed. "So you think she's a harmless old woman?"

"I would know if there was something awry. My wife would tell me. My friends would tell me. I am respected in La Jolla."

Eugenio observed Pepe as if he was not sure about this declaration. He laid his hands on the counter, now streaked with oil from the chocolate. "You know my grandfather. You know him from your stories about this village. He was the brave man who encountered the foreigner and the traitor child on the road from Lo Puerto. The foreigner made my grandfather beg for his life out on a lonely road to nowhere. And still, he murdered him. Murdered him in cold blood."

"I see why you feel the way you do," said Pepe. "But if I may ask, what is it you are seeking here now?"

Eugenio stood taller, adjusted his leather hat, licked his lips clean of bread and chocolate. "I'm looking for Robert Martin."

Pepe's head jerked back. He narrowed his eyes. "With all due respect, sir, the man is dead."

"Can you prove it to me?"

"Well, everyone knows, of course."

"That's not proof. Open your eyes, man. Have you seen the body? How many Moles have pushed out from hiding since the war? One doesn't have to conduct research to know they exist."

"Now, sir, I don't believe any of us have ever seen this man…"

Eugenio pounded his fist hard on the counter, startling Pepe. "Of course you haven't seen him. Have you not heard me? I said he is hidden. And he's hidden here in La Jolla. How can anyone see a man who is hidden?"

Pepe reached his limit. He groped for the wall behind him, knocking over several packages of chips and *pipas* in the process.

Eugenio stared at him a moment, eyes hooded. "I've made a mistake," he said. "You are not the right man for the job."

"Oh, now, now. I am the right man. My family's allegiance was always correct." He put a finger to his cheek, his eyes brightened. "I know who you must talk to. Our priest, Blas Alvarez. He knows most things and was a leader when the times were difficult. Yes, Father Alvarez will be the one to talk to."

"In the church?"

"Yes, he's always there."

"Ah," Eugenio said, nearly spitting. He wiped his hands on his pants. His boots creaked as he turned and walked to the doorway. The sun streamed around him with such intensity, Pepe had to shade his eyes. The figure framed before him was an eclipse of foreboding. Seeing movement to the side, Pepe glanced over and located his wife, leaning against the wall, dread covering her face.

"What have you done?" she mouthed.

§

Eugenio stood in the doorway of the church. This place was to be pitied, he thought. His footsteps echoed across the floor as he marched through the nave to the damaged painting. He touched the torn part, thought he might have felt the pain of the war pulsing through it.

"Welcome."

Eugenio startled at the sound, saw an old man, his wrinkled hands clenched in prayer. He removed his tricorne. "You are Father Alvarez?"

"Yes. And I can see that you are Gaspar's replacement." His eyes traveled the *Guardia's* body. "They have replaced well."

"And you were here during the war? You gave our soldiers succor?"

"Indeed." Father Alvarez bowed. "And now what succor can I give to you?"

"What I need is information."

"Ah." Father Alvarez squinted. "You seem vaguely familiar to me. Could we have met before? Perhaps when you were a child?"

"We have."

"I thought so. Can you refresh my memory?"

"I came to you once, Father, when my family was visiting the village."

Blas Alvarez's furrowed brow suddenly jumped.

"The children wouldn't play with me. They mistreated me, sent me to be alone."

"Oh, my word. You're..."

"That's right. I am Eugenio Robles Quintana. My grandfather was Francisco Robles de Casares." He waited for the acknowledgement, which came quickly.

Father Alvarez bowed again. "I remember you and I am in awe. No wonder you are so fit and regal. Your grandfather was a brave and valiant man."

"You knew him?"

"Most certainly. I knew him well. He was a blessed man. Filled with goodness. It was my honor to meet him. It was my shame to be posted to this village where he met his end."

"Funny how time passes, no?" said Eugenio.

"But today you are teased by no one."

"Life is better when you have no one."

"This I know very well."

Later, they sat across from each other in the small room that served as Father Alvarez's office. An old print of Jesus suffering under his crown of thorns adorned the uneven white wall. One window, perhaps half a meter square, with a deep well, lit the room. Ancient bars crossed in front of the glass.

"It is perfectly private here," Father Alvarez said. "This room has heard many confessions, many sentences."

"But not enough to save my grandfather."

"How can I make up for it?" Father Alvarez waited, hands folded. "Here we are two men, alone, waiting for someone to talk to."

"How private is your confessional?"

Father Alvarez squeezed his eyes together. "Why, it is absolutely private. It is a conversation between God and…"

"Don't be foolish," said Eugenio. "Remember, I came to you, sat on your lap, felt your caresses on my cheek. I know all about the confessional. Especially the confessional during the war."

Father Alvarez's face reddened. "My son, you seem troubled. Is there reason for this? Have I offended you?"

"I may be young, but I have studied. I know of you and your kind during the war. I know that you may have suffered yourself for the decisions you had to make, the wrongs you had to make right. What thinking man wouldn't suffer over such decisions?"

"To be sure. But…"

"And I simply would like to know about the decisions you made. That's all. I am not asking you to divulge secrets from the confessional. Am I? I certainly would never tell anyone of my experience in the confessional."

The priest snagged his lip with a tooth. "What is it you want to know?"

"Specifically, I would like to know what has been your relationship with a woman here, Maria del Carmen Escobar."

Father Alvarez raised an eyebrow and then fought to lower it, but not before Eugenio witnessed the struggle.

"I see. What can you tell me?"

Father Alvarez stood, secured his wrists behind his back and paced along the wall. He stopped in front of the window, turned to the *Guardia*. "Her family has a long history in this village." He paused.

"Go on," said Eugenio. "

Father Alvarez's lip trembled; his hand came up to steady it. "I am a weak man. Surely a strong man like you can see that. And I grow weaker. I am past the age I should be alive. I am alone."

He walked over and fell to one knee, putting a hand on Eugenio's leg. "My memory is not as sharp as it once was. But perhaps, perhaps, you would like to take dinner with me, drink with me, and maybe my memory can come back." He stood and walked back to his chair.

"Perhaps," said Eugenio. "But before I could dine with you, I must have the right information. I am looking for someone to provide it. You have heard the secrets of this village more than any other I am sure. I am prepared to offer you the world if you can find out for me where the man Robert Martin is hidden."

"Robert Martin?" Blas Alvarez squinted. "I don't..."

"Oh, but you do," said Eugenio.

§

Eugenio sat in his Land Rover at the *martirio*. He needed to go up the hill to Moclinejo and do his job, but he couldn't seem to leave this spot. The priest frustrated him, made a hard lump grow in his stomach. He was guarding information and it was no secret what he would like in return. Wouldn't it be good if the techniques the *Guardia* used back in the old days were still permitted today? He believed he would have his answers sooner and he would not have to compromise himself to get them.

He picked up his clipboard and read down the list. Thefts and injuries on *motos,* drunk drivers and shopkeepers without proper papers. All this could be done by lesser people. He was a carbineer, an expert, and his skills should be exercised regularly lest they go off. He threw the clipboard back down and picked at his eyebrow in the mirror. The tension inside him mounted.

Soon, a small rental car pulled up next to him and stopped. It was the woman from two days ago, the American. She turned off the engine as he rolled down the passenger window. "We should talk," he said.

"Why should we?"

"Now, now," he said. "You should have more respect for this uniform."

She opened her door, stepped out, leaned in his window. "You weren't very nice to me the other day. If you had been, I might now be more respectful."

He appraised the woman with her hair pulled into a braid down her back and briefly imagined himself pulling on it, getting a yelp out of her. But he tried to extinguish this idea. He couldn't have any distractions.

"You've returned," he said.

"That's right. I left something here." She leaned back from the window and brushed tendrils of hair off her forehead. "It's hot today."

"Why did you stop?"

"What?"

"Why did you not go down into the village instead of stopping here next to me?"

The truth played on her lips. "I stopped for the shade. Not for you."

"You know, we're trained to tell when a person is lying, and my training tells me that's a lie."

"Were you trained by a man or a woman?"

"Ah, yes. What is the French word, *touché*?"

"Close enough," she said, and he laughed for the first time.

She watched while he picked a clipboard up from his seat, studied it absently and then set it down again. His eyes wandered the distant hills and then came back to her.

"I used to play in these hills," he said.

"You lived here?"

"A time or two in the summer." He felt strangely whimsical as he disclosed his youth to her. What was it in her that drew this out of him?

"Let me guess... You were the boss, the bully."

"Now, why would you say that?"

A smile crept to her lips. "Because now you're alone."

He took another, closer look at her, felt desire rise up. "Would you like a refreshment?"

"Why?"

"As you say, you're hot. I'm hot."

"I have to find someone."

"Perhaps I can help."

She considered him a moment, thought he was too young to do her any real damage. "All right."

She started to turn, but he said, "No, leave it. I'll take you down."

She pulled her purse from her car before she slid into his passenger seat. The leather had held the heat, but she enjoyed the fragrance of cologne circling around her. "You better not be up to something," she said.

They ended up at the same bar where they met, across the square from *Boquete de José*. She ordered two Victorias, and he brought out three. All were cold. She took a drink and realized he was staring at her.

"Stop that," she said.

"What did you leave behind here?"

"Well... my partner."

"Did you have a fight?"

"Not a fight. A misunderstanding. It happens whenever we're on vacation together."

"You're on vacation, but here you are not together. And how do you know he's still in the village?"

She rarely talked to law enforcement and the familiar feeling of scrutiny crept up on her. "Aren't you a little young to be so inquisitive about an old woman like me?"

He took a drink and set it down. Unsatisfied, he moved it slightly to the left where a puddle of condensation rested. "And if you are as old as you say, then you are too old to be flirting with me."

She laughed, felt a tickle as she did. "Obviously, it's been a while since a woman has flirted with you."

"That's offensive."

"My apologies then." She was most of the way through her first bottle. "I thought maybe you had a sense of humor."

"Some things are humorous. Others are not."

"What do you find funny?"

He cocked his head and looked up into the umbrella that shaded them. A black bumblebee bumped against the canvas. "I think it is funny a woman like you, who is on vacation with a man, has lost him and has returned to find him. It fits from what I know of *Los Estados Unidos*."

"So, you have opinions." She drained her bottle. "As well as a very strange hat."

He touched his head and removed the tricorne, studied it from all angles. "I do believe the inventor of this was put to death."

"Ah, now I see your sense of humor."

He set the hat on the table and took another drink. "If you're looking for your companion, you could ask anyone in this village, any woman on her way to the *lavanderia,* any man on his way to relieve the trees of their almonds, and they would tell you if he is here or not. You know this about these villages, don't you? Everybody knows everything about everyone."

"Yes, but you're the *Guardia* here. And from what I know, the Guardia is in charge of knowing about foreigners who visit. I could ask you and get the same answer." She frowned. "What do you know about me?"

"I know you are American."

"But I told you that."

"I can see you have expectations, like Americans do. You speak with high expectations, you drink with the same expectations, you even flirt with them."

"I don't flirt." She reached for the other bottle. "I don't have to."

"Enough of this." His own bottle now sweated like a worker in the sun. It slowly slid across the table on its condensation. Eugenio grabbed it, held it tight around the neck. "Why are you really here? There are no sights to see. You could go to Granada if you're a tourist. You could see the Alhambra. You could see where Garcia Lorca was executed."

She thought this an odd thing to say and concentrated on his thick hand clutching the bottle. The fingernails were perfectly trimmed. "So, I could be on the atrocity tour to see all the assassination sites of the Civil War."

"Just answer my question please," he said. "As you say, it's my duty to keep track of visitors to this region."

The beer had given her a buzz. She glanced at her watch. "My partner came here years ago and he liked it and wanted to return."

"When was he here?"

"I don't know. I think 1969. After college. He was touring on a motorcycle. Unfortunately, the motorcycle didn't last as long as the tour. He almost died."

"But surely he's not trying to find the *moto*."

"No. We found it and believe me, it's better left to its bones."

"How did you find it? Twenty years is a long time to remember."

She rested her chin in the palm of her hand. "You are the one for questions, aren't you? I think maybe you're in the right profession. We had help from a woman he met when he was here before."

"What woman?"

"I don't know. Maria. Like every other woman here. That was her name."

He was interested now, grabbed for his hat and toyed with the leather. "Could I see your passport please?"

"Why?"

"To validate you. We both agree it's my job."

She hesitated before picking up her purse and pulling her passport from the side pocket. She held it out across the table and he stared at it a moment before taking it, flipping through its pages.

"It has one stamp," he said. "You're more travelled than that."

"It's new," she quickly said. "As you can see by the date. I had to renew it before I came or the old one would have run out."

"Antoinette Parks," he said with a crushing accent.

"Toni for short."

"Toni. That I can say better." He handed it back and when she took it, she got a static jolt from the rough edge of his fingers.

"Thank you."

"If you find your man, please tell him I need to see his identification as well. It's important if you plan to visit here often. Do you?"

"I don't. This place is trying to be something it isn't."

"And yet, here you are back again. It's the man you want to see, not the place, as you say." He stood then and retrieved his hat.

Delia had a brief fantasy of how he stacked up without his uniform, knew she wouldn't mind making it real. She focused on his holster, which squeaked as he shook his pant leg down to his boot.

He caught her looking. "You are a liar," he said.

"What?"

"You do flirt." He then strode away toward his Land Rover.

§

Delia didn't know how to feel about her meeting with Eugenio. She hadn't spoken with an officer for that length of time since shortly after the bombing. She ordered another beer and waited. The sun struck her on the shoulders and loosened her up. There was something about this one. He was two people, she could see that immediately. What man would tell you he used to play in the hills before he even knew you? That had to be the boy in him. But the man part loomed large as well. She knew she had to be careful, but could she be?

She watched the morning life around her, thought of her own small hours of the day, standing before a class, always expecting an order from a principal asking her to come to the office and speak to someone in uniform. That only happened twice. The first time, she simply picked up her bags, put on her coat and walked out of her classroom, the students watching, mouths agape. That was California. The second time had been in Oklahoma. She'd actually talked to the cop that time, provided him with identification convincing enough to get him to leave the school. That time she knew it would not be much longer before they would return. When you kill a peace officer, other cops become prosecutors. They moved as if everyone they met was guilty, and if not, they soon would be.

Three beers later and she was calmer. She heard bells. One from the church. One smaller one tinkling from down the street. Soon, a goat peeked around the corner, followed closely by others, their tiny hooves clacking on the cobblestones. Then came the old woman, and finally, Michael. His face was bright red, his hair pasted to his forehead.

"You need more exercise," she called to him.

As Mari Carmen moved on with her charges, Michael sat down. In spite of his promise, he quickly said, "You won't believe it. You were right. My uncle was alive when I was here before."

"Doesn't surprise me. I'm usually right."

"He was alive, Delia…"

She quickly glanced to the *Boquete*. "Toni," she whispered.

"Isn't that something? This is the wildest news ever."

"For you, sure. But not so hot for him. He had to be hiding. Where is he now?"

"She says if I stay, she'll take me to his grave."

"So, what does that tell you? Why won't she show you now?"

"I don't know." He rubbed his hands together. They were dark with dirt.

She leaned in closer. He could smell the alcohol. "Maybe he's still alive," she said.

For a moment, he wondered himself, but said, "You're drunk before noon. And what are you doing back here anyway? I thought you took off."

"I did. But obviously I came back."

"Why?"

"It's clear to me. I can't get enough of you, big boy."

"Why do you do that? Why do you keep making fun of me?"

"Because you're so damn easy to get to."

He stood but had to steady himself on the uneven cobblestones.

"Who's the drunk one?" she said.

"Nothing's changed. I'm staying a while."

"With the old lady."

"If she'll have me, I guess. There's still a lot for me to learn here."

"And what about your family? Your kids? They'll do their learning on their own?"

"I don't have much control over that now."

"Not from here you don't."

He pulled the chair out and sat down again, rubbing at his chin. "What would you do?"

"I think I'm the wrong person to ask. Like I said, I've never had a family. I don't know what you're feeling."

"I want to call my kids. I need to know how they're doing."

"I don't see any phone booths here. I've seen a few down on the beach, though."

"Can we go there?"

"Right now?"

"Please."

"You better drive," she said.

§

Carmen shooed the last of the goats into the pen. She arched her back, grabbed at her side. Now she'd done it. She told the man about his uncle. At least part of it, she told. Foolish of her, she thought. She might as well have set off a bomb right over the olive oil jar.

But didn't the American deserve to know? She had lied twenty years before. Why did she tell the truth this time? Was it the surety that her days were numbered? Who would take care of Robert when she could no longer do so?

"So, it's settled," she said to the pain in her side. "I've either got to find a replacement for myself or figure out a way to drag that man out of his hole. Or both."

She felt substantially better. But it was not just this decision that calmed her. She reached into a drawer and pulled out a long, curved knife, the one she used to butcher her goats. From behind it, she removed the old family whetstone, lined with cuts. This stone had served many times as her confidant.

Pulling out a chair, she began the process of wearing down the blade of the knife. One pull across the gritty surface, then another on the opposite side. Back and forth, almost like a gentle sway. And it was as if she were dancing, the way her head fell back and she closed her eyes. And she knew who her partner was. And he didn't even like the dancing. She was in a fantasy and wanted more. The time had finally come.

Chapter Twenty-One
Robert, Along the Mediterranean, 1937

Robert could speak for no one but himself. He had seen most of hell and all of its demons. There was no chance he would ever see the world again as a safe and happy place.

The German planes and the fascist ships were bad, to be sure. But the *Camisas Negras?* God help everyone.

Robert walked through the deserted town of Torre del Mar. The shop windows were boarded up, only a stray dog or two roamed the streets. Everywhere evidence of looting greeted him. Hunger had deserted him even though in his pack, he had some sugar cane left over, a couple of nearly ripe oranges.

The waves of refugees still rolled at him and he swam through them as before. These folks looked fresher, and indeed they'd started their run a day or two later than the early ones. They moved faster. They had brought along their animals. Chickens clucked, burros brayed, pigs squealed. After a while, Robert had a hard time distinguishing them from the sounds of humans. But there was fresh anxiety in the air. Robert soon learned that maybe they moved faster because something stalked them. The minions of hell who had been on everyone's lips all along the road. There was a new urgency to their advice.

"They are right behind us. Don't go any farther. The Fascists are here." And they didn't tarry. One word to Robert's ill-advised route, and they were off again, hurrying toward a future they couldn't possibly fathom, but away from a past that was already well-known to them.

Between Torre del Mar and Valle-Niza, Robert found blood and desperation. These were the slower ones, the ones unable to make up their minds. Stay or go? Robert shared a heart with them. They pressed on him the most of all.

"No farther!" they pleaded. "This is the end. The *Camisas Negras*, they are here."

The Black Shirts, he thought. Mussolini's elites. He saw the grim reality of them a half mile in the distance. Finally, he understood. Move or die. This was the way of the new world. He jumped from the highway and hid in an orange grove maybe thirty yards away.

And they did come, those Black Shirts, marching in step down the road. They carried their bayoneted rifles loose in front of them and from time to time, picked off stragglers on all sides. When they passed the bodies of the unfortunates, they kicked them off the road and marched on.

From his vantage point, Robert saw one refugee dig into his waistband and pull out a pistol. He turned and fired into the chest of one of the Black Shirts. Like a swarm of hornets, the battalion set on him. He fell in their midst. The rifles fired, the bayonets stabbed, and within seconds, the battalion stood back. One of them impaled the prone figure on the ground and brought up a head, which he now carried proudly on the end of his rifle.

The family around the dead man screamed and tried to run, but the Black Shirts moved quickly among them, stabbing and cutting, tearing off limbs. One of them chased a little girl into the sea and used the bloody arm of her father to batter his child to death. Robert felt his toes curl, could sense the people he hid with tightening their muscles, holding their breath, trying to keep quiet. One small child next to him, started to yell, and Robert slipped his hand over the girl's mouth.

The slaughter continued before them. The soldiers marched through thickening blood, kicked aside body parts and still used their bayonets to carve pieces out of human beings they had learned to think of as animals. How else, Robert wondered, could they act so without conscience amongst people they didn't know at all?

They were a deep group and were still passing by after a half hour, albeit now they had no ready victims. At this point, they were like soldiers in a parade, twirling their rifles, moving their heads from side to side, acknowledging the admiring crowd. In their black uniforms they resembled the battalion of death in every Spaniard's nightmares.

At last they passed, but the group in the orange grove hesitated. How far away must the killers get before it was safe to re-mount the road? The small girl next to him made the decision for all.

She broke loose and hurried up to the highway, stopped with her hands to her face. She turned and pleaded with Robert who had snuck up behind her.

"This is not the place for you," he said.

Meanwhile, the rest of the group now moved amongst the ruins of the bodies. Sadly, they picked up what was left of the belongings of the dead, a bag of clothing, a wallet with a few pesetas hidden in the lining. A watch. A comb.

The girl took Robert's hand and led him in among them all. She squatted and pushed back the hair on one, brushed drying blood off another.

Robert tried to pull her back, but she resisted, finally escaped his grasp. At the side of the road, she stopped at the headless body. She pointed.

"*Mi papa,*" she said.

Oh God, thought Robert.

She kept pointing around herself. "*Mi mama. Mi hermana. Otra hermana. mi hermano.*"

Apparently her entire family had been butchered by the Black Shirts.

She shook one sister's body, her mother's, her brother's. Quietly at first, but then with more desperation. "*Mama! Mama!*"

Finally, another man leaned forward and pulled her away. "They are gone, *bonita*."

She quieted then, looked up at Robert. She took his hand again, leaned against his body. Her thumb found her mouth.

"Where will we go now?" the man said.

"Málaga," said Robert.

"No, we can't. The rebels have taken over the city."

"But I have to get there," Robert said.

The man pointed to the little girl. "And what about her? Will you take her too?"

Robert looked down, felt the girl's firm grip, realized she had no plans to ever leave his side. A fly lit on her hand and Robert waved it away.

The man looked back from where they'd come. "If we keep behind them, maybe there's a chance."

"They might just kill you," said Robert.

The man flicked his head toward the mountains to the north. "Perhaps you can hide in there. Not every village has been taken over. It will give you time to plan." He reached out and rubbed Robert's uniform. "And you can fight the enemy with better odds."

"But how?"

"There's a road and an *arroyo*. Better to move along the *arroyo*. There are more of these heathens in Málaga. Don't go there." He settled in front of the girl. "You can come with us. It's your only hope."

Reluctantly, she let go of Robert's hand, took one last look at the remains of her family and then joined the small group that started heading to Torre del Mar.

There were no other refugees coming from Málaga. Robert imagined spots along the road that looked like the collection of parts laid out before him now. Málaga would have to wait. Perhaps he could go inland for a while, find a path with no monsters on it, and make his way west again. He picked up his pack, shouldered his rifle and headed north.

Chapter Twenty-Two
Michael, Delia and Carmen, Andalusia, 1989

Michael located a phone booth on the edge of the sand that led down to the beach in Rincón de la Victoria. The booth stood there all by itself, like a lighthouse to guide him. Delia did the talking with the operator, but when the connection to the States was made, she began walking along the beach.

Danny answered in a sleepy voice. "What?"

"Son? It's your dad."

"Dad? It's not even light yet."

"Oh God, I forgot about that. Is anyone else awake?"

"No. Why are you calling? Where are you?"

"I'm still in Spain. You know, in the place I always talk about."

"Mom's not happy," Danny said.

He let it go. "But tell me how you are. Talk to me. I miss you."

There were muffled voices on the other end, a loud bang.

"What are you doing, Michael?"

"Eva. I'm talking to my son."

"Who can barely keep his eyes open. You woke me from a sound sleep. Is there an emergency?"

"No, sorry. I forgot about the time change. I always get it backward. It's morning here."

"What is it you want?"

"He was alive, Eva. Uncle Robert. When I was here in sixty-nine, he was alive."

"Oh, gosh. So the trip's been worth it?"

"Yes." He felt infused with joy. "And I found my old beat-up motorcycle and…"

"Oh Michael, it's so early here. Maybe you can tell us all this when you get back."

"Please."

"It's late," she said. "And we're not going to solve anything with one late night call. You didn't say when you're getting back."

"Uh, I may not be coming home as soon as I thought."

"Did you not remember you have children who need to see you? This is not helping the problem at all."

"I'm sorry. I'm just so excited."

"Is there a number the kids can reach you at?"

"Not exactly."

"A hotel?"

"Not really."

"This is no time to play coy. It's tiresome to say the least. And Michael?" She paused and the moment was devilish for him. "There's something I really, really need to talk to you about."

"So tell me now."

"It's not for over the phone."

A lump took form in his throat. "Okay. For a minute there I thought you were going to tell me about a divorce."

"Oh, Michael."

"All right. I'll call back then, at a reasonable hour. Give the kids my love."

"Of course."

The line buzzed and he hung up. Only now did the sound of the lapping waves enter into his awareness. He thought of walking off but decided to make another call.

Arlene answered after a million rings. "This better be good," she said.

"My wife wants a divorce."

"Who is this?"

"Sorry. I'm just checking in and the time issue is screwing with me. How's it going?"

"Is that true about Eva?"

"I'll tell you later. Right now I want to know how my clients are."

"You called my home phone, Michael. What are you doing?"

If it had been Mason on the line, of course Michael would talk about his news, but with Arlene it wouldn't have the same impact. "So, nothing's falling apart there?"

"No, they're all just working overtime so you can go off on your mid-life jaunt. What could possibly be the problem with that?"

"I promise I'll make it up to everybody."

"I know you will. Can I go back to bed now?"

After hanging up, Michael took off. At the edge of the sand, he removed his shoes and held them each by two fingers as he walked down toward the water. A warm breeze caressed him and he turned his face up to it. He smelled the salt and dying crustaceans, saw plastic bags with peaks of sand holding them fast to the shore, and, further on, a dead dolphin rolled back and forth by the waves.

He saw Delia in the distance, or Antoinette, Toni, rather, and the fact she was now going by an alias brought him back to reality. The call to Eva was like waking up after a night of debauchery. Regrets crowded his thinking. But no one besides Mason had died. There was no new, great crisis. It would be easy to book a flight out to Seattle, go to Eva and hear what she had to tell him. He had a good idea what it was. Eva was a good woman. She wanted him to know everything.

Up ahead, Delia stood where the water could lick at her ankles. She was a mystery, but he was aware he had always longed for a woman like her. He wondered if it wasn't simply leading an interesting life that won it for you in the end. Maybe he needed to ask Delia how it was done. He walked toward her again.

When he got close, she said, "Were they glad to hear from you?"

Her feet looked healthy, young even. Foam crept in and out between her toes.

"Yeah, sure," he said.

"You don't really have the chops to be a decent liar. They're mad at you, aren't they?"

"Yes."

"It's a trade-off," she said, turning toward him. "Life is. You can't have it all at the same time. In the end you can, but you have to take it in steps. A serial life."

"And how would you know that?"

"Because I live what I preach. I don't have kids because I couldn't manage this kind of life if I had them. It wouldn't be fair. I practice pre-emptive sacrifice."

"It's a little late for me to change. Should I go back?"

"You're asking me? I've never gone back. Never. Something tells me this is what your marriage must be like on a daily basis: 'Please, Eva, tell me what to do.'"

"We share decision-making."

"Do I have to remind you that you're here and she's there based on separate decisions you each made without the help of the other? Marriage is bullshit and you can't convince me otherwise. Kids are bullshit, too, for that matter."

"Hang on now."

"You can't go."

"What? Just yesterday you were on your way to never seeing me again."

"I changed my mind. I may have my own hunting around to do."

"Here, or in Madrid?"

"Here, I think. I met someone."

"Why does that not surprise me?"

"Asshole."

"What I meant to say was, good for you. And I don't much care for the idea of you taking off anyway."

"It's settled then. We stay. I take what I said back now. This marriage thing is a piece of cake."

§

But when they got back to La Jolla, Carmen said she had no room for them.

"We'll pay you," Michael said. "You can make some extra money."

"I am not interested in your money," she said. "I have a private life and always have. It's simply the way I like to live."

"But where will we stay then?"

"Well, since the Germans started coming to the village to learn Spanish, there are many places. I can help you find one because if you ask someone like Pepe of the *Boquete*, he will charge you large fees."

They ended up with an apartment in a house on the opposite side of town from Carmen. A window overlooked the ravine that separated La Jolla from the hill up to Ventura. There were two bedrooms, newly painted a brilliant white. The ceilings were home to a family of geckos, making short work of the extra insect life.

"This is amazing," Michael said, staring out the big window.

"It'll do," Delia said.

It would do, but it set her nerves on edge. When Michael left, she walked to the bar at the square and came back with an armload of cold Victorias pressed against her chest, making her nipples come to point. At the apartment, she started in on them and had three down within minutes. Drinking mollified her, tamped down her panic, allowed her to see her life more clearly. It was one of the ironies that pushed her to drink more.

§

It was full night and the relentless stars blanketed the sky, allowing for a smattering of light along the hillsides of La Jolla de Málaga. Carmen needed it when she stumbled here and there, caught her jacket on thorns as she wended her way up to Ventura. Her own flashlight remained dark until it was absolutely needed.

The moon came out when she reached Ventura, but like her, it was only half of itself. Still, it provided enough luminescence for her to proceed easily to the jar. Before opening the lid, she sat on a piece of concrete for a moment and listened to the night. She wondered what Roberto was doing down below.

Conversing with Franco himself? Perhaps that bastard Queipo? The one who loaded the people into trucks like Jews on a train and ordered them to dig their own graves and stand politely, their hands bound at the wrist by barbed wire. Each of the men was shot in the back of the head. Blas Alvarez was one step ahead, giving last rites to the condemned before their turn came and they tumbled into nothingness deep in the soil of the *patria*.

Carmen shook her head. No, Robert would not be speaking with these men. Although she was no stranger to his conversations with those long dead. She wondered if he now preferred it to speaking to those still alive.

She stood once more and set to work. Soon, she had the lid laid aside.

"Robertito?" she whispered.

There was a rattle and bump below and the top of the ladder leaned against the opening. She tested it before stepping down.

It was completely dark now; they were used to not seeing each other at this time of night.

"Your brother was here," Robert said before she reached the ground.

"*Ay, mi vida*, not now. We must talk about something important."

"We've already talked about that, haven't we? I'm not coming out."

"Not that. Something has changed."

He searched with a blind hand for the back of a chair, dragged it over and sat down. "I'm ready," he said.

"Very well." She sat opposite him and held one of his knobby hands. She could follow the trail of one big vein that stood out in bold relief from his skin. "Your nephew has returned," she said.

"My nephew? Who is that? I don't have a nephew."

"Michael is his name. Remember when I told you about the young man who wrecked his motorcycle in the river? That was him. And now he is back. And, *mi corazón*? Forgive me, but I told him you were alive when he was here."

"You did what?" he roared but she quickly covered his mouth.

"Please indulge my thoughtlessness."

He pushed her hand away. "Now they'll come and haul me off to slit my throat from this ear to that one."

"No, no. That will not happen. Listen closely, Robertito, I told him you were alive twenty years ago. I said nothing about today. But I fear I may have to."

As so often happened now that he was older, he was unable to contain his anxiety. His hands worked in and out of each other. He rocked like an autistic child. "But why?" he said, his voice trembling. "Why have you done this to me? To us?"

Us, she thought. How long had it been since he referred to the two of them? "Because it's time."

"But Efrain was telling me what they do. Mari Carmen, I can't face it."

"Let me tell you this one more time, Don Roberto. It is true that many years ago when Franco said there would be amnesty for those who wanted to return, that they should come out of hiding, yes, he was lying then. He did murder those trusting souls. But twenty years ago, a decree was made promising that nothing bad would happen to those who wanted to return to the *patria*, and Roberto, they came back and resumed their lives with no consequences. And that was when the monster was still alive. Now he is gone. You are free to be released from this cell."

"But don't you see, Mari Carmen, it's a trap? It's always a trap, no matter what."

"My brother is dead. It pains me to tell you this over and over again. Please stop talking about him."

"He warns me," said Robert. "He keeps me safe."

"I am thinking of telling your nephew that you are up here. That he should come visit you. That he should care for you."

"No, Maria. Please. It'll kill me."

"I'm the one who's dying, Don Roberto. It's me who hasn't much time left."

He didn't respond to this.

"Did you hear me? I have a lump in my side. I can feel it grow every day."

"No. That can't be. You're going to live forever."

"It's the truth. I've never lied to you." There was a quiet on his part deeper than she had ever heard from him. "Roberto?"

"I'm here."

"How could I not tell you? Was I going to not show up someday because of my death and leave you here with no one to care for you, with nothing?"

"I have nothing, as it is…"

"How dare you. How can you say that when here I sit as I have for a lifetime catering to your every need?"

"I won't survive."

"Listen, *mi flor*, he's a young and sturdy man with a family. Relatives for you. Children. Are you hearing me? I said children. Haven't you always wanted that? All the things that make a life, this nephew has. He could help you when I no longer can."

"Please don't say that."

She reached out and captured one of his hands. It burned like ice. She rubbed at it. "Haven't we always known this day would come? Haven't I always been clear that life will change? It has to, don't you see? Imagine, you could be free."

"Mari, Mari, Mari Carmen. Don't talk. Please."

And she didn't. For a few minutes at least. She imagined herself as a girl. When the future with all its promises beckoned. She sang a young girl's song:

Vengan a ver mi granja que es hermosa.

Vengan a ver mi granja que es hermosa.

El patito hace así, cua, cua.

El patito hace así, cua, cua.

Like the song about her little farm, so lilting was her life. To be replaced by:

I am a Falangist and will

Be a Falangist 'til I die.

An indoctrination song from Franco. Work, work and more work. Clean hearts and clean souls. Good little Fascistas.

But Carmen much preferred what children sang behind the dictator's back:

Franco, Franco, que tiene el culo blanco,
Porque su mujer lo lava con Ariel.
Franco, Franco, his butt is very white
Because his wife washes it with Ariel.

Oh, my goodness, she thought with a sudden intake of breath. Her eyes brimmed. What has happened to my life? To our lives? It is now fifty years since the end of the war, fourteen years since Franco died, and here we still are, sunk into the ground.

"I have to tell him," she finally said. "Otherwise I am already dead. You have to trust me, Robertito. You must."

"But your brother..."

"My brother was tortured to death because of you. Eight years old and they took his life. You protected him once, I protected you, and now..." Here she paused. Had this lump injected its venom into her thinking? "And now, *mi dulce*, I don't exactly know why I've done this. Yes, you killed one of the enemy, but now, after all this time, his bones have grown moldy and dull. No one would stop to see what you've done now. No one would clap you on the back and call you a hero. It's a new day. The world has moved on. Except for my dear brother. And us."

There came a sound overhead and the two of them grew still. Carmen could feel his blood speed up in the big vein on his hand. It was a small noise, like an animal on a night hunt. But, you could never know. Her breath came in tiny puffs. He was looking up as well, she could sense this, felt the energy leap along his wires. Even now, the poor man feared being caught. But why was she nearly without breath and feeling a rash of fear herself? She had heard that after time had passed, couples who had been together took on the mannerisms of each other. The speech patterns, even the looks. But the emotions? Was that what this was? She knew that the new *Guardia* could come to do him harm now, but why was her own heart triggered to thrash about in her chest? Did she fear him as well?

The sound disappeared and the two, as one, breathed out. Gently, he slipped his hand from hers.

"This is the news I've brought you today," she said.

"All bad."

"But news all the same."

Chapter Twenty-Three
Eugenio, Delia, Carmen Michael and Robert
Andalusia, 1989

At the Guardia Civil precinct, Eugenio undressed in the locker room. Two other men sat on benches. They didn't speak to him; he was developing a reputation but was not aware of it. He was the intense man, the loose cannon, some might say slightly crazy. The others didn't understand him. They came from elsewhere, he thought, from radio and television propaganda that led them down more modern, more liberal paths. He overheard them joking with each other but dismissed it.

Naked now, he strode away from the lockers, towel draped at his shoulder. He hung it on a peg and stepped into the communal shower tiled with Arabic mosaics. Eugenio moved to the far end and turned the water on. When he ducked in under the heat, he immediately thought of the American woman. He was not sure why and was surprised. She was older and not the type he usually gave a second glance. What was it that made him now forget his quest for the moment and focus on her? Was it her eyes, the way she spoke his language, her breasts perhaps? Her audacity? Her future helpfulness?

To be truthful, he had not had much time for women, or they for him. A trio of short-term affairs in secondary school, all called off by the girls. A baby scare he quashed two years before. Women seemed always to be disappointed in him. Later, they would ridicule him. So that what he was usually left with were brash images that swam in his brain when he woke in the middle of the night, his body in a relentless state of yearning. It sharpened his plans to revenge his grandfather, but left him a lonely man.

When the other two men came into the shower, Eugenio had to turn toward the wall and let the water cascade down his back. He was embarrassed, unable to control his arousal. His body quaked with a delicious beat. He couldn't touch himself now, had to focus on something else. He closed his eyes, tried. He stayed so long that when he could finally turn back around, the other two were gone.

He quickly rinsed himself and shut off the water. Disappointed, he grabbed the towel and retreated to his locker where he dried off, partially hidden by the open door.

Naked or not, he now felt vulnerable, too easily distracted. A crack had opened on the surface of his world. Yes, it was this woman. This creature. He was certain of her dubious morals, her bold and brazen nature. She was not cowed by him. And, far from making him angry, he continued to be strangely drawn to her. He quickly dressed, sensing the fabric of his clothing as it glided across his tingling skin.

"Focus," he whispered. "I must focus."

Now dressed, he went to his desk and turned on his computer. He typed in, Antoinette Parks. United States citizen. And her birthdate. He tapped his finger on the tabletop, hoping to hit the jackpot.

§

Eugenio made a visit to Moclinejo the next day. The mayor wanted to know what he planned to do about the young strangers who were infiltrating the village and turning bored teenagers against their parents and tradition.

He was still distracted. He shouted at the mayor, "This is your problem! Are there drugs? Are the girls prostituting themselves? Pull your thumb out of your ass and come to me when you have a job I can do."

Eugenio was unpopular in most of the villages he visited. But his mind animated on something else today. As soon as he started up his Land Rover and left town, it was only the woman he could think of.

In fifteen minutes, he was in La Jolla. He walked into *Boquete de José* and once again found Pepe as obsequious as ever. "You have information for me?"

"I do," said Pepe. But he glanced toward the back and made a quiet sign with his finger at his lips. He slipped out from behind the counter and parted the curtain, sticking in his head. "All clear," he whispered.

"Get on with it, old man."

"I have heard the American couple have rented an apartment from Virgilio and now occupy it." He waited a beat and raised an eyebrow.

"The man and the woman? But how does this information help me?"

"Well, sir, it means they plan to stay a while. Doesn't that interest you?"

"What interests me is that I have placed my confidence in you to help me and you come back with stories of suspicious foreign romance. Is this something you pick up from the *telenovelas* on morning TV?"

Pepe brought himself to full height. "I do not watch morning TV."

"Then, unless there's something else, you have failed me once more."

"No, no. That is only one piece of information. I have saved the best for last." He rubbed his hands together, blew into them. "I have heard that the man, the American, is herding Carmen's goats." He snapped his head down.

"What?"

Doubt creased Pepe's face.

"You tell me about a man who is learning to be a goat herd?"

"Yes. Why would a tourist want to learn such a thing?"

"Where?"

"In the hills, of course."

"No, idiot. Where is the apartment?"

Pepe pointed down the street and gave him directions. When Eugenio turned to go, Pepe said, "Bollycao?"

But Eugenio had already stepped outside onto the cobblestones. In minutes, he was at the apartment door, knocking. He was surprised when Delia opened it, standing in her robe. She held it closed with both hands.

"Hello," she said.

"I must speak to you. May I come in?"

Before she could answer, he was already past her. She closed the door and leaned against it. "Sorry, it's not cleaned yet."

"Who are you?" he said.

"What?"

"You may be legal, but something's off. So, who are you?"

She walked over to him, stood so close that he could smell her morning bath. "You've been checking up on me?"

"I could arrest you and take you down to the precinct for questioning."

"Or you could question me here like you're doing now."

He could not resist looking at her body. He longed to reach out and stroke it.

"Do you want to look at my passport again? My other identification?" She moved away, but he grabbed her by the arm. She stared into his eyes. "I am who I say I am."

"There's no record of you."

"Of course not. I've done nothing wrong."

He let go, considered what she'd said.

"Admit it," she said. "You were just looking for an excuse to come see me."

"My job is more important than that." But he felt the truth of her words build in him.

"From my experience, there's nothing more important than testing what you're interested in."

He glanced around. "Where is the man?"

"Gone. Does that make a difference?"

"How can you be living with him? You're not in love."

"Are you always so girlish with your questions?"

"Do you know who you're talking to? I could have you deported. Is that what you want?"

Without looking at him, Delia walked to the other side of the room and opened a door. Through it, he could see an unmade bed. She turned around. "It's still warm, I'll bet." Her voice had changed; it was now honeyed and low.

For the first time, he seemed uncertain. He stepped forward, then stopped. Sweat formed at his hairline. He couldn't take his eyes off her. Desire continued to grow large.

"What are you waiting for?" She slowly slid the robe off her shoulders, exposing her breasts.

"I am..."

"That's right." She held out her hand, crooked a finger and beckoned him. She then turned, dropped her robe the rest of the way and glided toward the bed.

§

He lay naked and adrenalized. A sheet barely covered his midsection; one leg was thrust out and hung over the edge of the bed. Only now, he could feel the nips all over his body from her sharp teeth. They stung, teetering between pain and pleasure. And that was the question: Was this pleasure or was it pain? He couldn't tell, and maybe that was the answer. Pleasure and pain together sounded like, well, love. No, no, he thought. I cannot bring that into it. But it persisted. The end of loneliness?

Regardless of what it all meant, he had been unable to come down from a high he had never experienced before. Now that he knew he wouldn't fall victim to the feeling, he was driven to repeat it. He turned on his side and moved up next to her.

"Still want to deport me?" she said drowsily.

"Not now, no."

"Good."

Her flesh was soft and supple, and he wondered why he did not indulge himself with more of this. The power he felt lifted him up to a heady cloud. "Man, oh man," he said.

"You're nice to stare at."

"I don't disgust you?"

"No. Should you?"

"Yes. Men's bodies are so ugly."

"All right… Then I am thoroughly disgusted." She turned toward him, could smell his breath, mint from some spray. She found a place on his arm where she bit him and rubbed it with the point of her finger. "Young men," she said.

"What?"

"You're so strong." She pressed harder. "And quick."

He sucked her nipple into his mouth, at the same time pushed his tumescence against her leg.

She whimpered, pushed back. "Harder," she said, and when he thrust again, she said, "No. My nipple. Bite it."

He caged the nipple with his teeth and she quivered with anticipation. He gently pressured it.

"No. Please. More." And at his ear. "Harder. Ahh," she said when he clamped down. But when he tried to withdraw, she held his head close and said, "No. Okay. *Más*."

He was humbled by his desire, his loss of control. He thrust at her leg while he devoured her breast.

"Yes," she urged.

"You are golden. Nothing matters but you."

"No, I am not golden."

"Golden. Golden." He rammed once more against her and burst apart from the inside out.

She grabbed his head and tilted it up. "What happened?"

"Sorry," he said, breathing heavily. He smiled for the first time in weeks.

But she let go and slapped him on the cheek. "Never apologize. Don't do that."

He winced, once more couldn't decide whether there was pleasure or pain in what she'd done, but it truly didn't matter. He pulled her toward him, mounted her, and plowed inside so quickly that she sucked in an intense breath.

"More like it," she said, and began a rhythm that pulled him in closer and harder and with a violent need.

I am home in this land, she thought. At last.

§

She was asleep now, at least he believed she was. She had not moved from her position for the last few minutes; her breathing was deep and regular. Gently, he lifted the sheet and slipped out of the bed.

He tiptoed to the doorway, stopped a moment, remembered the tile that moved in its crumbling mortar and avoided it. He recalled where she left her purse and stepped over to the sofa. He squatted and pulled her purse down to the floor. He began to rummage. Gum, a tampon, tissue, coins, a wallet, which he gently slid out. He snapped it open and flipped through credit cards, her passport, a folded stash of *peseta* notes. Frustrated, he tossed the wallet on the sofa.

Now that his senses were back, he was certain of his suspicions; he had never been wrong about them. There was evidence of her somewhere. She might be excellent at hiding, but he was better at discovery.

He picked up her purse once more and spilled the entire contents on the sofa. He was about to toss the purse itself aside, when he felt something odd. He ran his thick hands around the cloth, then around once more, always coming back to a place with a slight bulge. He rubbed it with his fingers, then opened the purse.

Looking closely, he noticed the stitch marks. Carefully, he picked at one until it loosened and, holding the thread tightly, pulled on the whole thing. The lining had been cut about four inches across. He dug in his hand and felt the prize he had been looking for.

He stood up, holding three different passports in his hands. Three different names. It thrilled him. But something was wrong. This should have been better than filling her with his flesh. Better than making her shout his name. He was happy, for sure, but there was a damper there. A disappointment as well.

"No. Stop," he whispered.

He walked back to the sofa and quickly stuffed all but the passports back in her purse. Not having a needle and thread, he tucked the lining back in on itself. It would have to do.

He was mad for doubting himself. He cleared his throat, shook his head. No, he wouldn't let her take him over. Even if it was the most exquisite pleasure he had ever known. No. He would build his plan before she noticed what he had done.

§

Carmen waited in the anteroom of her doctor's office in Rincón de la Victoria. She was sorry she made the trip. Why pay so many *pesetas* to receive an answer she already knew? Professional opinions be damned, the pain was getting worse.

She had been subjected to large noisy machines that took pictures of the inside of her body. She was handled roughly, ordered to do this, to do that. Lie still. Don't breathe. Follow directions. She was twelve again and they were trying to make her one of them.

Her doctor knocked politely and came into the room, her arms laden with charts, which she dumped on her desk.

"I wish there were more hours in the day," she said. She was much younger than Carmen. There were family pictures on her walls, children with smiling faces, a man who could be either her husband or her father. Her fingernails were painted crimson and stood out against the papers she now shuffled through.

"You don't need all those to tell me," Carmen said.

The doctor stopped, smiled, then set the papers aside.

"I just need to know how long I have."

"I'm not sure since we found it in the pancreas, and this is not good in terms of prognosis. I have been surprised a few times and let down another few."

"So, you spend a lot of money and time to tell me what I already know?"

The doctor leaned against her desk, crossing her arms. "You cannot make long-term plans. I know that much."

"How long?" said Carmen.

"It could be tomorrow; it could be…"

"You're not worth much, are you?"

"I'm sorry."

"Platitudes I can do without." She felt well-armed now, more confident as she stood.

"I wish I had better news for you," the doctor said.

§

At exactly 3:30, Carmen was at the bottom of the hill with Victoria when the school bus arrived. It was jammed with kids, some hanging out the windows. She boarded with the plastic bag of fruits and vegetables she'd bought from the hole-in-the-wall store next to the stop. She pointed Victoria to a window seat now occupied by a boy she knew. He tried to ignore them, but Carmen kicked at his feet and he surrendered the seat so the two women could sit together.

The bus smelled like exhaust and sweat and Carmen reached into her bag and pulled out a half-peeled orange, removed a slice of peel and passed it to Victoria. She then carved out another for herself. She squirted the essence in front of her nose, thus dulling the noxious smell and easing the clutch in her stomach as the bus wound up to the village.

"I can tell the news is not good," Victoria said.

"The news is what I expected."

"Tell me."

She squeezed the orange peel once more and a tiny puff of fragrance was released. She looked out at the landscape of her home – dry brush and the stumps of Muscat grapes topped with a flurry of green and yellow leaves. The children around her fought and played without once looking out at the land. They were the background noise as Carmen told her friend, Victoria, about the doctor's verdict.

They passed the smoking dump and Carmen gave herself an extra squirt. Now the children screamed and complained and plugged their noses, yelling "*Que peste*" as they always did when the bus passed this spot. Carmen pulled her shawl up around her neck as Victoria patted her leg. When the distant Sierra Nevada appeared, Carmen glimpsed her goats about fifty yards from the road with Michael Virtue desperately firing rocks at them.

She had no time to fight with herself. "Stop!" shouted Carmen. "Let me off here."

The driver braked and opened the door. Carmen handed Victoria the rest of the orange peels before she gingerly made her way down the steps. The door clacked closed and the bus chugged off. She could hear the children fighting until it disappeared down the hill.

She walked along the road to a high point where she could push across and up a small incline. From there she could watch her goats pop their heads up, one by one. The lead shook her head, setting off her bell. Carmen's first thought on seeing this was that she must now decide when to sell them to the butcher.

It was a moment before Michael saw her, so she studied him. He was earnest, she would give him that, but he had a long way to go where technique was concerned. There was a disadvantage to being born out of country and out of time. When the goats headed in her direction, he finally noticed her and waved.

Carmen leaned down, gathered a stone and elegantly tossed it near the lead goat's feet. That stopped the animal in its tracks. Then she negotiated her way until she reached the goat, pulled on its ears, and scratched behind them.

"We have to go," she told Michael.

"Where?"

"Come with me."

Together they walked back to the road, waited for a truck to pass, then directed the goats across to the other side where they hopped down the slope.

"I think they're starting to pay attention to me," Michael said. "I think I'm getting the knack of it."

"What is this word, *knack*?"

"It means I have an aptitude for it. I'm getting better."

"They are looking for a leader is all," said Carmen. "You must be that leader."

"The head goat then?"

"What does that mean, the head goat?"

"I'm trying to be funny," he said.

"Goats do not understand humor."

As they walked, Carmen wondered if the doctor's news hadn't somehow penetrated her bones. It felt harder to dip and climb. She flagged quickly and had to rest more often. During one of those rests, she sat close to Michael.

"I have to tell you something. You must listen to me."

"I'm all ears," he said.

She didn't bother to ask the translation of that phrase, but rather took a deep breath. "I have told you a lie before. Remember. I lied to you about your uncle."

"You didn't really lie."

"Please, let me talk. It is a lie by, how do you say, omission?"

"Don't feel bad about that," he said.

"I want now to take you to a place. Will you go with me?"

"Of course, I will. It's his grave, isn't it? But are you sure? You look so tired."

"We must go now. Today." She let him help her stand. "Come." And she led him away from the stone, up across the ridge from where they could see La Jolla de Málaga, which indeed did shine like a jewel as they traversed the slopes.

"That is Ventura." She pointed up to the village on one of their rests. It took them another half hour to arrive. Not only was she tired, but Carmen also shook with fatigue. They stopped near the blown-up factory.

"I lied to you when you visited in 1969, and I continue to lie to you until now. I must tell you something very important. And you have to promise me you will never say a word to anyone about it. If you're unable to promise, then I cannot tell you."

Michael's mind whirled with the possibilities. He promised before but told Delia. He was not trustworthy. But this secret filled him with a delicious hope and he wanted to know it now. "I promise."

"Your uncle... Robert Martin. He still lives."

It was as if his body had lifted and floated high above the two of them standing there. He could see the rubble below, the crumbling sides of the buildings. He believed he could see for miles. "But..."

"I am about to show you, but you have to be prepared. And this is most important because as a foreigner you stand out from the crowd and are easy to spot. It's the daytime. You must learn how to hide. You must learn how to pretend." She stopped herself. For, unlike Michael, she felt stuck to the earth, unable to move in any direction. The glue was a sadness that swathed her tightly. She quickly wondered if her decision was wrong. Did he really understand what she was saying? Michael would stand out like the dark mole on her eyelid. His mere presence would cause the *Guardia's* flame of suspicion to ignite an even stronger flame. "I may have just destroyed my life's work."

Michael finally found his voice, made sure he was planted firmly on the ground once more. "My uncle is still in hiding?"

"Okay then. I will tell you. He is a *Topo*."

"But he doesn't need to."

"This will be your opportunity to tell him that."

"But where?"

"Underneath your feet."

He picked up one foot and then the other, as if heat were building there.

"Look around you," she said. "Study the area. Do it now and tell me what you see."

"The goats."

"And what are they doing?"

"They're climbing that little hill."

"Are they running away from us?"

"No, they're staying in one place."

"Yes. They've learned."

She set about clearing the area near the jar. Michael soon took over and removed all the litter.

"Look up," she said. "What do you see?"

"The goats."

"Anything else?"

"No, just them."

Carmen took his face in her hands and leveled his eyes to hers. "Now, who do you see?"

"I see you."

But she shook her head. "No, you see fifty years of doubt over whether I've done the right thing."

"I see."

She squeezed his cheeks until he yelped. "No, you don't see. You never will because this is not your home. But you are my best chance so you must listen to my every word if this is to be successful."

He nodded.

She let go. "You will come at night normally. It's easier to hide yourself."

When she put Micheal back to work, it was as if he was uncovering an archeological find. Layer by layer, he dug, hoping with each swipe of his hand, he would find treasure.

"Now," she said, when they were ready. She put her lips next to the lid. "Robertito?"

Hearing this, Michael dropped down next to her. He heard movement, like a forest animal scurrying for cover.

Carmen placed her knuckles on the lid and rapped quickly two times. Then again. Then came a voice from Michael's dreams.

"Mari Carmen?"

Carmen glanced at Michael, slightly nodded her head. "Help me."

Together, they grabbed the lid and pulled it to the side. The light shined down into the jar, but only a small area was visible.

"It is best I go down first and prepare him," she said.

"What?" said Robert.

"I am talking to myself as an old woman would."

Michael nearly fell backward when the edge of the ladder bumped against the lip of the jar. He watched, entranced as Carmen turned herself around and slowly descended. He reined in the impulse to hang over the edge and watch her progress. He heard voices below. The ladder scraped once or twice against the edges. After five minutes, Carmen said to him, "Look around. What do you see?"

"Nothing, The goats."

"Come down then."

§

Eugenio gathered his clothes and sneaked back out to the living room where he dressed rapidly. He saved his boots for the doorway and slipped them on before leaving the apartment.

He stood outside, looked up and down the street. Two older women in black were installed at one end, huddled together, chatting. When they saw him, they turned their backs. In the other direction, he saw Victoria leaving the Boquete de José. She passed by Eugenio, staring straight ahead. She hurried to the two women and now their three heads came together. Eugenio walked back up to the square. Before he could get to his Land Rover, Pepe ran out.

"Sir," he said. "Forgive me." Then he lowered his voice. "I have news. Do you want to come in?"

"No. Tell me here."

"I have just overheard a conversation with my wife. It's Carmen. She has a tumor. She is dying."

"Who is this person?"

"Maria del Carmen Escobar. The woman you told me to pay attention to, of course. She went to the doctor today and received the bad news." He paused. "Or maybe good news for you."

"She is the woman whose brother the American took the bullet for?"

"Yes, she's the one."

"Where can I find her?"

"She may be out with her goats. It is time for that. But she may be at home."

Eugenio studied Pepe, watched the drop of sweat as it traveled past his bulbous nose. "Just tell me where she lives."

Eugenio decided to take his Land Rover even though Carmen's house was only a few blocks away. He parked out front. Below the street, he pounded at her gate. More loudly the second time.

"You won't find her home."

He saw the three ladies who were talking in the street before. "Where is she?"

"She has cancer. She is returning from the doctor," said Victoria.

"Or she is with her goats," said one of the others. "It's that time."

Eugenio walked up the incline a few steps and planted himself with one foot in front, one hand grasping his knee. "What can you tell me about her?"

One woman started to open her mouth, but Victoria placed a hand across her arm. "She has goats."

"And nothing else?"

"What more does she need? Goats are plenty of work. True, less work than a husband, but work nonetheless."

When Eugenio climbed closer, all three ladies took a step back, but when they saw that he was not stopping this time, they took off in different directions.

Eugenio watched them go. He was tired of this village. He patted his pocket now filled with the passports. But life would change here very soon, he thought. And that made him at least partly happy.

§

Michael carefully stepped down each rung. His feet trembled. At the bottom, Carmen balanced the ladder until he arrived at the last step and then she moved to the side. There was a smell that Michael couldn't place, a bit sour, certainly lived in. He hit the floor and wiped at his hands as his eyes grew accustomed to the darkness.

"Here we are," Carmen said. "Robert isn't happy with you being here."

Michael stared into the gloom on the other side of the jar. He could make out a form, but it was ill-defined. "Hello?" he said.

"Trap!" Robert yelled, and suddenly this undefined figure was across the space and upon Michael before he could defend himself. Robert hit him in the face with a sharp object and pushed him to the floor.

"Roberto!" Carmen shouted. "No."

Michael rolled on the floor with his attacker. They crashed into the table and chairs, sending the table rocking on three legs and finally snapping to the ground. Michael was astonished at his uncle's strength, and it took him longer than he thought it should to get the upper hand, to roll Robert over and sit on his belly. When he had his arms secured, Robert spit in Michael's face.

"Get away. It's a trap," he hissed. "He's killing me, Maria."

"No," Carmen said. "No, Robertito, it's not a trap. This is your nephew, Michael." She was straightaway aware that the jar lid was still open and she set to pulling down the ladder and then taking the branch to slide the lid back over into place. The jar quickly darkened.

"Should I let him go?" Michael said.

"Yes," Robert said. "And then I can kill you."

Carmen fell to her knees. She took his head in her hands. "Robertito, please listen to me. I would never betray you. This man has come all the way from the United States to see you. He is your family."

Robert's groan suffused the whole jar. Michael could feel his tension loosen. "If you are my family," Robert said, "when did I leave my hometown?"

"December, 1936."

"Where did I attend high school?"

"Lewis and Clark."

"What is my mother's name?"

"Loretta."

Robert calmed now and even more so when Carmen caressed his cheek. Feeling blood, she said, "Have you hurt yourself, *mi vida*?"

"I think it's mine," Michael said. The cut on his face was bleeding. He touched it. "He got me good."

"Let him go," Carmen said. "He won't try anything now."

Michael slowly released Robert's arms. "I'm sorry, Uncle Robert. But you scared me." He stood up and brushed off his pants. He used the sleeve of his shirt to wipe the wound.

"Are you hurt?" Carmen asked Robert.

"No." He finally sat up, resting his arms on his knees. He glanced over at Michael. "It's a hard time," he said. "Why are you here?"

"He comes with good news," Carmen said. "Don't you, Michael?"

"Yes."

"He's come to tell you the war is over, Franco is dead and it's safe for you to leave your hiding place."

"All of that, yes," said Michael.

"I won't talk to you," Robert said. "I can't."

"Of course, you can," Carmen said.

"No."

"But why not. He's your family."

Robert bowed his head. His fingers drummed on his knees. "It's all wrong. This can't be the truth. I have no nephew. No nephew named Michael. And if I did, he would be small. It's all wrong, Maria. You have brought me the wrong man. I have to talk with your brother. With Francisco. With the others."

Carmen leaned into him and held his head again. She talked to Michael. "Maybe it's too late. I've waited too long."

"I won't listen to this man," Robert said. "Make him go. Where is my rifle?"

Michael looked to Carmen for direction, but all he saw was a heavy sadness.

"*Vaya,*" she said to him. "We have much to work out." Then she patted Robert on the shoulder. "You don't need your rifle this time. We'll have him go instead."

Chapter Twenty-Four
Michael and Eugenio, Andalusia, 1989

Michael stood on the outside of the jar, hearing the sound of the grating lid as Carmen closed it once more from the inside. Across the abandoned road, the goats still milled, bleating, waiting. He wandered over; they were accustomed to him now and didn't shy away. He decided to take the animals back down the hill and wait for Carmen to return.

They followed him along the rutted road. His mind drifted; he tucked his hands deep in his pockets. He wondered if his presence had set off a chain of events that would lead to the destruction of a carefully built secret. He touched his face and flinched. His cheek swelled with each step. This was the kind of moment where he would get next to Eva and share the exciting news. This was monumental. Gigantic. Unprecedented. He ached for his wife right now. Who could he tell here? No one. He'd been warned about that. He understood Carmen's reasons for the admonition to keep quiet, and it left him lonely.

Wasn't he supposed to be happy, thrilled even? Here was the stuff of dreams. His uncle, safe all this time. But what of Robert after their brief time together in the jar? Michael's first glimpse was not promising. His uncle was paranoid and it seemed he had been plagued with hallucinations. The man needed help, the sooner the better.

As Michael traveled down the hill, he took the easiest, most exposed path. Sensing the way, the goats diverged to pass him, then remerged as one once they were in front. He could smell them now, and it helped him disengage from his thoughts. This was not a bad life here, he supposed. It was simpler. The people were mostly friendly and accepting. He felt stronger as he led the goats up and down and across the hills.

His thighs started to ache. He stopped to sit for a moment. He picked up a few pebbles and rattled them in his hand. Below him, he caught sight of the Land Rover as it turned a sharp corner on the road out of La Jolla. He watched it until it disappeared behind a hillock, only to reappear some seconds later. It moved more slowly now.

After a few minutes, Michael continued down the hill. He picked up a limb, tore off several protruding leaves and used it as a cane. Below him, the Land Rover had stopped. As he approached it, the sun sparkled off the windows, blinding him briefly. As he got closer to the *Guardia's* vehicle, Michael felt some trepidation. The first chance he got, he made a left turn toward another ravine.

But just as he made the turn, the door to the Land Rover opened and the *Guardia* jumped out. He reached in for his tricorne and placed it squarely on his head. Michael picked up his pace, imploring the goats with his tongue snapping at the roof of his mouth. They, too, divined his urgency and scattered across the ravine.

He stopped and checked on the *Guardia*. The man was walking along the raised edge of the roadway, studying the terrain around him. Now, when he saw Michael, he took off his hat and waved it at him. By instinct, Michael waved back.

Eugenio cupped his hand and in a downward beckoning motion, entreated Michael to come to him. But Michael stayed put. Around him, the goats picked up on the change. They stopped spreading out and grazed quietly instead, save for the lead's bell, which jingled at each turn of her head.

Eugenio dropped down from the edge of the road and walked in Michael's direction. Little devils of dust rose and whirled around his feet. He grew larger as he closed in on Michael.

"What are you doing?" Eugenio said in Spanish.

“I don't understand.”

“*Y Maria*?” Then, in strained English. “Where. Is. Maria del Carmen?”

“Uh, I don't know.”

“But you have her goats. Her. Goats.”

Michael shrugged and held up his hands. “*En* her *casa* maybe.”

“I want your identification,” Eugenio said. “*Pasaporte*?”

“Not here,” said Michael, patting at his pockets.

“But you must have it. You must carry it at all times or you can be subject to arrest.”

Michael simply smiled and shook his head.

“She is not at home,” Eugenio said. “*No está en casa, Maria del Carmen.*”

“Then, well, I don't know.”

“But here you are with her animals. Have you left her somewhere? Where is she now?”

And Michael did understand that, or rather understood the tone. This man was not interested in him or his passport. He wanted Carmen. And he wanted her now.

“I don't know,” Michael said once more.

A goat came up to Eugenio and nibbled at his pants. Eugenio kicked it away. Then chased it and kicked it again. It screamed and limped off. Eugenio turned. “Do not think that you can get away with pretending not to understand. I know you understand. How do you talk with Maria del Carmen if you cannot speak Spanish?”

“I'm sorry. I don't know what you're saying.”

Now Eugenio grabbed him by his shirt collar. “He is around here; I already know it. And I will find him. And those who have protected him will pay the price.” He waited a moment, still clinging to Michael's shirt. “And that includes you.”

“I don't understand.”

Eugenio pushed, sending Michael reeling backward to where he stumbled over a goat and fell to the ground.

Now Eugenio shaded his eyes and scanned the landscape from which Michael had just come. "He is out there somewhere," Eugenio said, barely audible. He turned to Michael. "I know who you are," he said before he walked back to his Land Rover. "And we are not finished."

§

Michael stayed down long after Eugenio had driven away. Finally, he sat up and looked around. The sun beat down on his face and he could feel a burn as it penetrated deep into his flesh. The goats were not far away; he could hear the lead's bell just over the rise. He could also see a man in dark pants, wearing a beret, on the next hill over. He was clucking at the goats and they were gathering before him. The lead came into view and the man directed them over toward Michael.

"I know you," the man said. The sentence came out slippery. His mouth had only three teeth, widely spaced, and the words issued through the spaces.

"I can't speak well," said Michael.

"Is she okay?"

"Who? Me?"

"Maria del Carmen."

Stuck with a dilemma, Michael simply shrugged. "I don't know."

The man scratched his head under the beret. "*Mejor morir de pie que vivir para siempre en sus rodillas.*"

"Say again…"

"Better to die on your feet than live forever on your knees." The whispered voice came from behind him. Michael spun his head around and there stood Maria del Carmen, holding a baby goat.

"What does that mean?" Michael said.

"They are the words of a great woman, *La Pasionaria*. Here it means there are some things worse than death."

"Why would he say that to me?"

"He is concerned about you. He says you had a run-in with the Guardia and that he pushed you down. He's telling you not to be afraid. There's nothing the *Guardia* can do to you."

Michael thought differently when he considered the ease with which the man had pushed him, but he kept quiet.

"It's time to go back," Carmen said. "I need to rest."

Michael stood and brushed the back of his pants. "He says he knows who I am. How does he know me?"

"You forget where you are. Everyone knows everything."

"But then…"

"Those who can be trusted know everything," she said again. "And now you do as well."

She stumbled a bit as she set off and the man reached out to steady her.

"*Gracias*, Casimiro," she said, and she leaned on him for a few more steps while all around them the goats took up their dancing.

§

When they arrived at her house and the animals were penned in, Carmen lay down in her bed and quickly fell asleep. Michael took the opportunity to slip off and walk to the apartment. He found Delia asleep with her bedroom door open. She stirred when he knocked on it lightly.

"Oh," she said. "I thought you were him."

"Who?"

"The *Guardia*."

"Why would he come here? I just had a run-in with the guy. He tried to strong arm me."

"That's funny. I had the same kind of run-in with him. Tell me, did it hurt?"

"I don't trust him."

Delia yawned and threw the covers off, struggled to sit up. Michael turned sideways and stared at the wall.

"Oh, come on," she said. "I think we're too far along for you to get all schoolboy on me." She stood and quickly put on her underclothes.

"I'll wait out there," he said, and retreated to the ragged sofa in the living room.

As she came out, she tethered her hair into a ponytail. "What did you mean you had a run-in with him?"

He filled her in on the incident, and when he finished, she said, "I don't really trust him either."

"Finally, we agree on something."

"But it's also what attracts me to him," she finished.

"So, he was here?"

"Yes."

"And you two…?"

"Yes."

"God, I wish you wouldn't do that, but if you're going to, please don't bring him here. He's up to something." It occurred to him he could tell her about his uncle and that might make a difference, but he also was aware he couldn't actually trust her either after her disclosure about the *Guardia*. Telling her anything more could make it all go bad. But he was pushed to say something. "I think that guy is looking for my uncle."

"Your uncle? Why?"

"He thinks he's still alive. He said he's sure he's out there somewhere."

"Maybe not. You know how your Spanish is."

"I understood that part. You should have seen the look in his eyes, though. It was almost demonic. He's off – I'd say likely certifiably so."

"Yeah," she said. "I think I've seen it."

"And he knows who I am. He said that too… 'I know who you are.'"

"It's his job. The *Guardia* are supposed to keep track of visitors in their region. Especially in these small villages. I wouldn't make a big deal out of it."

"So did the other guy who was there. He said he knew who I was. And he said something really strange. Better to die on your feet than live forever on your knees."

"He said that?"

"Yes."

"Wow. Some things are never forgotten."

"What do you mean?"

"It was a famous saying by a communist activist back in the Civil War. Dolores something or other. They meant it then, they mean it now. But not to worry, Mikey. It's all going to be okay.

§

Eugenio was still angry by the time he made it to his office. He slammed his gun belt down and pulled out his chair. When it caught on the carpet, he yanked it harder and it fell backward. Sergio, his boss, stood in the doorway.

"You sure you don't need a partner?" he said.

"No." Eugenio righted the chair and sat in it.

"What's up?"

"Nothing."

"You come in like a cyclone and there's nothing wrong?"

"It's the people in these towns. No respect. Not like the old days."

"What would you know about the old days? You're still waiting for the other testicle to drop."

Eugenio just stared at Sergio. It was the kind of look that, in spite of all the years Sergio had spent as a Civil Guard and the criminals he had run across, made his blood run frigid in his veins. He had seen it before, but not on this side of the law enforcement fence.

"There's something up with you," Sergio said. "You're obsessed. You're on your computer constantly. What are you looking for?"

"Nobody we've talked about."

"You've been spending a lot of time up in La Jolla. Is there a reason for that?"

"It's on my route."

"So is Periana, but I don't see it much on your daily logs. Is it a woman?"

"A woman? You know better."

"Do I? You wouldn't be the first man to fall prey to it."

"I'll be in Periana tomorrow. Good?"

"And, Eugenio... Just between you and me, a couple of the men have complained about you. They say you anger easily and have no sense of humor."

"Does this job require a sense of humor? If so, I'll start laughing more. Good?"

"Try to loosen up, will you? And keep your affairs to yourself."

"Yes, all right." Eugenio kept staring at him until he reached his office.

Eugenio started up his computer again as he carefully pulled the passports from his pocket. The picture inside of each was clearly of Antoinette, yet each name was different. He studied them, one after the other. Three pictures of this woman, this Delia Parks, this Rachel Dawson, this Susanna Fine.

He set them next to the computer and began his search. It did not take long to find one of the names and he whistled.

"Murder," he said out loud. Then he took a deep breath and held it. "Murder of a federal security guard twenty years ago."

He kept searching through the Internet, looking up the different names. Delia. Rachel. Susanna. Then another. Sonia. How many more women was this Toni? A contact number with the FBI loomed large at the bottom of each page.

Eugenio leaned back in his chair and swiveled it. He stroked his chin. So, if she was wanted, was the man with her also under investigation? He liked this. Not that she was a killer. But this information might lead him where he wanted to go.

He looked through the glass to his boss. He couldn't really afford to skip going up to Periana again. He would have to put it off for tomorrow. But La Jolla was once again on his new urgent to-do list.

Chapter Twenty-Five
Carmen and Eugenio, Andalusia, 1989

Carmen sat up abruptly. A noise had jarred her awake. Outside, she could hear the wind blowing. Had the swaying trees scratched against her house? She had no idea how long she'd slept, but she knew it was not just the noise, but the pain in her side that had awakened her. She rubbed at it, but that only made it worse. She stood, wobbly at first, and then went into the kitchen, fired up the butane and put on a pan of water to boil. There was a knock on the gate outside her house.

"Carmen!"

She recognized the voice and sat down to put on her shoes.

"Carmen!"

"Coming." She walked outside, clucked to her goats when they rose up and batted against their cage. At her gate stood Maria del Mar, a syringe in her hand.

"I'm sorry, but I thought I could hold out until I saw you today, but I can't. And I can't reach it myself."

Carmen took the syringe and escorted her friend inside. Maria del Mar quickly pulled down her undergarments and leaned over a chair. Carmen stuck in the needle and pushed the thick liquid into her flesh.

Maria del Mar winced, but breathed out heavily in relief. "God will pay you," she said.

"One day you must learn to inject yourself."

"Never. I could not deny you the pleasure of doing it for me."

"I have coffee," Carmen said. "Perhaps it will keep you awake on your way back home." She went to the boiling water and poured it into a pair of cups whose bottoms were filled with freeze-dried coffee. She returned to the table, spoons rattling.

"You don't look well," said Maria del Mar, dropping in two healthy teaspoons of sugar and stirring briskly. "I know you went to the doctor. Have you hurt yourself in the hills?"

"No. But yes, I did go to the doctor." She paused a moment and studied her friend of a lifetime. "The news is not good."

"So Victorita told me. It is I who should be caring for you."

But Carmen waved her away. "How could you possibly care for me? That *cochino* husband of yours is a full-time job." Then she laughed, shaking the table, nearly spilling her coffee. "Remember when he was chasing you? What were you, fourteen? He was so clumsy and so horny."

"Mari Carmen!" But Maria del Mar also laughed with the memory. "In spite of that stupid auntie who was our *duena*, his mess was all over the place, night after night. That boy could float on all his seed. And now..." She sighed.

Carmen patted her friend's hand.

"*Ay,* Mari Carmen, remember that night?"

"What night?"

"You know what night I'm talking about. What were you, twelve?"

Carmen nodded. "Yes, that night."

"You were so in love with that older man."

"I was not. How could I be? I was twelve."

"Twelve-year-olds can't fall in love?"

"We can't talk about this."

"What do you mean? The beast is dead. We're almost dead." She threw up her arms. "We can talk forever."

But Carmen grew serious. "Listen, Marimar, this new *Guardia* comes with a weight on his shoulders. Heavy with the past."

"Yes, I hear him through the curtain talking to my Pepe."

"And I suppose Pepe is still giving him information."

"He thinks he is a spy." Maria del Mar shook her head.

"Pepe's father was worse."

"I know. I'm sorry."

"Don't be silly. A wife cannot control her husband. You had nothing to do with those executions."

"But, still..."

"Why can't the past just be the past? Shouldn't the dead be left to molder in peace?"

"He watches you," said Maria del Mar. "The young *Guardia* is looking for you to make a mistake. He will find things out and it will not be good."

"It has never been good." Carmen took a sip of her coffee. "What can he find out?"

"Whatever he wants. He is strong and there are some here who are weak." Maria del Mar rubbed at her eyes. "Enough of that. Tell me what the doctor said. Specifically."

"Nothing much. I am dying. Like the rest of you."

"*Ay, Carmen. No.* What will you do?"

"What do you mean? I will die, of course."

"No, no, not that. What will you do about...?"

"I have no idea what you're talking about."

"I would take over; I promise you I would. But I can barely walk on flat ground as it is."

"I said I have no idea what you're talking about. And besides, we were discussing your husband. What has he told the *Guardia*?"

"I am sorry to say he has told him about you."

"What?" Carmen sat up straighter. "What has he told him?"

"Who you are. You probably can expect a visit from the young man."

"What else?"

"The *Guardia* already had your name, so it wasn't Pepe who gave him any ideas. He just asked Pepe to report on your comings and goings."

"Does he think this is 1950? What does he want?"

"Revenge."

"For what?"

"For his grandfather, of course. Turns out, revenge lives on both sides of the line."

"I don't like this," Carmen said, tapping her cheek. "I thought we were done with it."

"When the last *Topo* comes out, it will be over."

She waited for Carmen to look up. "It's time, Carmen. Certainly now with your death on the way."

"He won't come out," Carmen said.

"He could be forced."

"You want to try? You could end up with a scar on your cheek like the American."

"The woman or the man?"

"The man."

"Because if it is the woman, I would call you a liar. I think she would have gotten her scar from the young *Guardia*."

"No."

"Yes. And how would the man get a scar from Roberto?" Maria del Mar paused and her eyes grew big.

"Yes. As it turns out, the American is his nephew. He has a right." She grabbed the back of a nearby chair and pulled herself up.

Maria del Mar seemed in a dreamland now as the drug took effect. "I am always shocked by your life."

"Do you think this is the right thing to do?" Carmen said. "If the nephew is to take my place, doesn't the fact that he is a foreigner make him vulnerable to those like the Guardia? I fear I may be wrong and putting Roberto in danger."

"But hasn't he always been in danger?"

Carmen nodded.

"Every teenage girl's dream. A few hours with a man twice her age."

"What about your Eusebio? His danger was real."

Now, Maria del Mar snapped out of her dreamland. Her wrinkled cheek quivered.

"I'm sorry," Carmen said.

"The bastards."

"Such a man with a good future and strong arms."

"Someday I'll find him again." Maria del Mar rubbed at her face and when her hands came away, her cheeks were wet. "I heard the shots. I think the grave is between here and Benaque."

"I think maybe we are too old now to nurture the past."

"But, Carmen... The past is all we have."

§

Later that night, it was 1937 again. Carmen awoke with strong arms pulling her out of bed, dragging her across the floor. She felt every bump of the uneven tiles as she was towed out of her room. She was not sturdy enough to put up a fight, much like the ancient night when they came to snatch her family and hurried away, with her younger brother calling out to her: *"Carmen! Mi Carmencita!"*

She could hear it now as she fought to orient herself before she was slammed into a chair by her table. A lamplight flashed on and drowned her face. She blinked furiously, rubbed at her eyes. "Who is this?"

"Where is he?" came a voice, harsh with anger.

Her skin prickled. This was how the *Guardia* talked. This is how they always talked.

"Efrain?" she said, battling for composure.

"You know who I'm looking for. Will you tell me or will I have to dig into your brain for it?"

Now, anger brought her back. She felt an urge to bite him. "What are you doing in my house?" she screamed.

Eugenio slapped her hard, wrenching her head to the side.

This young man is alive with crazy, she thought. He exists in a time long past.

He grabbed her hair and yanked up her head. "Look at me."

She finally did. He was in uniform, perfectly pressed. His eyes, though, wandered through the darkness like those of a night beast. "Let me go," she said. "I have nothing for you."

He did let go, but dragged over another chair and sat down with his face so close to hers she could smell strong cologne. "I know you have him."

"Who?"

"The deserter. The murderer."

Her anger roiled. "You have no right to break into my house. You have no right to question me. Get out now and I won't report you."

"You may have others fooled. But not me. You're only hiding the truth. I have worked forever to put the pieces together. I am not wrong about this."

"It can't be that long. Your age betrays you."

He slapped her again. "Where is he?"

"Check the lists. You have them. You'll find his name there. That is, if you can remember where you buried the bodies."

"He is on no list."

"That is your problem then. Not mine. If I were in the business of genocide, I would at least keep an accurate account."

He stood up and kicked his chair behind him. He wondered if he could actually be mistaken. That the Civil Guard captured Robert Martin and carried him out into the *campo* and put a bullet through his brain. And maybe they were so proud of themselves, they clapped each other on the back and went off to awaken the local *taberna* owner to pour them drinks until they were blind drunk.

He hated this doubt and shook his head violently. These kind of thoughts were Toni's fault. "No," he said. "He got away."

Carmen sat up taller. Her face ached, her side screamed out. "My father? Dead. My mother? Raped and changed forever. My brother? Swung like a metronome on the hooks of the church wall and used for target practice by filthy traitors like you. Why should I be afraid of you? Kill me now or get out of my house."

"Who is this American who everybody sees you talking with? He was out with your goats."

"Who are *you*?" she said. "A man who thinks he can break in and wring lies from me. What business is it of yours?"

Eugenio sat back down in the chair. "I am Eugenio Robles Quintana. My grandfather was Francisco Robles de Casares. That's who I am."

"That means nothing to me."

"Now I know you're lying. That name means everything to everyone in this village."

"Why? Because he tore through us, loaded the men into trucks and took them away because they didn't give the answers he was looking for? Why? Because he treated the women and children of this village like animals? Is this why we should know his name?"

"But you were animals. What but an animal would kill a man who was only trying to be kind to a child?"

"I was there. You were not. He was never kind. He tried to kill a boy not yet ten. My brother."

Eugenio nodded his head, smiled wickedly. "So, we both have players in this game."

"Yes. But I know where my brother is. He lies in a pile of bones along with his baby friends. Get out of my house."

"You couldn't have been that old. What happened to you? Did no one think to question you about Robert Martin?"

"Get out."

"I have talked with others. I already know what happened to you. I know why it is that you have no husband. That you have no children. People who withhold information pay a high price."

"You know nothing. If you did, you wouldn't be here to question me. You may know facts, but you know nothing of the real lives. Get out."

Eugenio stood up again. He lifted Carmen's chin and examined her face. Both cheeks were bright red. In her place, he saw his mother, crying as he left her house without kissing her goodbye.

"I don't know why," he said to Carmen. His big thumb rubbed away a drop of tear. Carmen saw the thumb shake.

"You must leave me," she said.

But Eugenio dropped to his knees, buried his face in her lap. She could barely make out what he said. "I don't know why I'm made of this." He looked up. "I'm sorry for hitting you," he said.

"Go."

Chapter Twenty-Six
Michael and Delia IV, Andalusia, 1989

Michael Virtue sat quietly drinking coffee by the window that overlooked the back of the village. Up high to the hills, he could make out Ventura, the lost town. He was trying to reconcile his uncle being in a hole in the ground for over fifty years, but everything seemed surreal. People just didn't do this kind of thing. At least they didn't do it and not suffer the psychological consequences. People didn't hide away their lives for a cause, or did they? What was his uncle's cause? Was he a communist or a socialist? Was this why he was barely talked about in his family? Perhaps he was more than just a guy from Spokane who had once won a dance marathon.

He stood and paced with his cup in one hand. He had already drunk too much. He needed to be calm when he called his family again. He needed to be self-assured when the kids asked him for money or for the use of his car. He knew Eva well enough to know that she would ask him for nothing. He was finally starting to admit that she was finished with him. Who could blame her? She was always sharper, stronger, more adaptable. She got along with everyone.

He wanted to go outside. He wanted to take Carmen's goats and follow them up the hillside to a place where he could sit and think clearly.

He heard Delia rustling around her bedroom and soon she was at her doorway, yawning and stretching her arms high over her head. My God, she's beautiful, he thought. His eyes roamed her body until she caught him.

"Perv," she said.

"Where's your boyfriend?"

"Busy, I'm sure. And recuperating."

"We need to talk."

"Oh please, I don't need any more lectures."

"No lectures, I promise. I just need to know what the plan is."

She glanced at him sidelong, a frown creasing her face. "I thought this was *your* big adventure. I thought we were out here to uncover the remains of your uncle."

"You're right." He hesitated, but then plowed forward. "And I have."

"What does that mean?"

"I found my uncle." As soon as it was out, he wanted to suck it back in. But he knew now that Delia had her own secrets and might actually be the one person he could trust. "But don't tell your boyfriend. God knows what he'd do with the information. Do you promise?"

"Yes, of course," she said. "But tell me."

He retreated into the kitchen and poured her a cup of coffee. When he came back out, she was sitting on the sofa, most of her legs peeking out of her robe.

"Okay, here's the deal," he said. He still couldn't sit down, so he took up his pacing again as he told the story.

Delia's mouth fell open and stayed that way as she listened. The coffee grew cold in her hands. It wasn't until she was aware he'd stopped talking that she looked up at him. "Didn't I tell you?"

"Well, you said he was alive twenty years ago. But now? You should have seen him, Delia. Look at my face. He still has this massive strength. He attacked me and I fell like a rock."

"But what about, you know, his mental state? It's a long time to be alone."

"Not good, I think. He's impulsive, isolated. Paranoid."

Now Delia's face wrinkled in worry. She set her cup on the coffee table and stood, wrapping her robe more tightly. She walked over to the window Michael was at earlier. "I haven't exactly been honest with you." She closed her eyes and reminders came to her. Darkness, explosives, screams, and running, endless running.

"I know."

"You know? How could you know?"

"Because we didn't leave the states under normal circumstances."

"No, we didn't."

He walked over, picked up her coffee on the way and offered it to her. "You want to tell me what the deal is with you?"

She just stared at the cup. "I'm afraid. I'm afraid for your uncle. What's going to happen to him now?"

"Nothing," said Michael. "He comes out. The war's over. Franco's dead. He's the only one holding himself back. He just has to understand that and things will be all right for him."

"It may be you who doesn't understand. It's never over. The coast just looks clearer. But it's never over."

He decided to take the route of the shrink. "I want you to imagine telling me what your secrets are. Just imagine it. Close your eyes."

"Fuck off."

"Just do it, please. For me."

She frowned but did close her eyes again.

"Now picture yourself telling me everything that you want to keep to yourself."

"And?"

"What does that feel like?"

"Wrong," she quickly said.

"Keep imagining. Don't stop. Now think about telling me what it is you're running from."

"You're the shrink. You should already know that it's myself I'm running from."

"Yes, but we all have a reason for running from ourselves. What's yours?"

"Okay. I manned a getaway car. There. You happy? That's my reason."

"I don't understand. There was a robbery or something?"

"Or something." When he still looked confused, she said, "I'm an accessory, for Christ's sake. Good God, I didn't have to be so specific with Mason."

"An accessory to...?"

"To murder. We made the mistake of trusting a guy with blood in his teeth and this is how it played out. I was manning the car during a bank robbery and the guy used explosives because he loved explosives and a cop ended up getting killed. Now, that's all I'm saying. And if you breathe a word of this to anyone, especially to that precious wife of yours, I will tear your nut sack off your body and stuff it down your throat."

"But why? I mean how? How does a person get into trouble that bad?"

"Were you ever young? Did you ever have ideas about the world that seemed so perfect that you would go to the ends of the earth to see them through?"

"I've been in love. That can make you crazy."

She grabbed the cup from him and threw it to the floor where it shattered into shards. She stared at it and spoke through gritted teeth. "I don't think you're getting what I'm saying."

"I do get it. Your thinking changes over time. When you're young, you're wild, when you're old not so wild. It's normal. It's the progression of things. You once were young and idealistic and now you're not."

"You make it sound trite when it's so much more than that."

"I don't mean to. I actually admire you."

Now she turned again and looked him in the eye. "I'm a murderer. I made it possible for someone to be killed. I didn't care at the time, I mean, I did care, but I could justify it then. What's the consequence of the death of one ant on the whole hill? I can't justify it now. And when I read things like what the cop's daughter said to a journalist, that she doesn't care what the times were like, she doesn't care that it had a political motivation, all she cares about is that a group of people took her father out of her life and she won't be happy until we're caught and justice is served. And you know what? I agree with her. I think she's right. We should be caught and punished to the full extent of the law."

"But..."

"We killed someone in cold blood. End of discussion."

"What are you doing here then? Why did you come with me? Why didn't you just give yourself up?"

"I've thought of it more than once... But it's not that simple. You get used to being on the run. You get used to a paranoid existence. You make decisions based on that. I should turn myself in, but I run and they don't catch me and somehow that feels like a victory, like it must be right. I guess when I stop getting a charge out of eluding the big guys, then I will turn myself in." She bit at one of her fingers. "I can't help but think, though, that this time I've made some kind of mistake. A fatal error."

"Wow," said Michael.

"I shouldn't have told you. You shouldn't have told me."

"No. I'm glad you did. Now I know. Now you make more sense."

"So, given what you just heard, what are you going to do about your uncle?"

"Keep him hidden until I can get him some mental health help. It's not good, even after all this time, for him to roam free."

"He's not wanted for anything, I guess. But Eugenio is a problem. He's looking for your uncle and... I know his type. He will not give up. It doesn't matter if the government's more liberal here now. This young *Guardia* is his own government."

"I don't think he's well." Michael thought about what he'd just said. "Eugenio or my uncle. Delia, both of them are mentally ill."

"Don't call me that," she said.

"Toni."

"Practice it."

"I will."

"What's the solution then? Let him die in a hole in the ground?"

Michael rubbed at his hair. "I don't know. Maybe bring in people to talk to him. Government people. Before Eugenio can get to him. He would be interesting to them; don't you think? A guy who hid out from a monster for all this time and still doesn't trust the world enough to come out of hiding? It's a hell of a story for some journalist."

"Yes," she said, thoughtful again. "It is."

"I'm going to talk to Carmen. See what she thinks. She's part of the story, too."

But Delia just waved him off. She was back at the window, barefoot, carefully avoiding the broken cup. She wished she could float above it. Behind her, she could hear Michael as he walked down the hall to his room. He's so naïve, she thought. In her life, naiveté had been tantamount to idiocy. It was guys like Michael who ended up getting everyone else in trouble. But now, at this late date, wasn't she longing for his style of earnestness? Not if she looked at her recent behavior. Same old Delia. Same old patterns of self-deceit. She kicked at one of the larger broken pieces on the floor. Better to disrupt things, keep people off-guard than come up with great answers, she decided. She'd always been good at that.

§

Carmen wasn't home when Michael tried her gate. But it was not locked and a simple push let him in. Immediately he could sense something was wrong. The door to the goat pen was nearly off its hinges. Her house hung open to the elements. He sneaked inside.

Her dining chairs were on their backs, one of them broken.

"Carmen?"

Nothing.

"Carmen?" he called again, then tore back outside the house and through the gate. He scanned the hillside across the ravine, didn't see her.

"Carmen!" Louder this time. He could hear the end of her name echo back at him.

He traversed the incline. Above her house, a trio of women watched him as he climbed and called out Carmen's name. A dog barked, setting off a cacophony of others that lasted nearly a minute. Coming to the impassible part of the hill, Michael climbed back up to the street, where he brushed the dust off his clothes.

One of the women, Victoria, walked toward him now. "Not here," she said. "If you are looking for Carmen, she's the other way." And she pointed back in the direction of Carmen's house. "She won't be far. It's hard for her to move this morning."

Michael thanked her and took off down the street. But before he had gone far, she called from behind, "You must be careful."

He turned, and she hurried to him.

"Listen to me. I have talked to Carmen. You must be careful."

"I will."

"No." She used her hands to talk. "I know what she plans to do. You must be very careful. There are traditions you don't know."

"What do you mean?"

"As life changes, everything remains the same."

"Is that a warning?"

"Advice. Nothing more."

He thanked her again but was not sure why this time. She stood motionless as he left her, was still standing there when he looked back once more before turning the corner. He nearly ran into the two other women who were watching him before. He raised a hand and nodded.

"Miguel," one of them said.

"*Sí?*"

"Even though you never will be, you must act as if you are a part of this village," the shorter one said. She smiled and was clearly missing the bottom row of her teeth.

"What? I don't understand."

But they moved off toward Victoria who still waited farther up the road.

Her words kept Michael occupied as he walked down from her house, around the corner past the *taberna* to where the street opened up to a vista of the valley below. Across it, he could make out the brown and white goats as they nibbled their way along the landscape. But he couldn't pick out Carmen. Starting out in a trot, by the time he hit bottom, he was going full speed.

It didn't take him long; he made his way along the riverbed until he found a track heading up. The whole hillside was covered in yellow oxalis that moved like ocean waves in the stiff breeze. The path doubled back on itself and soon he was halfway up the hill. He could already smell the goats as he got closer. The herd parted to let him pass. The lead took a bite of his pants and chewed while the fabric was still attached. He batted at her and looked around. He finally saw Carmen. She sat, her back to him as she looked out to the distant sea.

"Carmen?"

She didn't reply, so he walked up and grabbed her shoulder. She recoiled, nearly fell off the stone as she struggled to see who it was. He steadied her.

"I'm sorry," he said.

But still she didn't turn toward him.

"Are you all right?"

"I'm fine. Why are you here?"

He tried to step around to face her, but as he did, she swiveled on the stone so that he could never quite see her face. "What's wrong?" he said.

Finally, she gave up and let him come around. He startled.

"What happened?"

"Please don't look at me that way."

"Did you fall or something?"

"Afterwards, yes."

"May I?" He got down on his knees and touched her face, which was swollen now and turning a bluish color. "Your goats?"

"A *cabrón*, yes. But not one you think."

"I'm not understanding." He leaned back.

"There is evil about in this village once more. One must be careful all over again."

"What can I do?"

"You can promise me something. You can promise me you will let no harm come to your uncle."

"I want that. Yes, I promise."

"I am serious, Michael. You are a foreigner here and this village has not always been kind to foreigners. The young Guardia, the one who shoved you, he is on a mission to find your uncle and he will focus on you."

Michael held up his hand, signaling like a Boy Scout. "I promise to protect him."

"Good then. And you must promise to treat my goats well. Never let the herd get too small or too large. How do you feel about slaughtering animals? Can you do it? It requires an understanding between the two of you. My goats, they understand me. I'm not sure yet whether they will understand you."

"Why are you telling me these things?"

"Because once in a while, the world turns over on itself. Do you understand? Those who are young make it do so. Events come round again and there are few left to remember caution. They think that they can do it again and the result will be positive. But it will turn out the same for people like me, for people like Robertito. Ay, Michael, what is the use of learning, of even having a brain if we cannot accept the results of bad ideas and fashion better ones?"

"I'm sorry. I don't think I get what you're saying. My Spanish, you know."

"But I was speaking in English." She caught herself then and was not sure. Her side was hurting badly now. She couldn't find a position that relieved it. "Be careful of the young *Guardia*. That's what I want you to remember. He's lost his way and I fear he won't find it until it's too late."

"You're really worried about him."

"Yes, I'm worried about what he can do. He is after Roberto who shot his grandfather. He has harbored a resentment all his life. These are the most dangerous kind of people, those who are so deeply involved they can't see what they are doing. So don't take him lightly. He will stop at nothing."

"How do you know?"

"Because I have already lived a life of looking over my shoulder and hoping I have chosen the right one to look over. Please, be careful." The pain caught her again and this time she couldn't hide it in her movements.

"Something's wrong," Michael said.

"Like always, it's more than one thing."

"What can I do?"

"How long do you plan to stay in La Jolla?"

"I'm not sure."

"Then the first thing you can do is learn to tend the goats."

"I've been doing that."

She looked at him a moment before she nodded. "More practice would be of benefit. And most important is that you must learn how to make your uncle your friend."

Michael slowly sat down on the grass. He took Carmen's hand. "You're very sick. Am I right?"

"I'm slowing down. That's true."

"Your hands are cold."

She looked down on them. Her veins ran in all directions like burrowing animals. Her skin was bruised and speckled. "Please tell me you will be able to take care of your uncle when I am unable."

Michael, too, studied her hands, remembered her from twenty years ago when he thought even then she was an old woman. He only now realized she was then very close to his own age now and that humbled him. The faces of his wife and children, his clients, the people who relied on him passed through his mind. He wanted his daughter to appreciate what he'd done for her, wanted his son to be more open to different kinds of people and ideas.

Wanted Eva to be happy, yes, no matter where that wish might lead her. He thought of Mason, the man of mystery in his life. More to him than ever met the eye. Turned out to have been not only a top-notch shrink but a kind and courageous man as well.

"That's really it," Michael said. "Being courageous enough to be of some value in the world."

"What?"

"Like you. You're a brave woman. Were a brave girl."

"Really? In your mind it must take so little to be brave. I've done nothing that anyone else wouldn't do. It's the job of women to keep life alive. Since I could never do it in the normal way, I did it differently."

"You're terminal, aren't you, Mari Carmen?"

"I am. But I knew this time would come."

He squeezed her hand and felt a slight one back.

"When the end comes, we must be ready. Who can you trust? This woman you are with?"

"Yes, I'm pretty sure I can."

"Then enlist her aid. You can't do this alone. The first thing you must do is convince your uncle to come out. He has a chance if he is out in the open. If not, it is the war all over again and he has no chance." She tried to stand but failed.

"Let me help you," he said.

"I will sit. I have not taken enough time to appreciate what I have." She pulled stones out of her pocket and handed them to him. "For practice."

"Will you be able to make it up to my uncle again?"

"Not today. It must be you who goes. Be kind. Be gentle. And be careful."

Michael manipulated the stones in his hand as he turned from her and walked along the edge of the hill. Most of the goats followed him, but a few hovered near Carmen; one nibbled at the hem of her dress.

She rubbed at its neck as its ears flopped forward and back. Then, abruptly, she pushed it away, kicked at it so it would follow the others behind Michael.

Michael waited for them to catch up. He thought of himself in his office, growing softer behind his desk as he listened to the misfortunes of people. But here he was standing at the lip of a hill, surrounded by yawping animals who could not care less about the bleating of those clients. All they wanted was to find delicate morsels so they could live another day.

Like real life, Michael thought. Then he tried to click the roof of his mouth and tossed a stone too far from the goats, realizing he had a long way to go.

Chapter Twenty-Seven
Michael, Robert, Carmen and Blas, Andalusia, 1989

The first mistake Michael made was to buy a flashlight from *Boquete de José*. And Pepe had no batteries so Michael had to go to the other side of the village to find some that worked. That done, he herded the goats together at the *martirio* and led them up the hill toward the ravine thick with canes that would hide him as he climbed. He carried a canvas backpack, military green, old and smelly, now filled with food and fresh clothing pulled from Carmen's line that stretched high across the goat pen. He felt a mix of trepidation and excitement, which favored more dread than not. He stopped at every rise and checked the road, the streets of the town, and the landscape, as Carmen had taught him.

It took him forty more minutes to arrive at Ventura, and he was sweating and breathless by the time he got there. He found the jar easily and pushed aside the detritus. He rapped on the lid and waited, but heard nothing back. Then he remembered. Of course, two quick knocks, pause, two more quick ones, and then...

"Mari Carmen?"

Michael briefly entertained disguising his voice, but steered clear of the possible consequences. Instead, he worked at moving aside the lid, found it more difficult than he thought and again marveled at how valiant and strong Carmen must have been to do this day after day. When the lid slid aside, he poked in his head.

"Uncle Robert?"

Silence.

"It's me. Your nephew, Michael."

"I have a weapon," Robert said.

Well, he can't have one, Michael thought. Otherwise he would have used it the last time. But he'd done pretty well with the shard of terra cotta.

"Carmen's sick. She can't make the walk anymore."

"Then I'll die here. Go away. Leave me to rot in peace."

Flummoxed, Michael dug for anything that might help. "The Cougars," he said. "They beat the Huskies in football last year."

Silence again.

"Uncle Robert? I've food for you. No one else is here. I promise."

Now there was rustling below and soon the ladder fit against the edge of the opening. Michael quickly stepped down into the pit. At the bottom, Robert held the pole for him and Michael used it to slide the lid over into place. It was dark as night now. Michael sensed Robert looming next to him. "You're a liar."

"No, honest, Uncle Robert, I'm alone."

"Not that. Washington State College never wins."

Michael dug into his bag and pulled out the flashlight, snapping it on. "You always sit here in the dark?"

"Not always. When Mari Carmen visits, I light the candles." Now, he went to the table and started doing just that. Soon, the cave's dank walls were alive with flickering light. Robert now turned and studied his visitor. "Are you really my nephew?"

"I'm Little Loretta's grandson."

"Loretta... Little Loretta. My sister. I've wondered about her."

"I'm afraid she's passed."

"Dead?" Robert's head snapped to the ceiling. "Of course, she's dead. Everyone's dead. Except for that vicious son-of-a-bitch."

"Franco's dead too, Uncle Robert."

Now the head came back down and leveled on Michael. "You brought me supplies?"

"Yes, I did." Michael slid the pack off his shoulder and handed it over. Robert quickly rifled through it, pulling out cheese, chunks of kid swaddled in paper. Robert unwrapped it and stuffed a piece in his mouth.

Meanwhile, Michael looked around the space. He could see where one of the sides of the jar had been torn away and the earth behind it chipped out. It made the space wider, longer. Lengths of wood had been thrust into the dirt and now supported cups and plates and a framed photo. He walked over and shined the light on it. The sepia toned piece looked to have been folded more than once, as if it had spent time in someone's pocket. It was a young woman in a graduation cap and gown, smiling casually out at the camera. "Who is this?"

"Maggie."

"Who is she? I've never heard of anyone named Maggie."

"That's my girlfriend. You haven't heard anything from her, have you? Is she dead too?"

"I don't know her, Uncle Robert. So much time has passed, you know."

"You can go now. Tell Mari Carmen she has to come next time."

"But she's sick, very sick. I don't think she can come anymore. She can barely walk. Haven't you noticed?"

"She always comes. You don't know what you're talking about."

"Uncle Robert, please, can you sit down for a minute? We need to talk."

Robert looked around his home, nodded, then sat down. He crossed his legs and one foot started a repetitive motion.

Michael sat across from him. He clasped his hands, then decided to speak with them. "You have to listen to what I'm saying. I've come from America. I got a good education. I know things. And one thing I know is that Franco is dead. His government is dead. The Socialists rule Spain now. I know that's probably hard for you to believe and I understand why it is. But, I wouldn't lie to you. It's safe for you to come out. The horror, all the terror is over."

Robert's leg stopped its restless movement. "If I believe you, what happens?"

"You could come out of here. You could take in a breath of fresh air. I could take you back to the States. You could live out your life at home."

"And my home. Is it still there? On Eighteenth?"

"I don't know. I never knew where you lived. But we can certainly find out."

"And my parents?"

"I'm sorry. I don't know." But he did, of course.

Robert's face lit up. "I have an idea. I wonder if you could do something for me." He shambled to one of the sides where he'd picked out the walls. From his canvas bag he pulled out a pile of paper of different sizes. He came back, cradling them. "I never got around to mailing these and I really should have. Some of them are very old, some are more recent. But if you could please mail them. My parents will be worried."

Michael took the handful and set to arranging them by size. He noticed some of the dates as he did so; 1943, 1957, 1968, and on and on. "You just kept writing…"

"I promised them I would."

"All right. I will."

"My parents will be happy to finally hear from me."

"Does this mean you're not going to come out?"

"It's like this," Robert said. "I have information to the contrary. I have people who come and tell me the truth about the war."

"Who are these people and what do they say?"

"It's war, young man. I can't tell you that. How can I possibly trust you?"

"Carmen trusts me. And the war is over."

At her name, Robert grew solemn. "You have no idea about this girl. She's a miracle. I don't know for sure, but I think she suffered for me. There was a time when I almost starved, I didn't see her for so long. Soon after I got here. When she finally did show up, I could see in her eyes the light had left her at only twelve years old." He drifted off briefly. "Her hair. I thought she was a boy."

"But if it's true she suffered for you, then you should listen to her. She can be trusted."

"Yes, but the way she's been talking lately tells me she's not comfortable."

"Her health…"

"Yes, yes, she told me about that. But it's something different. Tell me, are there still the men in the typewriter hats?"

It took Michael a moment and then he grinned. "Yes. And they do look like typewriters perched right on their heads, waiting to be used."

"As long as there are men like that around, you need to be careful."

"Can I ask you something?" Michael said. "These people, when they come to talk to you, do their voices come from inside your head or outside?"

"Outside, of course." He narrowed his eyes. "What are you asking? If I'm crazy?"

"But Uncle Robert…"

Robert came right up to his face and Michael feared he might hit him again. "What I've seen with these eyes, it still plays out in my head. I fight to get rid of it but it's always there. It never ever ends. Listen to me. Your life can completely change just by getting a letter in the mail. Maybe as simple as changing shifts early or late. Your best friend can be murdered if you're not careful. Have you ever really seen what one human can do to another? With knives and guns and boats in the water? I never knew until I came to this country. If you are to survive here with me, then you have to listen. You have to listen." Robert grabbed Michael by the arms and shook him. "Trust no one all the way."

Michael was troubled after he left the jar and led the goats back down to La Jolla. What was he to do now? The natural thing would be to seek out a local shrink and figure out how to get medication for Robert. He very much needed it. But that, of course, opened up a can of worms Michael might not have been ready for. Questions would be asked. His uncle would be poked and prodded.

Back in the village, he penned Mari Carmen's goats back up, and found her in the house. She slept on top of her unmade bed. Carefully, he lifted up the blankets and placed her legs underneath. She opened her eyes briefly, but just stared past him.

He locked her gate and walked back up to the apartment. Delia was gone. No note. No anything. He checked her room and her bed was military perfect. He walked into the kitchen, heated up some water and made a cup of coffee. While he stirred it, he shook his head. He couldn't get the smell of the jar out of his nose, his clothes. He knew that he would be crazy within days if he had to spend any time in that tiny jail.

Shivering in his own bedroom, he stripped down and crawled under the covers even though light still shined through the window.

He pulled the stack of letters out of his pack. Some of the pages were water stained, some crusted with dirt. He started reading the first one. Would that he had the opportunity with each one of his patients to get to know them so well before he began treatment.

§

As Michael read, outside of the apartment, Blas Alvarez was just passing by. His hands twirled at his lips and he spoke quietly into them. It could have been Last Rites, it could have been Our Fathers. He didn't often mingle, but he had something to do, someone to convince. Perhaps he was practicing as he whispered into his hands.

The hem of his robe brushed the cobblestones as he moved along. He'd traveled these streets many times over the years. Both he and the stones had stories to tell. One or two of these tales had kept Father Alvarez up at night but not since the death of Franco. It was calmer in La Jolla now, albeit less reverent. The village had always been good to the priest. He came there as a very young man fresh out of the seminary and just in time for the start of the war. He enjoyed built-in respect and used it wisely. Quickly he knew where the protection was going to come from. And certainly not from the likes of women like Victoria, who approached him now and passed without comment.

Women like this, well, they deserved what they got, didn't they? Soon, he arrived at the house of Maria del Carmen. Only she was climbing up to meet him so he waited. She stopped when she saw him.

"I must talk to you," he said, and without another word, he passed her on the way down to her house.

"I am busy," she said.

"This is important. It concerns your immortal soul."

"My soul is not immortal," she said. "When I die, it dies with me."

"Quiet. God will hear."

"Then it would be the first time."

Frowning, Father Alvarez strode back to her. He pointed a finger and shook it. "You should pay attention to me. I am offering you an opportunity to cleanse yourself before the end."

She eyed him briefly before putting out her own hand and grabbing his finger. She twisted it sharply and then let go.

"I want you to come to confession," the priest said.

"I will never confess to you."

"You and I both know that you have much to confess. And you and I both know that you have received bad news. The time is now. God is trying to get your attention, Maria del Carmen. Listen to him."

Carmen rubbed at her elbow, felt the pain. She thought of the years she had witnessed this man do the opposite of what she thought a priest should do. She looked at his lined face, his shaky hands. "Who do you confess to, Blas Alvarez? Who is saving your soul?"

"I report to the Archbishop," he said. "And my confession is not your concern."

"Then we have nothing to talk about. Until the day you are willing to confess to me, I will not be entering your confessional." She turned then and began the grueling walk up the street.

Chapter Twenty-Eight
Robert and Carmen, Andalusia, 1937

"God help me, I've killed a man."

The man's horse swayed several yards away, its bridle dragging the ground. Robert wondered if he could jump on it and ride into the mountains, far away from this place. But when he tried to stand, the pain in his side knocked him back down. He felt under his shirt. The blood still flowed, but slower now. He could not feel a bullet, so it must have gone all the way through.

He was grateful the boy escaped. Surely, that was a good outcome. He picked up the man's rifle, inspected it as best he could. It would add more weight, though, so he placed it back down at the side of the body. He searched the pockets, found cigarettes, a thin French brand. He was about to light one up, but froze when he realized a flame might give away his position. He stuffed them in his pocket and sat back, trying not to look at the man whose life he took.

A half hour later, he wanted to move. He did not think he should be found next to a dead man when dawn arrived. But when he tried once more to roll over, he gritted his teeth to keep from crying out. Not only was the wound worse, but he also felt fainter when he moved. He lay back down. That's when he heard the noise.

At first, he thought it might be the horse, but the animal now grazed nearby. No, this sound was tinier than a horse, more the sound of little feet trotting quickly. With great difficulty, he rose up. Coming at him from the other direction, a donkey cantered. When it drew close, Robert picked up his rifle.

With his improved Spanish, Robert said, "I killed a man; I can do it again."

"No, don't." It was the voice of a girl, perhaps a young woman. "I'm here to help." She slid off the donkey. "What is your name?"

"Robert."

"I am Carmen Escobar, Roberto. You must go. The man you killed will be missed. It's not good what will happen to you." She leaned in close to him, smelling of lavender and blood. She looked down on the dead man and suddenly spit on the body. "Good," she said.

Again, Robert tried to move and managed only to roll up to his knees.

"Are you injured?"

"He shot me. It hurts."

She quickly moved behind him and put her arms around his waist. "Up now. Quickly. Your pain is meaningless if you don't get away."

Agony shot through him with every step. Soon they were at the donkey's side. She pushed while he tried to climb, and the combination of both got him on the animal's bony back. He lay himself flat against its neck. When he bit his lip to keep quiet, he tasted fresh blood.

"*Conozco un lugar*," she said. "I know a place."

With Carmen steering from the side, they took off, and it was as if Robert were a fly. As the burro began to trot again, he bounced and felt every movement at the site of the wound.

Ahead of them, he could barely make out a village situated on a hill. He believed they would go there, but instead, she urged the burro to take a narrow path up a different hill. The uneven surface continued to pound at his wound. He leaned further forward to ease it.

Up and up, they climbed. The girl was mostly silent except for the time or two she had to talk to the burro to get it to go the way she wanted. It was nearly dawn by the time they arrived at a town that looked, even in the bare light, to have suffered the worst of it. All around them lay rubble and the donkey had to slow down and pick its way or risk throwing them both down the incline into the debris. They finally stopped and the girl helped Robert slide off. In the new light, he could see he'd left a trail of smeared blood on the animal's hide.

"*Aquí, aquí,*" she said, and set herself to scurrying about, moving rocks, pulling things from the donkey's pack. Finally, she came to him and put a hand on his shoulder. "*Puede ver aquí. Venga. He preparado un sitio.*"

"You've made a place for me?"

At that she shrugged and helped him stand before she guided him about ten yards through the exploded adobe to a hole in the ground. A ladder poked out of the top.

Pointing to the hole, she said, "*Si puede, por favor, bajar abajo. Vuelvo por la noche.*"

Robert knew enough language to understand that she wanted him to go down the ladder and hide. She would come back in the night, she said. But he was still skeptical.

"What is this?" he said.

"*Es el sitio donde se va a esconder hasta que esté terminado la guerra,*" she said. "*Es mi idea.*"

"What? Hide until the war is over?"

"*Sí.*"

And not unlike the difficulty with getting on the burro, it took a while to place him on the ladder. It was rickety at best, but sturdy enough for him to step down into an inky cavity. If he hadn't known better, he would have thought he was descending into hell itself. But he eventually touched bottom and stepped off. She peeked over the rim of the hole.

"*Hay comida y agua.*" She handed down a sack on a long string until he could grab hold of it. "*Guarde la escalera con usted,*" she said. And when he had pulled the ladder in, she said, "*Adiós*", and pushed a top over the opening.

Chapter Twenty-Nine
Robert, Ventura, Andalusia, 1937

February(I think). The exact date, I don't know, La Jolla, Spain
Dear Mom and Dad,

I am no longer afraid to die. The last few days (week?) have been wrenching. I tried to rig up a place to sleep, but there's only hard ground with my pack as a pillow. I used my pick to break up the dirt some, to make it softer, so it's not exactly been like sleeping on a rock, but close. But that's only part of it. This blasted wound has gotten the best of me. Once the girl left and the shock of it all wore off, it started hurting, and I mean hurting. A throb a lot like a toothache, but bigger. So much bigger that I had thoughts of taking my pick and digging out that part of my body, like pulling a big tooth so I could get some relief. Having no light, I wanted to save my candle for letters to you, but I had to get a look at it and what I saw was disheartening to say the least. The hole itself was sunk into a swollen expanse of my flesh. Red lines radiated out from it like a sun. In the very middle, a black crust was rimmed with yellowing pus. Sorry to be so graphic but I want you to know what I'm going through. I know enough about biology (remember my only A that semester?) to recognize blood poisoning. Maybe the bullet is causing it or maybe the thing went clean through, but in any event, it hurts like hell and I need to do something about it. I wait and wait for the young girl who brought me here, but she hasn't come again. I think once in a while about climbing out and making a run for it, but how do I know they aren't waiting for me on the outside?

I don't know anything for sure anymore. I'm running out of water, which I know is good for infection, so I drip a few drops on my tongue every hour to preserve what I have left. Miraculously, the pain has subsided and that's a blessed relief. I sleep a great deal of the time. I eat bits of a cheese the girl left with me. I am starved, but the weeks before all this prepared me I guess. Although I sure could go for one of those fresh oranges off the tree or a big stalk of sugar cane. Now those meager things seem like sumptuous banquets. I am... Hold on, I hear noises above me. There is a God, and her name is Mari Carmen. Although like all those biblical Marys, I fear she's suffered mightily. The noises above me were her. She tapped on the lid of the jar and when I didn't answer, tapped again. Then I heard the smallest voice, speaking slowly so I could understand better. "Don Roberto, it is Carmen Escobar. The ladder. The ladder, Don Roberto?" Mom, Dad, it was like the voice of an angel and I didn't care one bit if I had died and gone to heaven. But soon I heard the grinding of the lid, and while I expected sun to come spilling in, it was as dark on the outside as it was in the hole. And cold. I placed the ladder solidly against the top and in a moment, the girl descended down to me. Since my eyes were now underground eyes, I needed no adjustment to see that something horrible had happened to her. Her hair was as short or shorter than a boy's. There were recent wounds all around her face. When she finally hit the ground, I could see she was unsteady on her legs. She had difficulty setting down the pack she'd come in with. In a moment, she recovered herself though and looked around. Meanwhile, I lit what was left of the candle. "No light," she said. But I couldn't help myself; I had to see my angel closer. I guess I must've been a little too intense because she shied away to a corner of the jar. "Here. Food," she said. The look on her face was not unlike the looks I've seen on the faces of the people in dance marathons after a few days have passed. Hope was absent. Spirit broken on the inside. Or maybe I was just looking in a mirror at my own miserable face. "You are hurt?" she asked.

I lifted my shirt and by her reaction I could tell it was bad. "Here is lino for you," she said. "I don't know what lino is," I said. But that didn't deter her. Turns out to be a potion of flaxseed. In a moment, she removed what looked to be some kind of poultice from the pack. Using a long strip of cloth, she laced the medicine over my injury and then wound the cloth around my middle so that it made a good solid fit. I watched her as she worked. "What happened?" I asked, pointing to her hair. But she bowed her head and kept it down, even after she finished dressing my wound. "Maria del Carmen?" I asked again. This time she tilted her head and simply shook it. I accepted that. After my time on the road to Málaga, I knew what she meant. She did tell me the date; she had been gone for over a week, and I think she said changes had come to her town but there was hope now that things would settle down. "What you did is a problem. Now they look for you, you must be careful. We will have a signal so you know it is me. Any other noise, you do not answer. Do you understand?" I nodded my head. I hope I did understand her, although it was still so hard to put words together. "Why are you doing this?" I asked in both English and Spanish. She just shrugged. Maybe she didn't understand, maybe she didn't know. She noticed the pack of letters I had ready to mail. She picked one up. "I send only one," she said. "It is a risk." "Then don't," I said. But she took one anyway and quickly stuffed it in her dress. She stayed only a moment longer. This person, this little girl, actually, has all the guile of someone twice her age and experience. I am glad we are on the same side. I will keep writing but I must get some sleep. Already I can feel the healing power of the poultice.

 Your loving son,
 Robert

§

Michael lost himself in the letters. His own problems faded into nothing. While he was reading, Delia finally came home. She knocked on his bedroom door and then stood there.

 "What are you doing?" she said.

He held up a fistful of the notes. "These. It's like reading magic. All my uncle's letters."

"Interesting," she said. "Listen, I have a date so I won't be home tonight."

"I see."

"You can fend for yourself, can't you?"

He held the letters up again. "It runs in the family, fending for ourselves."

"You may be forgetting about Carmen," she said. "I'll see you tomorrow then."

"Are you taking the car?"

"Nope. My date's picking me up in style."

He stared for a moment at the doorway she'd just left before he turned back to the letters.

After a while, Michael saw a slight change in them. It happened over months, maybe even a year. He sifted through them and made a diagnosis then and there. His uncle needed mental health treatment and Michael would be the one to find it.

Chapter Thirty
Carmen, Andalusia 1989

Carmen prepared to go out, maybe for the last time. She packed a bag, thought of the foreign women she had seen with their many suitcases and their cosmetics and their sharp self-awareness. She laughed. All you need is one bag to hold all you require in the world. So much movement, though, tired her, made her pull out a chair and sit down. She was to see Robert tonight, as she had for so many nights. The usual routine. Oddly, she now thought of that time back in 1943 when it wasn't so routine.

It was her father's blanket, made from sheepskin by her mother in the months before their wedding. Soft and pliable. Whenever she thought of her poor dead father or her dear mother, she would pull it out from its hiding place in the wall, hold it against her cheek, and allow herself to weep.

Why did she pack it now? For the first time since she was left for dead in the alley, she felt a flame slowly kindling inside her. And the nights had been colder of late. She might need a cover. Roberto might need a cover.

The pack was heavy when she secured it over her shoulder, but she was a young woman now, not a feisty girl; she'd been tempered by adversity. It was late when she left the house; the streets were empty. She stopped for a moment at the *martirio*, said a prayer for the fallen and continued on.

The world of La Jolla seemed vast at night and it all belonged to her, from the ground she walked on to the firmament above with its grinning stars.

Once at the jar, she set down the pack and slid the top aside. As soon as she did, a candle flickered alive, then another, and she could see this man as he stood in the midst of the glimmer.

"Don Roberto," she said.

"I've set the wood for fire. How is the news?"

"I'll go then. The purge continues. The lies continue. The innocent are still being sent across the great divide."

In a moment, she had walked down the half block to the old Moorish well. Most thought it was still poisoned, but the water now was sweet. She lowered a makeshift bucket down into the water and brought it back up. She struggled to hold it straight as she returned to the jar.

She watched from above as Robert set a kettle over flaming logs. Then she lowered the bucket and climbed down the ladder. On his bath night, they had to leave the lid open partway for the smoke. They sat together and after some minutes, watched the bubbles form inside the kettle.

"He has given permission for the Nazis to transfer Spaniards from France to the camps in Germany."

"Of course, he has."

"They're winning."

"Is there no good news?"

"I have three baby goats just born," she said. "There will be food for a while longer."

"Congratulations."

Today was a day he was dressed as a soldier. He had lost weight and the uniform hung loosely from his gaunt frame. But he wore it so infrequently and moved so little, it still maintained a rather fine press.

"I'm hungry, but I'm not, you know?" he said.

"I am..."

But he held out his arm. "Did you hear that?"

She stopped, cocked her head. After a moment, she said, "I hear nothing."

"I thought I did."

"Why are you dressed like that today?"

"I'm afraid I'll forget. I don't want to forget why I'm here."

He talked so little of the war, of his reasons for coming to Spain. She was hopeful one day he would in a way that would make sense to her. He never seemed like a man who hungered for war.

The water began a full boil, and she reached into the bag to take out a pair of rags. "You should get going on your uniform."

He stood and started to unbutton his shirt, which he now removed with no pain from the old wound. But Carmen jumped up to examine it. It had long since healed over. Her hand lingered there; a finger rubbed at it.

"What?" he said, pulling slightly away.

"I am remembering this now. I feared the infection would set in and I would lose you."

He touched it too, felt her fingers there and caressed one of them. "You saved my life."

"I hope there is water left in the bucket."

"There is." He used one of the rags to take the kettle off the fire and pour it into the bucket. He tested it with a finger and poured a little more. Then he began his routine.

He turned his back and unsnapped his trousers. He ran a finger along the waistband of his shorts. From behind him, she dipped a rag into the warm water and offered it to him. Her hand lingered just above the skin of his back. He palmed a thin piece of soap she brought him. He wrapped it in the wet rag and started washing himself, first under one arm and then the other.

Carmen watched him. She liked the way the muscles in his back rippled as he moved. Soon, he stopped and waited.

"All right," she said. She turned away from him, but this time she peeked. He had pulled out the waistband of his underwear and was washing himself down there. She decided at that moment, to turn back.

"I need the other rag," he said.

She grabbed the used one from him, but instead of giving him the fresh one to rinse off, she stepped over and in one motion, pulled down his underwear.

Robert jumped, trying to pull his shorts up. "What are you doing?" he sputtered.

"It would be so much easier." But she noticed his problem with pulling his shorts back up was not with the fabric. He was aroused.

He looked down and blushed.

"No, no," she said. "It's normal. It's all right."

He had turned away again. She came up behind him and put her arms through his and held him at his chest.

"This isn't right," he said. "You're so young. You were twelve when we first met."

"And now I am eighteen. Angelita, she is one year younger than me and she is pregnant with her second baby." She withdrew her arms. "Just let me clean you."

He hesitated a moment and then slowly pulled his shorts all the way off. He stood, shivering, his hands clasped to his mouth.

Gently, Carmen ran the rag across his back in slow ever-expanding circles. She paused to dip the cloth in the water once more and continued on. Without being asked, he turned toward her, gathered her in his arms and pulled her close.

"If I must do this, so must you."

She stepped back a moment and took him in. Then said, "I am shamed by my body. Things were done to me."

"I'm not ashamed of you. You're so gorgeous. You're perfectly lovely."

So, she did. As he watched, Carmen removed her clothes, placing each piece neatly on the table. The candlelight formed a kind of halo around her, moving as she moved, like in a dream.

When she stood before him, he saw what had been done to her. He traced a scar that ran from just under one breast to the other side of her body. On her legs, there were old healed burns each the size of a quarter that would never completely disappear.

"I'm speechless," he said, drinking her in.

"Please," Carmen said. "Just hold me."

He did, and he was like stone against her. Now she knew why she brought her mother's blanket. "Not down here," she said.

"Are you sure?"

"We could die tomorrow."

He stepped around the jar and blew out each candle, but when he turned around, she was gone.

"Please," she said from up near the edge.

When he climbed to the top of the ladder, he hesitated. Was that a gunshot? Was that the sound of a snapping stick? "Mari Carmen," he whispered.

"Here."

"Again."

"Here."

He followed her voice and finally saw her sitting on a thick blanket. He crawled out and tiptoed carefully to her. He spread himself out beside her. He leaned in, kissed her for the first time on her lips. He could feel her quiver.

"You must go like this," she said. "Carefully. Slowly."

"Then you are a virgin?"

"Right after I brought you to this place, I was, what is the word, tortured. I do not function now in the same way as other women. I am told that I cannot have children."

"Maybe we shouldn't do this."

"No, I am not saying that. I'm just asking you to be gentle."

He turned on his back, placed his hands behind his head, looked up at the stars.

"What are you waiting for?" she said.

"I don't want to do anything wrong. I don't want to hurt you."

"Ay, Robertito, how could you ever hurt me worse than I've already been hurt? There is worse pain in my loneliness. Please take away my loneliness for just this little time."

He turned on his side again, cupped a hand under her breast. "Mari Carmen, you are beautiful."

She put her arms around his neck and said, "Show me how beautiful I am."

§

Eugenio and Delia sat in the parking lot of the local *Guardia* office. She had expected he would take her to his house, but he came to the village and drove them here and was now simply staring ahead through the windshield of the Land Rover.

"Want to tell me what you're doing?" she said.

"Making up my mind."

She tried to move closer, but he elbowed her away. "Why are you in my country?" he said.

"I'm hoping that's not a real question because the answer would be I'm looking for you."

"I don't believe you. You are a woman who lies."

"I'm not lying. And I know another thing. You are looking for me. I know because we feel the same thing. People pass all around us but we don't see them. You and I are lone wolves. But even wolves need other wolves."

"You talk nonsense."

"Maybe, but you know it's true."

He finally looked at her. "I know who you are, Lone Wolf."

"I don't get it. Is this part of your game? Because if it is, it's a little tiresome. Just a note to you. You already have me."

"No game. You came here under a false passport. I could take you in and put you behind bars right now if I wanted."

She moved away, ears ringing, grabbed hold of the handle. But he seized her arm and pulled her close once more. "Do you think that's a good idea?" His fingers pressed into her wrist with alarming ferocity.

"What do you want?"

"Information maybe."

"What kind of information?"

"This partner of yours, the American. He bought a flashlight at Pepe's store. Why?"

"Are you kidding me? This is the information you're after? You're pathetic."

He squeezed harder. "Don't be a fool. Tell me where the old American is. Robert Martin."

"What old...?" But he squeezed so much harder that tears came to her eyes. "Let me go."

He saw her tears and stopped the pressure. "I don't want to hurt you. I don't even want you to go to prison. I just want you to help me."

"Fuck you." She tried to pull away, but his powerful grip held firm. In a second, he had unhooked the handcuffs from his belt and snapped them on her wrists.

"What are you...?"

"Shut up now. You had your chance." He opened his door and dragged her across the seat and out on the pavement.

Her first thought was that she'd been here before and with far crazier men, but Eugenio's kind of crazy frightened her more than any of the others. She stumbled along with him as he led her to the entrance of the building and inside. They stood together at the front desk. The cuffs already had made a deep red impression on her wrists.

"The keys," he barked, and the man behind the desk produced a heavy set. Eugenio grabbed them and pulled Delia along once more, through a pair of doors and back into a wing filled with iron bars. He unlocked the handcuffs and threw her into one of the cells, slammed the door shut. Delia scrambled up from the floor and stepped back, rubbing at her wrists. "Bastard," she said.

"You're not this Toni. You're a woman with too many names. This will give you time to think about it." He slapped the bars and walked away.

Delia sat on a cot against the far wall. Her hands dropped between her legs. She thought she had this one. He fell so quickly for her, so lustily. She was wrong. Obviously. This one had a competing, more ardent desire. Different needs. All her adult life she had walked a tightrope and that in itself had given her pleasure, but this man had jerked the rope even tighter, and she'd fallen off. There was a solid chance she would hit the ground unless she could give him what he wanted. She knew, of course, what it was.

§

Maria del Carmen could barely walk. The pain today had no antecedent, except for perhaps the pain of recollection. She thought she could borrow some painkiller from Maria del Mar, but she wanted a clear head right now. Up all night, she sensed she had little time left. She must have her faculties sharp so she could parse her duties well.

At her gate, she patted her dress, making sure she had what she needed. The bulge in her pocket was hidden by her shawl. After her mission was completed, she would return to the place where her happiest memories occurred.

In five minutes, she stood in the doorway of the church. Her heart ached. She wanted time to move backward, to when was it, to 1932.

"It will all be good now," said her father, leaning on his spade in his dirty overalls. Already two of his teeth were dark, one missing. "You'll see what happens when we are in charge. You are a lucky girl."

And she felt like it. She had studied for her Confirmation, or as much as any seven-year-old could. "Has she reached the age of reason?" Blas Alvarez asked her mother.

"Yes, of course," said Carmen's mother, the most beautiful woman she had ever and would ever know. "She has more reason than children twice her age."

She recalled snippets of the event: A white dress, sweaty hands, scrubbed *alpargatas* to help her walk on the cloud she was riding. And devotion and admiration. For God, for her town, for her country, and for her priest, Blas Alvarez.

Now Carmen walked across the floor to the confessional. Yes, it was time. The pain told her so. Time to confess her many sins. But Father Alvarez was not there when she arrived. She took up a heavy cane and thumped it on the floor two times, then twice more. Finally, the priest emerged from behind the chancel screen. When he saw who had bothered him, he frowned.

"I have very little time," he called from across the floor.

"I've come to tell you that you have finally won," she said. "I am dying. I want to confess."

Father Alvarez's eyebrows gave rise to his delight. He shuffled over, hunched now, his vestments dragging. When he approached, he said, "Give me my cane."

Carmen handed it over. Without a word, she sneaked into the structure and slowly knelt before the screen. Father Alvarez entered and sat noisily, his body facing out, his head resting against the partition. Out of Carmen's sight, he rubbed his hands together.

"Bless me father," Carmen said. "For all my sins past, present and future."

"Future?"

"As you know, I am dying, and at some point I may not have control of my faculties and this may cause me to sin without knowing. I want forgiveness for that."

"You would already be forgiven for mistakes not under your own volition."

"That is very good to know, Father."

"What has caused this change of heart? Could it be me? Have you finally listened to me?"

"It is you, Father. Finally. You make sense and, as I've just told you, I am about to die and hell does not seem to be a favorable place to go."

"I believe you would not go to any hell. You would be cast into purgatory until such time as you have redeemed yourself."

"Hmm. Perhaps I've already lived in purgatory."

"Enough of this nonsense... Let's not waste any more time. My hope is that you will confess your sins, Maria del Carmen. All of them." He paused and placed his hand on the screen. "Do you understand what I mean when I say all of them?"

"If I must," Carmen said.

Father Alvarez made a slight nod of his head.

"I am very serious. My death is close. I want last rites."

"Last rites? But you must confess, you must partake of the Holy Eucharist."

"I am confessing."

"Not everything." He moved even closer to the screen. "You have not confessed about Robert Martin."

Not surprised, Carmen nodded. "That is true."

Blas Alvarez grunted. "You hid the man, didn't you? When is the last time you received the Host?"

"And when is the last time you gave extreme unction...?"

"Why, just a few days..."

"...that mattered to God and the church and not the *Fascistas*?"

Father Alvarez jerked his head sharply, rattling the screen.

And now Carmen, as she had planned, began: "Is anyone among you suffering?"

"Stop now. That is sacrilege. Those are my words to give."

"Let him pray. Is anyone cheerful? Let him sing psalms. Is anyone among you sick? Let him call for the elders of the church and let them pray over him, anointing him with oil in the name of the Lord. And the prayer of faith will save the sick and the Lord will raise him up."

"Blasphemy!" shouted Father Alvarez. "Carmen? Stop now."

"Did you really give all those men a prayer of faith? All those women? Those children? I saw you in the alley the night I was tortured. Hiding your face against the wall. You were afraid, Father. You feared the *Camisas Negras*."

"I shall leave you without blessing your confession. And you know that will sentence you to no good afterlife."

Carmen calmed. "You're right, Father. Forgive me. I have so many sins, I'm sure. But I will tell you my most sacred one."

"Please do proceed."

"In 1937 when the man came to our village and killed the lieutenant. I helped him to escape and hide." Here she told him the whole story, from the ride on the donkey, to the daily trial of providing for him to keep him alive. When she finished, she said, "I hope this confession will get me to the gates of whatever heaven awaits me."

Blas Alvarez thought he was already in eternal heaven. Her words drifted to him as if they were the very manna he had been needing for fifty years. This was the world to him. This would bring the young Guardia to his side, to his graces.

"And I have kept this as a secret for these fifty years, Father. I have sinned against everyone, especially God."

"You are right to confess this, child. You are right to give this to God. Now, I must devise a penance for you, a penance that will merit the severity of your sin."

"Must I suffer?"

"Of course."

"Please don't tell anyone else about this, Father."

"The confessional is as silent as the grave."

"As silent as your cowardice?"

"What?"

"As quiet as your betrayal of this village?"

"Enough."

"God does not and never has blessed you, Father."

This time Father Alvarez rose and stumbled out of the confessional. He steadied himself with the cane. "You *will* go to hell, Maria del Carmen Escobar."

"I have been there as well." Now out of the confessional too, she reached into her pocket and pulled out her bible. She opened it to a marked page. "'And if he has committed sins, he will be forgiven.'" She threw the book to the floor and the slap resounded throughout the church. "You have long sinned, Father. Those you let be killed have not. My father and my brother are frolicking in heaven while you grovel in the hell you've created."

"Get out!" Father Alvarez said. And then under his breath, "*Puta.*"

Carmen had had practice enough in her mind, and she made the move with ease. She pulled the curved knife from her pocket and lunged for Father Alvarez. She plunged the knife deep into his neck, severing an artery that had too long kept him alive.

The priest staggered in shock, grabbing his throat and bringing back thick blood. He took one more step and crumpled to the floor. Watching him as his eyes slowly closed and a lake of blood spread around him, Carmen pocketed the knife, crossed herself backwards, retrieved her bible, and walked out of the church.

§

"Do you know why we call this the *martirio*?" Carmen said. She had walked to the top of the village, taking slow painful steps. She had washed the blood from her hands and her garments. Now clean, she had put aside the sight of Father Alvarez dying on the floor.

"Because of the martyrs?" Michael said. He had spent the night poring over his uncle's letters and was left feeling worn out.

"Back in the war, this was just a tiny mesa on the way into our village, just far enough away from the houses for the fascists to hide their dirty work. Here is where they took our men, ordered them to dig long and wide pits and here is where they shot them in the back of the head so that they tumbled into their self-made graves. Some were still breathing when the first shovelfuls of dirt were tossed over them."

"Ah, Carmen, I am so sorry."

"And other trenches were for the ones already dead. Women, children who were not quick enough to come up with the right answer when they were asked questions about their loyalty. Now it is a parking lot. Still, underneath it the bones of my brother crumble into dust. My father. Sometimes it feels that even I am under all this rock and concrete. Franco did this, you know. One of his last orders. Pave over the graves so no one will ever know. Soon enough, those who remember will be gone themselves."

"What can I do?"

"Something is in the air tonight. If you could take me to the only man I've known, I would be very grateful. If I am to die, I need to be with him once more. I need to make a home. I need to lie down with him."

"But you can't walk very far now. It doesn't seem possible that it can happen."

"You've come for a reason. That means it can happen. Please, Michael. This is my whole life we speak of." She glanced over to the parking area of the *martirio*. The rental car sat with pepper leaves dotting its hood. Victoria stood next to it, a bouquet of deep red carnations rested in her arms. "And there is a way to get there that doesn't require me to walk far."

§

Eugenio paced back to her cell. Delia knew he was standing there, but she refused to look up.

"Are you ready to change your mind?" he said.

She shook her head slowly.

"Very well." He squatted and slid some papers under the bottom of the bars, then left.

When he'd been gone a few minutes, Delia picked them up. She barely had to look because she already recognized the logo at the top with the bold scales of justice. Her old friends at the FBI. Still wasting their time on people like her. She had it so good there in Spokane. A place so out of the way that she could live a normal life.

She took the papers back to the cot and began reading them. In the middle of the page, she found herself:

Subject is indeed the female suspect in the Ordination Bank hold-up in 1973. Subject has assumed an alias, one Delia Ann Parks, who attended the University of North Dakota beginning in 1973. Received a B.A. in Secondary Education in 1977. Spanish major. Took a teaching position at Mandan West High School in 1978. Surveillance indicates no contact with other suspects in this case.

Then down the page further, she read more:

While not believed to have set off the explosives, subject is known to have manned the getaway vehicle

and was seen on security video "high-fiving" two others who escaped the scene with her. Subject is believed to be capable of inflicting harm and should be approached with caution. Subject is a priority get.

Delia set the papers down and grabbed the edge of the cot, straightening out her arms. She could picture herself surrendering, always had been able to, and every time she pictured it, there came with it a profound sense of relief. It washed over her now. It would be the simple solution. It would most likely save the lives of Michael and his uncle. But she knew it had never been the act of surrendering that kept her on the run. It had always been about losing the fight with the authorities. It started in the forest outside of town as she tried to escape the man who had raped her and then told her he would have to take her life. She chanted over and over in her head that she had to keep ahead of him, could not stop. Stopping was losing. And dying. So, as she sat on the cot and considered her options, she tried to imagine herself dying. And she couldn't quite feature it. This with Eugenio might be like a stumble in that forest as a teenage girl, but she was an adult now. She knew she could pick herself up and end up winning. She had the skill. She closed her eyes and remembered how she learned that skill.

Buzz dropped her off in Dickinson, North Dakota. It seemed natural back then, but now, she was not sure why. Why couldn't she just go on with him and end up where he ended up?

"The more scattered we are, the harder it is for the feds," he said.

They had lunch in a main street café and he explained the ways in which she could make herself invisible. Ironically, the federal government was a goldmine of names and identities, he said. She had perfected the half-listen. She picked up everything he said, but her heart was resisting. She took one of his heavy-veined hands and rubbed it. What was she going to do?

"I have no worries about you," he said. "You could do this with your eyes closed."

As a joke, she closed them, but didn't like the way it made her feel.

"I'll get hold of you when the time is right," he said.

"But how?"

"How did we get together this time?"

"That was planned?"

"Well, no... more the will of the gods. Some things are just meant to be."

She stood on the street as he got into his car, their car, as she'd come to think of it. She wanted to run and hold him one last time in her arms, but causing a scene was bad business.

"See you, Toni," he said. "Susanna. Rachel. Whoever else." He smiled and waved through the open window. "Drink in the panic. That's what will keep you alive. The fear will keep you safe."

She stood for a few minutes on the very spot where Buzz's car was parked until an old man in a pickup tooted his horn and yelled at her to move.

But it didn't take long for her to get going. She found out she was smart enough to get a GED long before her class was expected to graduate. She found work. She found a place to live. She found a college and a goal. All the while laughing to herself. Here she was on the lam and not a soul except for Buzz even knew it.

Now, sitting in the jail cell, she knew she could do it again.

§

It was evening when they hit the top of the hill on the road out of La Jolla and Carmen stopped him. "There's a track here that is no longer used," she said. "If you get out and look along the edge, you'll find it."

Michael searched the crumbling verge of the road, avoiding the steep ditch until he came to a spot heaped with sweet pea and milk thistle. He stepped on it and it was solid, and wide enough for the rental to pass. He got back in, made the turn and soon the two of them were driving along the crest of the hill. Too easy to see, Carmen thought, but Michael was happy to find this way to bring his friend to meet up with his uncle.

There was an actual track cut into the soil long ago by wagon wheels that appeared and disappeared at intervals. About three kilometers worth. To one side, Michael looked out on the distant hazy Mediterranean and could actually see a smoky vision of the coast of Africa. On the other side, the road fell away, down in dry weed-choked runnels toward La Jolla and beyond. He could just make out the top of the church.

In minutes, they were at the edge of the abandoned village and they stopped next to a pile of mud and timbers and stones that was once a house. Michael carefully guided Carmen out of the car and she stretched her back, wincing all the while. She scanned the horizon. This world of hers that had always seemed small now opened up its arms. They carried the supply bag through the obstacle course of rubble as they came at the jar by a route they'd never tread.

When they arrived, Carmen sat down on one of the big concrete chunks bearded with dry green and black lichen. As Michael moved to the lid of the jar, she said, "Wait a moment." She smoothed back the recalcitrant tendrils at the side of her head. "How do I look?" she said.

"Beautiful."

"You lie about as well as you herd goats."

Michael walked to her and wove the strings of hair into each other, then patted her head.

"I'm nervous," she said. "I've come up to this spot almost every day for fifty years and now is the time for me to get nervous?"

"What are you afraid of?"

"I'm afraid he will not like me in the light of day."

"In a few minutes the sun will be gone. I think you're safe." He waited until she had arranged herself and nodded her approval.

He tapped on the lid. Twice. Then twice again. There came a tap back and Michael began the work of moving the lid aside.

Once he was successful, he peered down into the hole. "Hello, Uncle Robert," he said in a whisper.

"Where is she?"

"She's here with me, but it's hard for her to move and she for certain can't get down those steps." He pointed to the ladder Robert kept hold of at the bottom.

"What do you mean?"

"You'll have to come out to see her."

But Robert was already shaking his head. "That isn't possible."

"Please."

"They'll get me, young man. You don't know. They're waiting for my mistake. I know it."

"I read your letters," Michael said.

"What? You didn't mail them?"

"Not yet."

"Those are private. You had no right to read them."

"But I had to read them. I know for a fact you've been outside of this jar before. And I know that worry drove you back inside. I know you better now."

"I don't want you to know me better. What I want is for my parents not to worry. I want them to know I'm okay."

"I promise I'll mail them. Now, let me down there and I'll help you out." Michael dropped down the rungs.

At the bottom, Robert stood with his arms crossed. "It's not even dark yet."

"Then we'll wait a few minutes for the sun to go down."

Now Robert started pacing, his hands clenched behind him. He muttered as he moved back and forth. "Won't work. Can't work. Trap, I tell you. It's a trap."

"I would never do that to you. Carmen would never do that to you. Uncle Robert, the wars are over. Everything political here has turned on its head. It's not like before. No one is out to get you anymore. In fact, they would probably welcome you with some kind of parade. You're a hero. You survived when so many didn't. You have to come out of here if not just for those who didn't make it."

Robert stopped pacing; his hands trembled. "A hero?"

"Yes. At the very least, a survivor. People will want to know about it, how you did it, how you got through."

"The whole story?"

"Sure. Why not?"

Robert frowned and batted at his head as if to rid himself of something. "I'll need to consult. I'll need to check with my people."

"Your people, Uncle Robert? I'm not sure I know what you mean. You know, sometimes when a person has been through what you've been through and for so long, the world moves sideways a bit, and makes it harder to know if what you're thinking is really true. Maybe that applies to you and maybe not. But right now I just want you to come out and greet that world, even if it's only for a few minutes, for a breath of fresh air. Just a spin around the block."

"No."

From above came Carmen's voice. "Get up here, old man. I can't wait forever."

The men looked at each other. The tremble was building in Robert's hands. He took a deep hollow breath. "Can I bring my pack? My rifle?"

"Of course. Whatever you need to feel more comfortable."

Robert picked up his original battalion pack. It was now threadbare, stitched together haphazardly. Part of it was patched with thick silver tape. From it dangled his pick and shovel. He brushed at it and then lifted it over his shoulder. "If this is a trick," he warned.

"It's not. I promise."

"You first." Robert pointed to the ladder.

Michael quickly mounted it and scrambled out. At the top, Carmen still waited on the concrete. Soon, Robert's head appeared. When she saw his face, she noticed the look of fear.

"I can't find my gun," he said. It was all there, the uncertainty, the terror, the monster that kept driving him back in the hole.

"Hello," Carmen said.

"Hello."

Robert quickly glanced around and then did another turn with his head. The sun had crept behind the hills Ventura straddled. The light painted itself against the landscape in curls of glossy Van Gogh strokes that retreated up the slopes. Robert slapped his palm over his eyes. "I just can't."

But Michael held out his hand. "I'll help you."

Robert stared at it a moment and then carefully fit his fingers into Michael's. They were cold, slippery, but Michael held tight and pulled.

It was like the delivery of a child as Robert moved up the steps, one at a time, resting in between until finally, with a gentle tug, Michael pulled him out onto the rubble where he fell on his knees. Spit slung from his mouth and connected with the ground. After a moment, he wiped it from his lips with the back of his sleeve. He turned and faced Carmen.

"Welcome," she said.

But he couldn't make it stop, this trembling that gravitated from his arms to his torso. He looked up at Michael. "Help me, you fool."

Michael gave him a boost. Robert closed his eyes and took in a deep breath. Pursing his lips, he blew it out slowly. Then he ducked. "What was that?"

"Nothing, Uncle Robert. Here, let me take you over."

A baby on new legs, he took one step, then another, grabbing for Michael and then letting go. Finally, he sat down next to Carmen. "This won't do," he said.

Carmen lay her hand gently on his leg. "Look around you. Don't hide. Look, this was an olive oil factory once. People worked here. Other people lined up with their jugs to get a chance at part of the first press. It was exciting to watch them and to guess who would be lucky and who would go home without oil." She pointed across the old road. "I hid over there between those two houses, watching. This whole village was once my playground."

Robert followed where she pointed and nodded his head. "But the fascist beasts destroyed this place."

"The Italians, actually. You remember when you told me about the Black Shirts on the road to Almeria? It was them. They were good at sabotage. One bomb could have consequences that rippled far out from where it went off. Look around you. No village any longer, no line of people waiting for their chance for fresh oil."

Robert tried to speak, but nothing came out save for a deep cough. He put a fist to his mouth. His eyes were rheumy. All around, the night descended. Stars emerged from the nothingness overhead. Michael found a piece of concrete a few yards away and sat down.

"I can't stop shaking," Robert said.

"The air is warm though," said Carmen. "You shake because now you're free again."

"I should go back in. This could be bad for me."

"Remember?" Carmen said. "Don't fret. Just remember. Close your eyes and tell me what you see."

He did but could only see the inside of the jar. "I see nothing."

"Try harder. I'll help you. Let's see, I see two young people in the night. I see us holding tight to one another."

"That's enough," he quickly said. "I see it."

"Now open them. Open them and look around you."

Robert opened his eyes and gazed down the slopes of the hills. "I see stars, no, that's not right, I see lights. Those are lights."

"Beautiful lights," she said. Then she turned to Michael. "Do you think you could go for a walk?"

Michael jumped up. "Sure, sure. I should have thought of it myself. You'll be all right?"

"We'll be all right," said Carmen.

Michael took off, following a path he'd seen the goats take, behind one of the crumbling buildings and to a flatter piece of ground one street up. It wouldn't be long until it was completely black. He found a spot where the destruction of the houses had carved a cleft through which he too could see the lights of La Jolla so far below, and even those of other villages farther in the distance.

Carmen stood with difficulty. "Do you remember, Robertito, when I told you about the dances?"

"Yes."

"Before the war we would gather in the square and the musicians would play flamenco music. Not bad flamenco, but good?"

"Yes."

"And then I forced you to ask me to dance on our night out here?"

"I remember."

"Ask me again."

"But we can barely walk."

"Well, that certainly leaves out the *fandango*. And the *sevillanas*. The *bolero* perhaps."

"I know none of those dances."

She pulled him up. "Then we will have to make one up. Like we did on that good night." She held him close, closer than they had allowed themselves to be for decades now. She felt her breath come in waves that left her gasping.

"I can still waltz," he said. "I think."

She let him lead and to begin with, he nearly sent them falling over one of the pieces of concrete as he took the first step. But they stopped and walked further away from the jar and to the middle of the old street. Here, he took her hand again, placed his palm on her lower back and they began to move.

"At last," Carmen said. "Yes, at last."

"Have I told you I danced in marathons?" Robert asked.

§

It seemed anticlimactic for Michael, this meeting up of his uncle and Carmen. Sad even, but he knew his sadness most likely was complicated by his own marriage and family. These two had stayed together for over fifty years, hung in there, to use the vernacular, and even after all that time, they had something to talk about as simple as lights vs. stars. He envied them.

He wished he could persuade Eva, but did he really? He *should* feel a desperate need, shouldn't he? Maybe it was his children he was more melancholy about. As they'd grown and slipped through his fingers, he'd wondered what was the magic word that would keep them close. Did teenage kids really need a father anymore? Wasn't it too late to offer that one last bit of advice to keep them happy and safe?

"Damn you, Mason," he said out loud. "Why did you have to go and die on me?" He knew this struggle was just the kind of conversation starter that would have kept him after work for longer than he should have, picking his best friend's brain about questions with no answers. It might have led to yet another IDC night. He could hear Mason right now.

"Sometimes there are no solutions because it really isn't a problem to be solved in the first place. If it's not working, you just move on. Life is a series of unstructured events that we as humans try to mold into a structure piecemeal."

Mason's voice vanished, and Michael was struck with the similarity between him and his uncle. Wasn't it just moments ago he worried about Robert hearing voices and relying on the counsel of folks long dead? One thing he did know; he was a long way from IDC nights now.

"Turns out I do care," he said.

He walked to the wall, unzipped and began to pee. He admired the lights through the rift. The lights of La Jolla reminded him of stars, maybe satellites because some of them appeared to be moving. He finished and walked to the edge of the crumbling wall to get a better view.

They were moving. Could it be the headlights of cars leaving the town? But there were so few cars in the village and these lights were so small and they bounced, like fireflies jittering. He stood for a moment, then was startled by the thunk of a car door.

"God no," he said as he twisted and jumped down from the grassy slope and sprinted back toward the jar. When he turned the corner, he was bathed in a wash of bright light.

"Stop right there," said a voice he immediately recognized, and his body froze.

He couldn't see well because of the light, but once he'd stopped, it drifted away and now he could make out both his uncle and Carmen standing. Eugenio had a rifle pointed at the two of them. But his greatest surprise was to see Delia back in the shadows, clutching herself. She glanced to him. "I'm so sorry, Michael. I just couldn't do it."

"So here is the truth," said Eugenio. His voice had a ring to it like that of the winner of a long race. "As I knew. Didn't I know?" He looked around for affirmation, but Carmen's stoic profile was unchanging.

Now Robert focused on Michael. His face transformed into a sneer that reduced Michael to a clumsy unqualified youth. "I told you it wasn't safe," he said.

"What's going on here?" Michael said.

"We have found the killer," Eugenio said. "Isn't that right, Toni? Or is it Rachel? Susannah?"

Delia shook her head. "All of those, darling."

"She's shy," Eugenio said. "But she loves me." He waved the rifle in the air. "But no matter." He looked at Robert again. "You are the reason I've lived."

"It's me you want," Carmen spit out. "I killed your grandfather. He fell like a stone when I pulled the trigger."

"And that's why this *Topo* has been in hiding since my grandfather's murder? You are wrong, *chocho viejo*. You've saved no one."

A sense of impending evil welled up in Michael, erupting like bubbles from a deep toxic lake. "No, you can't do this. Not now. You have to stop."

But in one motion, Eugenio pointed the rifle at him and pulled the trigger; the bullet slammed into his shoulder, knocked him backwards against the wall that he slowly slid down.

"No!" Delia shouted as she jumped toward Michael. "Oh God, oh God."

"Anyone else want to test the strength of my backbone?" Eugenio said.

Delia stopped and shook her head.

"Good. Now, *maestro*," he said, jerking his weapon in the direction of the jar. "Would you like to go back home now?"

Confused for a moment, Robert thought he was asking about America and his spirit pitched at the thought. "Yes, yes. My parents are worried about me," he said.

"Are they now?" Eugenio moved the gun barrel again. "I want you to walk over to the edge of that hole."

"Don't do it," said Carmen.

"I will shoot you then."

"Go ahead. It's not me you want," she said. "It's not the young man over there bleeding against the wall, either. It's not even this man, Robert Martin. You want something that slipped through your fingers before you were born. You want the thing you can never have. Don't you know that?"

"You have no idea what I want. What I need."

"The part that consumes you the most is that you know I'm right. You suffer from a sickness of war and you don't realize we are no longer at war."

"Ah, *La Pasionaria* speaks," said Eugenio. He lifted his rifle skyward and pulled off two quick shots. "*Viva España!*" he shouted. "*Viva!*" Then he leveled on Carmen once more. "How do you choose to die?"

"I don't choose to die."

"Move, old man," Eugenio said to Robert. "Let's get on with this."

Robert blinked at him two quick times and started toward the jar, but Carmen grabbed for his arm. She turned toward Eugenio. "Just who do you think your grandfather was? A hero? Far from it."

"Shut up."

"Before his own death, do you know what he was guilty of? Do you?"

"Shut up. He was a martyr, a demigod, a paragon."

"But of what?" Carmen said. "Do you even know? What have you been told? Who has told you these lies?"

"You have one more chance to quiet yourself and save your life. Go back home, old lady. I don't want you. Nobody wants you."

"Now, stop." It was Robert, finally shaken from his gloom. "This woman is a saint."

"You have to the count of three to start moving, old man. One…"

"He killed children," Carmen blurted out. "He killed innocent women and children, your grandfather did. Not even members of the party. He tortured and killed children because it gave him pleasure. Much like our late priest."

This captured Eugenio for a moment. "Late?"

"Ah, I should have known you and Blas Alvarez are old friends."

"You lie, old lady. Old man? Two…"

Robert gently removed Carmen's fingers from his arm and patted her hand. Then he walked toward the jar once more.

"This man should at least have a trial," said Carmen. "He should at least have that right. This is a civilized society, is it not?"

"Trials," said Eugenio. He wiped his sleeve across his forehead. To the side, Michael moaned. "All right. Just like my grandfather before me, I will grant trials to the accused. He wasn't an animal, and neither am I. None of us is an animal."

Robert stopped now at the edge of the jar. He held his hands together in front of him and waited. His voice wavered. "I'm so sorry, Max. So sorry."

Eugenio set the rifle on its butt next to his leg. "Mr. Robert Martin," he said. "You are accused of the murder of one, Francisco Robles de Casares, Lieutenant in the Grand Army of the *Patria* of Spain. You shot him through the belly and he died alone."

"He wasn't alone," said Robert. "Not like Max, he wasn't."

"You are not allowed to speak until I give you permission. But I can tell by those very words you are guilty by admission of your presence there. Is that not true?"

"Your grandfather was about to shoot an innocent boy. I couldn't let that happen."

"You have evidence for this?"

"I have my word as evidence."

"Your word?" Now Eugenio broke into gales of menacing laughter. "Do you know how much your word is worth? A single *peseta*, maybe less." He laughed again.

"Darling?" It was Delia. "Darling, we still have a chance to run off together."

Eugenio turned and it looked as if he was considering it for the smallest moment. He saw her beauty, her loyalty to him.

She smiled and held out her hand. "It's me you've always wanted."

He squinted, shook his head and turned back. "After," he said. "When it's finished, we can run away together."

"My brother was there," said Carmen. "He agrees with what Don Roberto is saying."

"And where is your brother now?" Eugenio asked.

"Dead," she said flatly. "Killed by your purification system. Killed by the Black Shirts."

"Then he cannot testify for us, can he?"

"He told me what the truth was. I can testify."

"You are not an eyewitness. Your testimony means nothing. Is there anyone else who cares to contribute to the proceedings? You there, over against the wall? Would you like to say something?" He was speaking to Michael who had continued moaning since the bullet struck him.

"No? Then I believe this court is ready to hand down a verdict." He unhooked the handcuffs from his belt and walked over to Robert. "Turn around." He waited while Robert slowly did an about face. He grabbed hold of Robert's arms and pulled each one back violently.

At that moment, Delia made a move toward Eugenio, a simple step. Carmen held her breath. But Delia, like the expert she had always been, ever so slowly retreated back into the darkness, then turned and ran down the hill away from Ventura.

Eugenio grabbed for his gun, but fumbled for a moment because of the handcuffs. He followed Delia's sounds down into the darkness. He turned back to the others. "Why would she leave me like that?"

"She's scared," said Carmen.

Eugenio shook his head violently, once, and then once more. "I will find her. Just like I found you." Focused again, he popped the cuffs on Robert's wrists and stood back. He looked to Carmen. "Are you satisfied you have witnessed an official trial?"

"Don't do this. Please." She spit out the last word. "His nephew may be dying over there. Another innocent."

But Eugenio ignored her and turned back to Robert. "Sing it for me first," he said.

"What?"

"Sing it. The *Internationale*. Your anthem. Sing it once before I pronounce your sentence."

"I don't know it," Robert said.

Eugenio suddenly struck the back of Robert's head with the rifle, sending him to his knees. "Of course, you know it. All your kind know it." Eugenio began to hum, then sang a few lines: "*'So comrades, come rally, and the last fight let us face. The Internationale unites the human race.'* Go ahead, you know it. Sing it one last time."

Robert shook his head. "I'm sorry. I don't know it."

"No? How about this? *'Onward squadrons, to victory. A new day dawns in Spain.'* Do you know that song?"

Carmen spit on the ground, then spit again. "Like all the others. You have no spine. Look at you. You cannot yet be twenty-five years old and this man nears seventy-five. Does this give you a sense of power to shoot him in the back of the head and watch him fall? Will this be the crowning achievement of your life?"

A storm gathered in Eugenio and he raised his rifle high. "Toni!" he shouted. "Toni...!"

A shot rang out, and then another, tearing into Eugenio's chest, spinning him around.

"No!" he cried. "Oh, Grandfather!"

But he kept spinning and staggering until he fell into the very jar where Robert had been living for over half a century. Shocked, Robert fell over. Only Carmen remained standing. She turned and waited as, one by one, people sliced through the old rubble from the explosion of the olive oil factory, led by her friend, Victoria, a rifle with a warm barrel in her hands. Men and women came, some children, each carrying a light and a weapon. They gathered silently near Robert's inert body. Carmen nodded at Victoria.

"Forever is never too long to wait," said Carmen as she carefully picked her way through them and stood at the edge of the jar. She borrowed one of the lights and held it over the opening, seeing clearly Eugenio's body displayed as if he were ready to run, his face forever frozen in a rictus of disbelief. "Let this be the last."

Chapter Thirty-One
La Jolla Townsfolk, Andalusia, 1989

Without a word being spoken, the people of La Jolla now set themselves in motion. A small group hurried over to the wall to check Michael. Two strong men bent down to gently pick up Robert who, once they had him upright, was able to walk on his own. One man scurried down the ladder and went through Eugenio's pockets, finding keys and money. He also took the ammunition from his belt and grabbed the rifle.

"Is there anything else Don Roberto needs?" he said.

Carmen sat on her haunches and shook her head. "We have his pack and his tools, but the only thing down there worth saving is now up here with me." She watched as the man slung Eugenio's bounty over his shoulder and scaled the ladder. At the top, he pushed the ladder back into the hole, where it fell onto Eugenio's lifeless body. Carmen was about to give instructions, but saw that people were already preparing to do it. By this time, some were lifting the debris they could manage, walking it over and dropping it into the jar's opening.

Carmen stepped carefully over to Michael. A trickle of blood had set loose from his nose, but his eyes were open, although his head was rolling back and forth against the old adobe side of the wall.

"It's his shoulder," said one of the men, now standing up. "Maybe nicked something."

"We'll get him to the car," Carmen said.

After the men had lifted Michael and carried him to the rental, Carmen walked back and used the key to unlock Robert's cuffs. He rubbed each wrist.

"See there?" she said. "Now you're free."

In the car, she sat in the passenger seat and checked on both Michael and Robert in the back. Michael's legs were spread out across Robert's lap, and he petted them absently as he stared out the window with the wonder of a young child. The driver followed the Guardia's Land Rover down to the *martirio*. Here they left the vehicle with the keys in the ignition. A group of women stood close by, each with an armload of deep-red carnations. Carmen noticed that carnations had been placed all around the edges of the *martirio,* the symbol of remembrance throughout Andalusia. She rolled down the window, took two from one of the women and handed them to Robert, who twirled one in his hand and lay the other across Michael's chest.

"We must go," said Carmen. "The *Guardia* will be missed."

§

Michael sat up in the bed in his apartment. His chest and shoulders were sore to the touch, but with every day, the pain lessened. The bandages made it hard to move. There was a knock at the door and he looked over to see Delia standing next to her suitcase.

"So here you are," he said.

"Yes."

"Won't they be looking for you now more than ever?"

"We'll see. I'm pretty good at this, you know."

"You could stay. It's not that bad."

She hurried over to the bed and sat. She patted his leg through the spread. "Michael, I couldn't be sorrier than I am for what happened with Eugenio."

"It doesn't sound like you had much choice."

"But I thought I had him. I thought he would listen to anything I said. I thought I could save you all." She bowed her head. "But I chickened out. Again."

"I think he loved you."

"That would be a first."

"For both of you, I'll bet."

"I've been thinking a lot about your uncle. He and I... This may sound weird, but I identify with him. Both of us being underground for so long. In different ways, sure, but keeping ourselves locked away just the same."

"You sound a little maudlin in your old age."

"Fuck you, Michael."

"So you're going right now?"

"Yes, a cab should be here any minute. I just wanted to see how you're doing."

He touched the top of her hand. "Someday I'll come visit you in prison."

"You know what they always say? A swift death is better than a lifetime's imprisonment."

"That's not an option for you," he said. "The swift death part, I mean."

"If you say so."

"I'm beginning to understand you."

"Listen, I never killed anybody. I promise. I mean, I didn't pull a trigger. I didn't set anything off myself. Believe it if you want. It doesn't matter." She rolled her eyes. "You want to know what the worst thing I did was? All those names I stole. They were once real people, real babies that somebody loved. I have no idea why now that seems like such a horrible thing to steal their identities, but it does. Jesus, they were already dead, you know. What difference did it make by then?"

"I doubt the parents ever knew."

"But I do. And that poor woman whose dad was the cop who died in the holdup. What must her life be like?"

"I know."

"I've got a lot of thinking to do, but like I said, my fantasies usually don't include me being led away by a bunch of feds." She pounded at her head. "I've just got to get rid of this, damn, this damn anger. Oh, Christ. It's rage, pure and simple. I don't know how. I don't even know if I want to but I've got to find a way to get rid of it or I don't stand a chance."

"Lean over here." He grabbed her hand and squeezed it. "Thank you for bringing me here. It's opened up my life."

She kissed him tenderly on the lips. "Goodbye, Michael."

"When will I see you again?"

"Never."

"I've heard that before."

"This time it's true."

"God, that sounds so final."

"Sorry, but that's the way it works. Son-of-a-bitch, and just when I was starting to get used to your sorry self. It's always the timing with me."

"Good luck. I mean it."

"Thanks." She stood. "It would really help if you would practice your Spanish."

"Always the sweet talker," he said. Then he saluted her and winced.

Later, Michael was down at the beach, sitting in a plastic chair, the public phone trailing down to his lap. He waited for Eva to get on the line. He had a speech prepared.

He had just talked to his kids and should have been feeling sad, but was surprised to find that he didn't. They seemed happy, involved. What more could he want for them? Sure, they missed him. Sure, he missed them. Those words were spoken out loud. He wanted to tell them about Robert, but he felt protective and didn't believe his family could keep so big a secret. They'd flock to him, a mass of journalists, onlookers, grifters even. His uncle would crumble into dust without Michael's help.

"Michael?"

"Hi, Eva. I want you to listen to me."

"No," she said. "I need to say something. I want to apologize. I'm sorry for those times when I was too tired or had too much work or just couldn't get close to you. It wasn't fair to you and it made you think that it was your fault. I've known for years who I really am, but I kept up the charade with you anyway. For that I am truly sorry."

"God."

"Can we at least be friendly?"

"We can be more than that. And thank you for telling me. It all makes more sense now. I love you." At that moment he knew it to be true.

"Likewise, only it's more of a Philia kind of love."

"I can handle that."

Later, he dialed his secretary's number. It rang and rang and he was about to hang up when Arlene abruptly came on the line.

"Ah, it's the star of The Great Escape," she said.

"Yeah, sorry I haven't kept in touch better. How are things?"

"Oh, you know. The same. Different faces but the same. When you coming back?"

"Well, that's what I wanted to talk to you about."

"That sounds ominous."

"I may not be coming back."

"Good. For a second there I thought you were going to say you're not coming back."

"I'm serious," Michael said. He adjusted his position slightly and jerked with the resulting pain. "I've found something here."

"Is it contagious?"

"Now, I need you to listen carefully," Michael said. "I need you to go over my patient list and send each of them a letter I'm going to dictate to you in a second. And then I'd like you to figure out if and how you can distribute them onto other people's caseloads."

"Oh, that sounds easy enough. I enjoy toying with people's lives that way."

"I'm really really sorry, Arlene."

"Just tell me one thing. It's a woman, isn't it?"

"No, as a matter of fact, it isn't. It's more a… It's more a change of heart. It's a new mystery of life I've got to solve. That's the best I can do."

"All right. I'll do it."

"I do have another question. That case of Mason's? The one when he died? Do you know what happened with it?"

"Yes. Bender told me. The father got custody."

Michael heard it but couldn't feel it. He briefly envisioned the girl back home with the guy who most likely took sexual advantage of her. Another lost to the failings of the court system. "Are you sure?"

"Positive."

"That sucks. I was really hoping it would go the other way."

"You win some..."

"You're telling me it's just life?"

"What else could it be?"

"You got a pen handy?" Michael asked.

A few minutes later, he hung up. He saw the *taxista* still waiting by the side of the road. He didn't signal for him quite yet, though. He slumped back in the chair. He sensed that maybe Mason died in vain. Of course, the outcome would have been different if Mason hadn't died. Like his Uncle Robert had said. People's lives were influenced by the slightest tilt in the axis of the world. Saying yes to a request to testify in court. Saying no to chasing a wife across the state. Saying yes when you got a letter in the mail begging you to go on an adventure.

He wondered where Delia was. Knew she could manage. Knew he could as well. He had a lot of thinking to do and knew just how to get it done.

He finally turned and motioned to the taxi driver to come get him.

Chapter Thirty-Two
Robert, Andalusia, 1989

August 22, 1989, La Jolla, Spain

Dear Mom and Dad,

At last, at last, I am out of my prison. And the good news? I can finally mail you all the letters. I'm sure you'll be happy to get the news that I am alive and well. Mari Carmen says there will be a time when I can go back and stay with you again, but not quite yet. She rests in her bed a lot now. She says it's because she's happy to have me close. She worries so much about her goats, but guess what? I have a nephew who came to visit, Loretta's grandkid, and he's taken over the job of herding the goats. He had to take a while to get over his injury from the battle, but he seems better now. There's a lot of the Martin family in that boy. One day I was out on the veranda and I saw him up on the hill, just sitting, like he was thinking of something very important. With those goats all scattered about him, it looked like a nice painting. He tells me he has family too, so that makes me feel like a lot has happened in my absence and that I have a lot to look forward to. I am learning so much I might as well be in college, which I know would make you happy, Mom. Today is one of those harsh middle of summer days that even in my old safe haven I used to be able to feel. Like osmosis, the changes outside always filtered through the skin of my secrets and told me the truths about life. Now, out here where I can feel the full brunt of the sun, it's both a blessing and a curse. And my dear, dear Mari Carmen, wise beyond her years, still guides me along the way. "Keep the windows closed during the hottest part of the day," she says. But I can't bring myself to close any window ever again. I think she understands, but she gets frustrated easily now. Even though she tells me it's safe for me to come out in the open, I prefer the comfort of her house. In my head, Franco still rules with an iron fist and from time to time I can hear him make a pronouncement that all is forgiven for those who fought against his rebellion, that they can come back to the country of their birth and resume their lives. But what happened before, when they returned, they were quickly rounded up and dispatched, leaving sadness and loss in their wake. He was always a wretched man, says Mari Carmen. Life here has settled some since the war, but she talks of a life that was different from the Spain she hoped to grow up in. There was freedom, she admits. There was freedom for men to stay out late and get drunk and work for mere pesetas a day. There was freedom to marry and have as many children as you wanted. There was freedom to attend the catholic schools led by the very clergy who stood by and watched as innocent Spaniards were cut down in their prime by wicked absolutists. There was freedom to walk the streets, to buy bread, to raise goats, to contract cancers and die, to love and be loved. But there was no freedom to make a mistake, to tell your neighbor that Franco once had your only baby murdered for the entertainment of foreign troops. You'd better never say such a thing as that or one day your neighbors, the people who you'd spent your entire life with, would notice you no longer herd your goats in the hills, no longer take your place in the communion line, would notice that you, in fact, had disappeared off the face of this blessed earth. Mom, Dad, now she says Franco is dead and there is all kinds of proof this is true, but you know, I am reluctant. It may take a while to get used to the fact I can venture out in the street and say hello to folks who all seem to know me even though I've never formally met them. Soon you'll feel able to do that, says Mari Carmen. There is always hope it will be soon. Meanwhile, I learn. La Jolla, says

Mari Carmen, is a village that never forgets. Fifty years have passed since the end of the war, and it is as fresh in the minds of the older citizens as if the bombs were still falling or the gunshots were ringing out. War, she says, stays with you long after it is over. The people who have lived through it share their experiences with a glance, with the hearing of an old song, with a mother calling for her child using the name of a loved one long dead. This sharing is strong, she says. But they're still not used to speaking it out loud. As a result, without a word being said, everyone knows what a neighbor is thinking. Everyone knows what a neighbor is doing. When I express my confusion about this, Mari Carmen will say, "It's like this. If, at the bottom of the village, you tell Rosario you are coming down with a cold, by the time you get to the top of the village, Asuncion will have a remedy ready for you." She also tells me that I have a part in the folklore of La Jolla, although I wish it were for something else I had done, in a different era altogether. She says I will always be remembered as the man who came in the small hours of the morning and obliterated the savage beast who was destroying their families. I may have done that, but I know I didn't do it on purpose. I had no choice. A child needed my help and I gave it. I tend to think that my presence may not have been fortuitous to the people of La Jolla, but Mari Carmen tells me I shouldn't think that way. She has a saying, "Smooth seas do not make good sailors." No matter the outcome, it needed to happen, she says, or the village might have fallen to its knees and let the nationalists take over without a fight. That, she says, would have been a fate worse than death. Maybe I'll completely understand it someday. Meanwhile, Michael brings me the latest edition of The International Herald Tribune. He pointed out a story and told me it reminded him of me. It's about a woman who was on the run for years and years who finally turned herself in to customs when she got back to the United States. Apparently, she taught high school Spanish in Spokane. You know her, he tells me, but maybe I do and maybe I don't. Anyway, I think Michael is convinced that by reading the paper,

I will start believing everything will be all right. I will close again, my beloved parents. Know that I think of the two of you every single day as I hope you still think of me. My health is good. The old wound acts up once in a while; Mari Carmen thinks the bullet is still lodged in there somewhere, which is a reminder of how close I came to losing my life. But I am very much alive now. I wish there was some way to let you know that in person. I don't want you to worry. Mom? How's your bridge group doing? Dad, I think I might actually be ready to go hunting with you some fall when I get back. I think I now know how to use a gun. Every Sunday, Carmen climbs out of bed and hobbles over to a small shrine she made years ago. We pray together for the safety of those we love but cannot see. Don't worry, I won't convert, but in some odd way, it's soothing to do the ritual. One more thing. Do you think you can find out the address of Max's parents for me? I have some bad news to tell them and I think it's better I do it now than later. I love you both.
    Your loving son,
Robert

The End

PREVIOUS BOOKS BY EDWARD AVERETT

Homing

The Rhyming Season

Three Star Private Nuisance

Cameron and the Girls

Scablands

The Yellow

Level IV

The New Prosperity Museum